MODERN

MAGIC

MODERN MAGIC

LOUISA MAY ALCOTT

SELECTED AND WITH AN INTRODUCTION BY
MADELEINE B. STERN

LARGE PRINT BOOK CLUB EDITION

THE MODERN LIBRARY
NEW YORK

This Large Print Edition, prepared especially for Doubleday Book & Music Clubs, Inc., contains the complete, unabridged text of the original Publisher's Edition.

1995 Modern Library Edition

 Published in the United States by Random House, Inc., New York, and simultaneously in Canada by Random House of Canada Limited, Toronto.

Jacket photograph courtesy of The Bettmann Archive

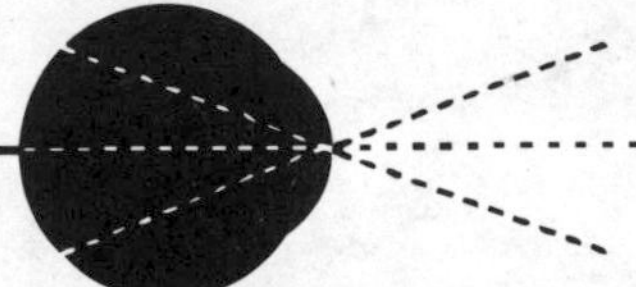

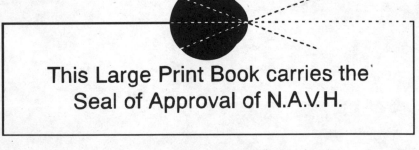

This Large Print Book carries the Seal of Approval of N.A.V.H.

ISBN 0-679-60171-6

Printed in the United States of America

Contents

Introduction

by Madeleine B. Stern

Louisa May Alcott's double literary life was first unveiled twenty years ago with the publication of *Behind a Mask: The Unknown Thrillers of Louisa May Alcott.* It was especially during the 1860s that the Concord Scheherezade, soon to become the revered Children's Friend, lived out her darker alter ego and produced the bulk of her blood and thunder tales. During that same decade, Alcott wrote, on the one hand—was it the right hand?—her realistic *Hospital Sketches,* her perceptive novel *Moods,* and her domestic family saga *Little Women.* It was then too that she imagined and shaped her anonymous and pseudonymous thrillers, those unacknowledged page-turners concerned with murder, madness, and mayhem. Surely they were the products of Alcott's left hand—those sensation stories that disclosed, behind the writer's mask, an image unfamiliar, shocking, intriguing, and often, and most surprisingly, intensely modern.

In one of her shockers the hero comments: "Human minds are more full of mysteries than any written book and more changeable than the cloud shapes in the air." Alcott's preoccupation with the mysteries of the human mind is traceable in many of her serialized narratives. In one story in particular she uses the theme in a remarkable way that recalls the eighteenth century and links us to the twentieth. The lead story of *Modern Magic*—indeed, the one that gives the collection its name, "A Pair of Eyes; or, Modern Magic," uses as catalyst the dangerous art of mesmerism. During the eighteenth century, the "great enchanter" Franz Mesmer developed a theory of hypnotism based upon some magnetic force or fluid that permeated the universe, a force he called animal magnetism. The theory, introduced to Boston, stirred a furor among proponents and antagonists. Poe, of course, was fascinated into writing his "Mesmeric Revelation." Emerson loftily observed that while mesmerism did indeed break "into the inmost shrines," it also "affirmed unity and connection between remote points." But it was Hawthorne's reaction that most influenced Alcott, Hawthorne's perception that the intrusions of the mesmerist might violate the human soul and result in the "unpardonable sin." The theme dominates "A Pair of Eyes," and the author writes as an expert on the hypnotic function of the mesmerist's eyes, the effects of hypnotic influence upon the subject, the use of mesmerism as an exercise in power.

It is in her treatment of mesmerism as mind control that Alcott allies herself most closely with the twentieth century, for her controller is not a man but a woman, the heroine of "A Pair of Eyes," Agatha

Eure, who uses those eyes to conquer and control her male victim. This is a variation upon Hawthorne's "unpardonable sin," a variation Alcott made peculiarly her own, one that sits comfortably with twentieth-century readers.

Just so, in "The Fate of the Forrests," the focal theme is a diablerie, but a diablerie based not upon mind control but upon violence. Readers of *Modern Magic* will not find Alcott's version of violence completely unfamiliar, although it was rooted in the remote theme of Hindu Thuggism. Surely in her search for shocking subjects the writer of sensationalism could find none more shocking than a "confederacy of professional assassins," worshippers of the Hindu goddess of destruction, who strangle their victims with pride and pleasure. This form of ethnic barbarism is interwoven in a tale that, like so many Alcott narratives, is concerned basically with the struggle between a man and a woman. Here, in "The Fate of the Forrests," the hero Stähl, representing Eastern vengeance and brutality, contends with the heroine Ursula who wins only through dying. In succumbing to Stähl but never returning his passion, Ursula becomes "both mistress and slave."

The struggle of slave and master, especially the power struggle between the sexes, runs like a scarlet thread consistently through most of Alcott's shockers. Alcott is drawn to the idea of conflict between men and women, a conflict in which, in varying degrees, the woman is victor. In Alcott's hands, involvement with sexual struggle becomes a productive literary theme. In addition, it is a theme that allies her to the twentieth century.

Nowhere is the motif of a woman's power more skillfully depicted than in "Behind a Mask; or, A Woman's Power," originally published over Alcott's pseudonym, "A. M. Barnard." Here, behind a mask, sits an actress supreme, Jean Muir, a woman filled with anger against the male lords of creation, a woman whose power triumphs in the end. When she first appears upon the scene in the guise of a young governess at the ancestral Coventry estate, an astute observer remarks: "Scene first, very well done." To this she replies: "The last scene shall be still better." And, as it turns out, it is.

Jean Muir is one of Alcott's most fascinating heroines, a femme fatale with a mysterious background, an ambitious manipulator with fatal powers. Proud and passionate, mysterious and mocking, motivated by thwarted love, she weaves her spell, achieves her ends, captures all prizes. Twentieth-century feminists may debate her motives and decry her methods, but they cannot fail to be intrigued by the versatile exercise of her "woman's power." Jean Muir was an adept in the sexual politics of any century.

Probably no theme is more ancient or more contemporary than the theme of drug experimentation. Alcott had familiarized herself, through the episodes of her life, her observations, and her readings, with mesmeric passes, Hindu Thuggism, and sexual power struggles. Just so, the effects of laudanum, opium, or hashish were no terra incognita to her. Tincture of opium was part of the pharmacopoeia of almost every nineteenth-century physician, and Alcott had undoubtedly used it as surcease from pain during a period of illness sustained when she was a nurse in the Civil War. Now, in a sweet short shocker entitled "Perilous Play" she used the experience as a narrative device.

Having sketched her dramatis personae with broad brush strokes, Alcott quickly presents her theme. To while away a long afternoon, Dr. Meredith produces a "little box of tortoiseshell and gold" containing "that Indian stuff which brings one fantastic visions." The good doctor proceeds to describe the effects of *Cannabis sativa* or hashish: "Six ["comfits"] can do no harm. . . . I take twenty before I can enjoy myself. . . . A heavenly dreaminess comes over one, in which they move as if on air. Everything is calm and lovely to them: no pain, no care, no fear of anything, and while it lasts one feels like an angel half asleep." When the trance comes on, "Your pulse will rise, heart beat quickly, eyes darken and dilate, and an uplifted sensation will pervade you generally. Then these symptoms change, and the bliss begins." An overdose, Dr. Meredith concedes, is "not so pleasant, unless one likes phantoms, frenzies, and a touch of nightmare, which seems to last a thousand years." And so the heroine is given her "taste of Elysium," and the experiment is made. Thanks to the author's ingenuity, it ends happily and the perilous players exclaim at curtain fall, "Heaven bless hashish, if its dreams end like this!"

If "Perilous Play" raises eyebrows today, the final story of *Modern Magic,* "My Mysterious Mademoiselle," may raise them higher, for in that narrative the young hero is presented in the guise of a girl. The author may have intended to create a mere delicious trifle but, despite the innocent explanations offered in the denouement, the tale cannot fail to convey to the readers of *Modern Magic* transvestite suggestions. An Englishman meets on a train "a slender girl of sixteen or so," a "demure demoiselle," who tells him she is "helpless." He kisses her hand "in true French style," finds her "a most captivating companion," and almost fancies himself "an ardent lad again." The Englishman confesses that "the idea of passing as her father disgusted" him. Rather, he pretends for a time that the young girl is his wife. When they part he asks for "an English good-by," that is, "a kiss on the lips." Sexual titillation punctuates the story until it turns out that the "mysterious mademoiselle" is in reality a "handsome, black-haired, mischievous lad" who has disguised himself to escape school authorities, and that the two protagonists are actually uncle and nephew.

* * *

Louisa May Alcott would have found herself at home in the twentieth century. Despite the enduring depiction of loving domesticity for which she is universally remembered, she was sufficiently absorbed by the perplexing mysteries of the mind to identify and be identified with a later period. Now, at the turn of yet another century, readers can recognize as a contemporary this writer from a Massachusetts village who took the world for her province. In her stories of mesmerism and mind control, Eastern violence and woman's power, drug experimentation and transvestism, she transcends her own time and bequeathes to us a corpus of intriguing, still-pertinent narratives. The enchantments she has conjured up are as modern as they are magical.

ORIGINAL PUBLICATIONS OF THE STORIES

"A Pair of Eyes; or, Modern Magic." *Frank Leslie's Illustrated Newspaper* (24 and 31 October 1863).

"The Fate of the Forrests." *Frank Leslie's Illustrated Newspaper* (11, 18, and 25 February 1865).

"Behind a Mask; or, A Woman's Power." *The Flag of Our Union* (13, 20, 27 October and 3 November 1866).

"Perilous Play." *Frank Leslie's Chimney Corner* (13 February 1869).

"My Mysterious Mademoiselle." *Frank Leslie's Lady's Magazine* (September 1869).

A Pair of Eyes
or
Modern Magic

Part I

I was disappointed—the great actress had not given me what I wanted, and my picture must still remain unfinished for want of a pair of eyes. I knew what they should be, saw them clearly in my fancy, but though they haunted me by night and day I could not paint them, could not find a model who would represent the aspect I desired, could not describe it to any one, and though I looked into every face I met, and visited afflicted humanity in many shapes, I could find no eyes that visibly presented the vacant yet not unmeaning stare of Lady Macbeth in her haunted sleep. It fretted me almost beyond endurance to be delayed in my work so near its completion, for months of thought and labor had been bestowed upon it; the few who had seen it in its imperfect state had elated me with commendation, whose critical sincerity I knew the worth of; and the many not admitted were impatient for a sight of that which others praised, and to which the memory of former successes lent an interest beyond mere curiosity. All was done, and well done, except the eyes; the dimly lighted chamber, the listening attendants, the ghostly figure with wan face framed in hair, that streamed shadowy and long against white draperies, and whiter arms, whose gesture told that the parted lips were uttering that mournful cry—

> "Here's the smell of blood still!
> All the perfumes of Arabia will not
> Sweeten this little hand—"

The eyes alone baffled me, and for want of these my work waited, and my last success was yet unwon.

I was in a curious mood that night, weary yet restless, eager yet impotent to seize the object of my search, and full of haunting images that would not stay to be reproduced. My friend was absorbed in the play, which no longer possessed any charm for me, and leaning back in my seat I fell into a listless reverie, still harping on the one idea of my life; for impetuous and resolute in all things, I had given myself body and soul to the profession I had chosen and followed through many vicissitudes for fifteen years. Art was wife, child, friend, food and fire to me; the pursuit of fame as a reward for my long labor was the object for which I lived, the hope which gave me courage to press on over every obstacle, sacrifice and suffering, for the word "defeat" was not in my vocabulary. Sitting thus, alone, though in a crowd, I slowly became aware of a disturbing influence whose power invaded my momentary isolation, and soon took shape in the uncomfortable conviction that some one was looking at me. Every one has felt this, and at another time I should have cared little for it, but just then I was laboring under a sense of injury, for of all the myriad eyes about me none would give me the expression I longed for; and unreasonable as it was, the thought that I was watched annoyed me like a silent insult. I sent a searching look through the boxes on either hand, swept the remoter groups with a powerful glass, and scanned the sea of heads below, but met no answering glance; all faces were turned stageward, all minds seemed intent upon the tragic scenes enacting there.

Failing to discover any visible cause for my

fancy, I tried to amuse myself with the play, but having seen it many times and being in an ill-humor with the heroine of the hour, my thoughts soon wandered, and though still apparently an interested auditor, I heard nothing, saw nothing, for the instant my mind became abstracted the same uncanny sensation returned. A vague consciousness that some stronger nature was covertly exerting its power upon my own; I smiled as this whim first suggested itself, but it rapidly grew upon me, and a curious feeling of impotent resistance took possession of me, for I was indignant without knowing why, and longed to rebel against—I knew not what. Again I looked far and wide, met several inquiring glances from near neighbors, but none that answered my demand by any betrayal of especial interest or malicious pleasure. Baffled, yet not satisfied, I turned to myself, thinking to find the cause of my disgust there, but did not succeed. I seldom drank wine, had not worked intently that day, and except the picture had no anxiety to harass me; yet without any physical or mental cause that I could discover, every nerve seemed jangled out of tune, my temples beat, my breath came short, and the air seemed feverishly close, though I had not perceived it until then. I did not understand this mood and with an impatient gesture took the playbill from my friend's knee, gathered it into my hand and fanned myself like a petulant woman, I suspect, for Louis turned and surveyed me with surprise as he asked:

"What is it, Max; you seem annoyed?"

"I am, but absurd as it is, I don't know why, except a foolish fancy that someone whom I do not see is looking at me and wishes me to look at him."

Louis laughed—"Of course there is, aren't you used to it yet? And are you so modest as not to know that many eyes take stolen glances at the rising artist, whose ghosts and goblins make their hair stand on end so charmingly? I had the mortification to discover some time ago that, young and comely as I take the liberty of thinking myself, the upturned lorgnettes are not levelled at me, but at the stern-faced, black-bearded gentleman beside me, for he looks particularly moody and interesting to-night."

"Bah! I just wish I could inspire some of those starers with gratitude enough to set them walking in their sleep for my benefit and their own future glory. Your suggestion has proved a dead failure, the woman there cannot give me what I want, the picture will never get done, and the whole affair will go to the deuce for want of a pair of eyes."

I rose to go as I spoke, and there they were behind me!

What sort of expression my face assumed I cannot tell, for I forgot time and place, and might have committed some absurdity if Louis had not pulled me down with a look that made me aware that I was staring with an utter disregard of common courtesy.

"Who are those people? Do you know them?" I demanded in a vehement whisper.

"Yes, but put down that glass and sit still or I'll call an usher to put you out," he answered, scandalized at my energetic demonstrations.

"Good! then introduce me—now at once—Come on," and I rose again, to be again arrested.

"Are you possessed to-night? You have visited so many fever wards and madhouses in your search that you've unsettled your own wits, Max. What whim has got into your brain now? And why do you want to know those people in such haste?"

"Your suggestion has not proved failure, a woman can give me what I want, the picture will be finished, and nothing will go to the deuce, for I've found the eyes—now be obliging and help me to secure them."

Louis stared at me as if he seriously began to think me a little mad, but restrained the explosive remark that rose to his lips and answered hastily, as several persons looked round as if our whispering annoyed them.

"I'll take you in there after the play if you must go, so for heaven's sake behave like a gentleman till then, and let me enjoy myself in peace."

I nodded composedly, he returned to his tragedy and shading my eyes with my hand, I took a critical survey, feeling more and more assured that my long search was at last ended. Three persons occupied the box, a well-dressed elderly lady dozing behind her fan, a lad leaning over the front absorbed in the play, and a young lady looking straight before her with the aspect I had waited for with such impatience. This figure I scrutinized with the eye of an artist which took in every accessory of outline, ornament and hue.

Framed in darkest hair, rose a face delicately cut, but cold and colorless as that of any statue in the vestibule without. The lips were slightly parted with the long slow breaths that came and went, the forehead was femininely broad and low, the brows straight and black, and underneath them the mysterious eyes fixed on vacancy, full of that weird regard so hard to counterfeit, so impossible to describe; for though absent, it was not expressionless, and through its steadfast shine a troubled meaning wandered, as if soul and body could not be utterly divorced by any effort of the will. She seemed unconscious of the scene about her, for the fixture of her glance never changed, and nothing about her stirred but the jewel on her bosom, whose changeful glitter seemed to vary as it rose and fell. Emboldened by this apparent absorption, I prolonged my scrutiny and scanned this countenance as I had never done a woman's face before. During this examination I had forgotten myself in her, feeling only a strong desire to draw nearer and dive deeper into those two dark wells that seemed so tranquil yet so fathomless, and in the act of trying to fix shape, color and expression in my memory, I lost them all; for a storm of applause broke the attentive hush as the curtain fell, and like one startled from sleep a flash of intelligence lit up the eyes, then a white hand was passed across them, and long downcast lashes hid them from my sight.

Louis stood up, gave himself a comprehensive survey, and walked out, saying, with a nod,

"Now, Max, put on your gloves, shake the hair out of your eyes, assume your best 'deportment,' and come and take an observation which may immortalize your name."

Knocking over a chair in my haste, I followed close upon his heels, as he tapped at the next door; the lad opened it, bowed to my conductor, glanced at me and strolled away, while we passed in. The elderly lady was awake, now, and received us graciously; the younger was leaning on her hand, the plumy fan held between her and the glare of the great chandelier as she watched the moving throng below.

"Agatha, here is Mr. Yorke and a friend

whom he wishes to present to you," said the old lady, with a shade of deference in her manner which betrayed the companion, not the friend.

Agatha turned, gave Louis her hand, with a slow smile dawning on her lip, and looked up at me as if the fact of my advent had no particular interest for her, and my appearance promised no great pleasure.

"Miss Eure, my friend Max Erdmann yearned to be made happy by a five minutes audience, and I ventured to bring him without sending an *avant courier* to prepare the way. Am I forgiven?" with which half daring, half apologetic introduction, Louis turned to the chaperone and began to rattle.

Miss Eure bowed, swept the waves of silk from the chair beside her, and I sat down with a bold request waiting at my lips till an auspicious moment came, having resolved not to exert myself for nothing. As we discussed the usual topics suggested by the time and place, I looked often into the face before me and soon found it difficult to look away again, for it was a constant surprise to me. The absent mood had passed and with it the frost seemed to have melted from mien and manner, leaving a living woman in the statue's place. I had thought her melancholy, but her lips were dressed in smiles, and frequent peals of low-toned laughter parted them like pleasant music; I had thought her pale, but in either cheek now bloomed a color deep and clear as any tint my palette could have given; I had thought her shy and proud at first, but with each moment her manner warmed, her speech grew franker and her whole figure seemed to glow and brighten as if a brilliant lamp were lit behind the pale shade she had worn before. But the eyes were the greatest surprise of all—I had fancied them dark, and found them the light, sensitive gray belonging to highly nervous temperaments. They were remarkable eyes; for though softly fringed with shadowy lashes they were not mild, but fiery and keen, with many lights and shadows in them as the pupils dilated, and the irids shone with a transparent lustre which varied with her varying words, and proved the existence of an ardent, imperious nature underneath the seeming snow.

They exercised a curious fascination over me and kept my own obedient to their will, although scarce conscious of it at the time and believing mine to be the controlling power. Wherein the charm lay I cannot tell; it was not the influence of a womanly presence alone, for fairer faces had smiled at me in vain; yet as I sat there I felt a pleasant quietude creep over me, I knew my voice had fallen to a lower key, my eye softened from its wonted cold indifference, my manner grown smooth and my demeanor changed to one almost as courtly as my friend's, who well deserved his soubriquet of "Louis the Debonair."

"It is because my long fret is over," I thought, and having something to gain, exerted myself to please so successfully that, soon emboldened by her gracious mood and the flattering compliments bestowed upon my earlier works, I ventured to tell my present strait and the daring hope I had conceived that she would help me through it. How I made this blunt request I cannot tell, but remember that it slipped over my tongue as smoothly as if I had meditated upon it for a week. I glanced over my shoulder as I spoke, fearing Louis might mar all with apology or reproof; but he was absorbed in the comely duenna, who was blushing like a girl at the half playful, half serious devotion he paid all womankind; and reassured, I waited, wondering how Miss Eure would receive my request. Very quietly; for with no change but a peculiar dropping of the lids, as if her eyes sometimes played the traitor to her will, she answered, smilingly.

"It is I who receive the honor, sir, not you, for genius possesses the privileges of royalty, and may claim subjects everywhere, sure that its choice ennobles and its power extends beyond the narrow bounds of custom, time and place. When shall I serve you, Mr. Erdmann?"

At any other time I should have felt surprised both at her and at myself; but just then, in the ardor of the propitious moment, I thought only of my work, and with many thanks for her great kindness left the day to her, secretly hoping she would name an early one. She sat silent an instant, then seemed to come to some determination, for when she spoke a shadow of mingled pain and patience swept across her face as if her resolve had cost her some sacrifice of pride or feeling.

"It is but right to tell you that I may not always have it in my power to give you the expression you desire to catch, for the eyes you honor by wishing to perpetuate are not strong and often fail me for a time. I have been utterly blind once and may be again, yet have no present cause to fear it, and if you can come to me on such days as they will serve your purpose, I shall be most glad to do my best for you. Another reason makes me bold to ask this favor of you, I cannot always summon this absent mood, and should certainly fail in a strange place; but in my own home, with all familiar things about me, I can more easily fall into one of my deep reveries and forget time by the hour together. Will this arrangement cause much inconvenience or delay? A room shall be prepared for you—kept inviolate as long as you desire it—and every facility my house affords is at your service, for I feel much interest in the work which is to add another success to your life."

She spoke regretfully at first, but ended with a cordial glance as if she had forgotten herself in giving pleasure to another. I felt that it must have cost her an effort to confess that such a dire affliction had ever darkened her youth and might still return to sadden her prime; this pity mingled with my expressions of gratitude for the unexpected interest she bestowed upon my work, and in a few words the arrangement was made, the day and hour fixed, and a great load off my mind. What the afterpiece was I never knew; Miss Eure stayed to please her young companion, Louis stayed to please himself, and I remained because I had not energy enough to go away. For, leaning where I first sat down, I still looked and listened with a dreamy sort of satisfaction to Miss Eure's low voice, as with downcast eyes, still shaded by her fan, she spoke enthusiastically and well of art (the one interesting theme to me) in a manner which proved that she had read and studied more than her modesty allowed her to acknowledge.

We parted like old friends at her carriage door, and as I walked away with Louis in the cool night air I felt like one who had been asleep in a close room, for I was both languid and drowsy, though a curious undercurrent of excitement still stirred my blood and tingled along my nerves. "A theatre is no place for me," I decided, and anxious to forget myself said aloud:

"Tell me all you know about that woman."

"What woman, Max?"

"Miss Agatha Eure, the owner of the eyes."

"Aha! smitten at last! That ever I should live to see our Benedict the victim of love at first sight!"

"Have done with your nonsense, and answer my question. I don't ask from mere curiosity, but that I may have some idea how to bear myself at these promised sittings; for it will never do to ask after her papa if she has none, to pay my respects to the old lady as her mother if she is only the duenna, or joke with the lad if he is the heir apparent."

"Do you mean to say that you asked her to sit to you?" cried Louis, falling back a step and staring at me with undisguised astonishment.

"Yes, why not?"

"Why, man, Agatha Eure is the haughtiest piece of humanity ever concocted; and I, with all my daring, never ventured to ask more than an occasional dance with her, and feel myself especially favored that she deigns to bow to me, and lets me pick up her gloves or carry her bouquet as a mark of supreme condescension. What witchcraft did you bring to bear upon her? and how did she grant your audacious request?"

"Agreed to it at once."

"Like an empress conferring knighthood, I fancy."

"Not at all. More like a pretty woman receiving a compliment to her beauty—though she is not pretty, by the way."

Louis indulged himself in the long, low whistle, which seems the only adequate expression for masculine surprise. I enjoyed his amazement, it was my turn to laugh now, and I did so, as I said:

"You are always railing at me for my avoidance of all womankind, but you see I have not lost the art of pleasing, for I won your haughty Agatha to my will in fifteen minutes, and am not only to paint her handsome eyes, but to do it at her own house, by her own request. I am beginning to find that, after years of effort, I have mounted a few more rounds of the social ladder than I was aware of, and may now confer as well as receive favors; for she seemed to think me the benefactor, and I rather enjoyed the novelty of the thing. Now tell your story of 'the haughtiest piece of humanity' ever known. I like her the better for that trait."

Louis nodded his head, and regarded the moon with an aspect of immense wisdom, as he replied:

"I understand it now; it all comes back to me, and my accusation holds good, only the love at first sight is on the other side. You shall have your story, but it may leave the picture in the lurch if it causes you to fly off, as you usually see fit to do when a woman's name is linked with your own. You never saw Miss Eure before; but what you say reminds me that she has seen you, for one day last autumn, as I was driving with her and old madame—a mark of uncommon favor, mind you—we saw you striding along, with your hat over your eyes, looking very much like a comet streaming down the street. It was crowded, and as you waited at the crossing you spoke to Jack Mellot, and while talking pulled off your hat and tumbled your hair about, in your usual fashion, when very earnest. We were blockaded by cars and coaches for a moment, so Miss Eure had a fine opportunity to feast her eyes upon you, 'though you are not pretty, by the way.' She asked your name, and when I told her she gushed out into a charming little stream of interest in your daubs, and her delight at seeing their creator; all of which was not agreeable to me, for I considered myself much the finer work of art of the two. Just then you caught up a shabby child with a big basket, took them across, under our horses' noses, with never a word for me, though I called to you, and, diving into the crowd, disappeared. 'I like that,' said Miss Eure; and as we drove on she asked questions, which I answered in a truly Christian manner, doing you no harm, old lad; for I told all you had fought through, with the courage of a stout-hearted man, all you had borne with the patience of a woman, and what a grand future lay open to you, if you chose to accept and use it, making quite a fascinating little romance of it, I assure you. There the matter dropped. I forgot it till this minute, but it accounts for the ease with which you gained your first suit, and is prophetic of like success in a second and more serious one. She is young, well-born, lovely to those who love her, and has a fortune and position which will lift you at once to the topmost round of the long ladder you've been climbing all these years, I wish you joy, Max."

"Thank you. I've no time for lovemaking, and want no fortune but that which I earn for myself. I am already married to a fairer wife than Miss Eure, so you may win and wear the lofty lady yourself."

Louis gave a comical groan.

"I've tried that, and failed; for she is too cold to be warmed by any flame of mine, though she is wonderfully attractive when she likes, and I hover about her even now like an infatuated moth, who beats his head against the glass and never reaches the light within. No; you must thankfully accept the good the gods bestow. Let Art be your Leah, but Agatha your Rachel. And so, good-night!"

"Stay and tell me one thing—is she an orphan?"

"Yes; the last of a fine old race, with few relatives and few friends, for death has deprived her of the first, and her own choice of the last. The lady you saw with her plays propriety in her establishment; the lad is Mrs. Snow's son, and fills the role of *cavaliere-servente;* for Miss Eure is a Diana toward men in general, and leads a quietly luxurious life among her books, pencils and music, reading and studying all manner of things few women of two-and-twenty care to know. But she has the wit to see that a woman's mission is to be charming, and when she has sufficient motive for the exertion she fulfils that mission most successfully, as I know to my sorrow. Now let me off, and be for ever grateful for the good turn I have done you to-night, both in urging you to go to the theatre and helping you to your wish when you got there."

We parted merrily, but his words lingered in my memory, and half unconsciously exerted a new influence over me, for they flattered the three ruling passions that make or mar the fortunes of us all—pride, ambition and self-love. I wanted power, fame and ease, and all seemed waiting for me, not in the dim future but the actual present, if my friend's belief was to be relied upon; and remembering all I had seen and heard that night, I felt that it was not utterly without foundation. I pleased myself for an idle hour in dreaming dreams of what might be; finding that amusement began to grow dangerously attractive, I demolished my castles in the air with the last whiff of my meerschaum, and fell asleep, echoing my own words:

"Art is my wife, I will have no other!"

Punctual to the moment I went to my appointment, and while waiting an answer to my ring took an exterior survey of Miss Eure's house. One of an imposing granite block, it stood in a West End square, with every sign of unostentatious opulence about it. I was very susceptible to all influences, either painful or pleasant, and as I stood there the bland atmosphere that surrounded me seemed most attractive; for my solitary life had been plain and poor, with little time for ease, and few ornaments to give it grace. Now I seemed to have won the right to enjoy both if I would; I no longer felt out of place there, and with this feeling came the wish to try the sunny side of life, and see if its genial gifts would prove more inspiring than the sterner masters I had been serving so long.

The door opened in the middle of my reverie, and I was led through an anteroom, lined with warmhued pictures, to a large apartment, which had been converted into an impromptu studio by some one who understood all the requisites for such a place.

The picture, my easel and other necessaries had preceded me, and I thought to have spent a good hour in arranging matters. All was done, however, with a skill that surprised me; the shaded windows, the carefully-arranged brushes, the proper colors already on the palette, the easel and picture placed as they should be, and a deep curtain hung behind a small dais, where I fancied my model was to sit. The room was empty as I entered, and with the brief message, "Miss Eure will be down directly," the man noiselessly departed.

I stood and looked about me with great satisfaction, thinking, "I cannot fail to work well surrounded by such agreeable sights and sounds." The house was very still, for the turmoil of the city was subdued to a murmur, like the far-off music of the sea; a soft gloom filled the room, divided by one strong ray that fell athwart my picture, gifting it with warmth and light. Through a half-open door I saw the green vista of a conservatory, full of fine blendings of color, and wafts of many odors blown to me by the west wind rustling through orange trees and slender palms; while the only sound that broke the silence was the voice of a flame-colored foreign bird, singing a plaintive little strain like a sorrowful lament. I liked this scene, and, standing in the doorway, was content to look, listen and enjoy, forgetful of time, till a slight stir made me turn and for a moment look straight before me with a startled aspect. It seemed as if my picture had left its frame; for, standing on the narrow dais, clearly defined against the dark background, stood the living likeness of the figure I had painted, the same white folds falling from neck to ankle, the same shadowy hair, and slender hands locked together, as if wrung in slow despair; and fixed full upon my own the weird, unseeing eyes, which made the face a pale mask, through which the haunted spirit spoke eloquently, with its sleepless anguish and remorse.

"Good morning, Miss Eure; how shall I thank you?" I began, but stopped abruptly, for without speaking she waved me towards the easel with a gesture which seemed to say, "Prove your gratitude by industry."

"Very good," thought I, "if she likes the theatrical style she shall have it. It is evident she has studied her part and will play it well,

I will do the same, and as Louis recommends, take the good the gods send me while I may."

Without more ado I took my place and fell to work; but, though never more eager to get on, with each moment that I passed I found my interest in the picture grow less and less intent, and with every glance at my model found that it was more and more difficult to look away. Beautiful she was not, but the wild and woful figure seemed to attract me as no Hebe, Venus or sweet-faced Psyche had ever done. My hand moved slower and slower, the painted face grew dimmer and dimmer, my glances lingered longer and longer, and presently palette and brushes rested on my knee, as I leaned back in the deep chair and gave myself up to an uninterrupted stare. I knew that it was rude, knew that it was a trespass on Miss Eure's kindness as well as a breach of good manners, but I could not help it, for my eyes seemed beyond my control, and though I momentarily expected to see her color rise and hear some warning of the lapse of time, I never looked away, and soon forgot to imagine her feelings in the mysterious confusion of my own.

I was first conscious of a terrible fear that I ought to speak or move, which seemed impossible, for my eyelids began to be weighed down by a delicious drowsiness in spite of all my efforts to keep them open. Everything grew misty, and the beating of my heart sounded like the rapid, irregular roll of a muffled drum; then a strange weight seemed to oppress and cause me to sigh long and deeply. But soon the act of breathing appeared to grow unnecessary, for a sensation of wonderful airiness came over me, and I felt as if I could float away like a thistledown. Presently every sense seemed to fall asleep, and in the act of dropping both palette and brush I drifted away into a sea of blissful repose, where nothing disturbed me but a fragmentary dream that came and went like a lingering gleam of consciousness through the new experience which had befallen me.

I seemed to be still in the quiet room, still leaning in the deep chair with half-closed eyes, still watching the white figure before me, but that had changed. I saw a smile break over the lips, something like triumph flash into the eyes, sudden color flush the cheeks, and the rigid hands lifted to gather up and put the long hair back; then with noiseless steps it came nearer and nearer till it stood beside me. For awhile it paused there mute and intent, I felt the eager gaze searching my face, but it caused no displeasure; for I seemed to be looking down at myself, as if soul and body had parted company and I was gifted with a double life. Suddenly the vision laid a light hand on my wrist and touched my temples, while a shade of anxiety seemed to flit across its face as it turned and vanished. A dreamy wonder regarding its return woke within me, then my sleep deepened into utter oblivion, for how long I cannot tell. A pungent odor seemed to recall me to the same half wakeful state. I dimly saw a woman's arm holding a glittering object before me, when the fragrance came; an unseen hand stirred my hair with the grateful drip of water, and once there came a touch like the pressure of lips upon my forehead, soft and warm, but gone in an instant. These new sensations grew rapidly more and more defined; I clearly saw a bracelet on the arm and read the Arabic characters engraved upon the golden coins that formed it; I heard the rustle of garments, the hurried breathing of some near presence, and felt the cool sweep of a hand passing to and fro across my forehead. At this point my thoughts began to shape themselves into words, which came slowly and seemed strange to me as I searched for and connected them, then a heavy sigh rose and broke at my lips, and the sound of my own voice woke me, drowsily echoing the last words I had spoken:

"Good morning, Miss Eure; how shall I thank you?"

To my great surprise the well-remembered voice answered quietly:

"Good morning, Mr. Erdmann; will you have some lunch before you begin?"

How I opened my eyes and got upon my feet was never clear to me, but the first object I saw was Miss Eure coming towards me with a glass in her hand. My expression must have been dazed and imbecile in the extreme, for to add to my bewilderment the tragic robes had disappeared, the dishevelled hair was gathered in shining coils under a Venetian net of silk and gold, a white embroidered wrapper replaced the muslins Lady Macbeth had worn, and a countenance half playful, half anxious, now smiled where I had last seen so sorrowful an aspect. The fear of having committed some great absurdity and endangered my success brought me right with a little shock of returning thought. I collected myself, gave a look about the room, a dizzy bow to her, and put my hand to my head with a vague idea that something was wrong there. In doing this I discovered that my hair was wet, which slight fact caused me to exclaim abruptly:

"Miss Eure, what have I been doing? Have I had a fit? been asleep? or do you deal in magic and rock your guests off into oblivion without a moment's warning?"

Standing before me with uplifted eyes, she answered, smiling:

"No, none of these have happened to you; the air from the Indian plants in the conservatory was too powerful, I think; you were a little faint, but closing the door and opening a window has restored you, and a glass of wine will perfect the cure, I hope."

She was offering the glass as she spoke. I took it but forgot to thank her, for on the arm extended to me was the bracelet never seen so near by my waking eyes, yet as familiar as if my vision had come again. Something struck me disagreeably, and I spoke out with my usual bluntness.

"I never fainted in my life, and have an impression that people do not dream when they swoon. Now I did, and so vivid was it that I still remember the characters engraved on the trinket you wear, for that played a prominent part in my vision. Shall I describe them as proof of it, Miss Eure?"

Her arm dropped at her side and her eyes fell for a moment as I spoke; then she glanced up unchanged, saying as she seated herself and motioned me to do the same:

"No, rather tell the dream, and taste these grapes while you amuse me."

I sat down and obeyed her. She listened attentively, and when I ended explained the mystery in the simplest manner.

"You are right in the first part of your story. I did yield to a whim which seized me when I saw your picture, and came down *en costume,* hoping to help you by keeping up the illusion. You began, as canvas and brushes prove; I stood motionless till you turned pale and regarded me with a strange expression; at first I thought it might be inspiration, as your friend Yorke would say, but presently you dropped everything out of your hands and fell back in your chair. I took the liberty of treating you like a woman, for I bathed your temples and wielded my vinaigrette most energetically till you revived and began to talk of 'Rachel, art, castles in the air, and your wife Lady Macbeth;' then I slipped away and modernized myself, ordered some refreshments for you, and waited till you wished me 'Good-morning.' "

She was laughing so infectiously that I could not resist joining her and accepting her belief, for curious as the whole affair seemed to me I could account for it in no other way. She was winningly kind, and urged me not to resume my task, but I was secretly disgusted with myself for such a display of weakness, and finding her hesitation caused solely by fears for me, I persisted, and seating her, painted as I had never done before. Every sense seemed unwontedly acute, and hand and eye obeyed me with a docility they seldom showed. Miss Eure sat where I placed her, silent and intent, but her face did not wear the tragic aspect it had worn before, though she tried to recall it. This no longer troubled me, for the memory of the vanished face was more clearly before me than her own, and with but few and hasty glances at my model, I reproduced it with a speed and skill that filled me with delight. The striking of a clock reminded me that I had far exceeded the specified time, and that even a woman's patience has limits; so concealing my regret at losing so auspicious a mood, I laid down my brush, leaving my work unfinished, yet glad to know I had the right to come again, and complete it in a place and presence which proved so inspiring.

Miss Eure would not look at it till it was all done, saying in reply to my thanks for the pleasant studio she had given me—"I was not quite unselfish in that, and owe you an apology for venturing to meddle with your property; but it gave me real satisfaction to arrange these things, and restore this room to the aspect it wore three years ago. I, too, was an artist then, and dreamed aspiring dreams here, but was arrested on the threshold of my career by loss of sight; and hard as it seemed then to give up all my longings, I see now that it was better so, for a few years later it would have killed me. I have learned to desire for others what I can never hope for myself, and try to find pleasure in their success, unembittered by regrets for my own defeat. Let this explain my readiness to help you, my interest in your work and my best wishes for your present happiness and future fame."

The look of resignation, which accompanied her words, touched me more than a flood of complaints, and the thought of all she had lost woke such sympathy and pity in my frosty heart, that I involuntarily pressed the hand that could never wield a brush again. Then for the first time I saw those keen eyes soften and grow dim with unshed tears; this gave them the one charm they needed to be beautiful as well as penetrating, and as they met my own, so womanly sweet and grateful, I felt that one might love her while that mood remained. But it passed as rapidly as it came, and when we parted in the anteroom the cold, quiet lady bowed me out, and the tender-faced girl was gone.

I never told Louis all the incidents of that

first sitting, but began my story where the real interest ended; and Miss Eure was equally silent, through forgetfulness or for some good reason of her own. I went several times again, yet though the conservatory door stood open I felt no ill effects from the Indian plants that still bloomed there, dreamed no more dreams, and Miss Eure no more enacted the somnambulist. I found an indefinable charm in that pleasant room, a curious interest in studying its mistress, who always met me with a smile, and parted with a look of unfeigned regret. Louis rallied me upon my absorption, but it caused me no uneasiness, for it was not love that led me there, and Miss Eure knew it. I never had forgotten our conversation on that first night, and with every interview the truth of my friend's suspicions grew more and more apparent to me. Agatha Eure was a strong-willed, imperious woman, used to command all about her and see her last wish gratified; but now she was conscious of a presence she could not command, a wish she dare not utter, and, though her womanly pride sealed her lips, her eyes often traitorously betrayed the longing of her heart. She was sincere in her love for art, and behind that interest in that concealed, even from herself, her love for the artist; but the most indomitable passion given humanity cannot long be hidden. Agatha soon felt her weakness, and vainly struggled to subdue it. I soon knew my power, and owned its subtle charm, though I disdained to use it.

The picture was finished, exhibited and won me all, and more than I had dared to hope; for rumor served me a good turn, and whispers of Miss Eure's part in my success added zest to public curiosity and warmth to public praise. I enjoyed the little stir it caused, found admiration a sweet draught after a laborious year, and felt real gratitude to the woman who had helped me win it. If my work had proved a failure I should have forgotten her, and been an humbler, happier man; it did not, and she became a part of my success. Her name was often spoken in the same breath with mine, her image was kept before me by no exertion of my own, till the memories it brought with it grew familiar as old friends, and slowly ripened into a purpose which, being born of ambition and not love, bore bitter fruit, and wrought out its own retribution for a sin against myself and her.

The more I won the more I demanded, the higher I climbed the more eager I became; and, at last, seeing how much I could gain by a single step, resolved to take it, even though I knew it to be a false one. Other men married for the furtherance of their ambitions, why should not I? Years ago I had given up love of home for love of fame, and the woman who might have made me what I should be had meekly yielded all, wished me a happy future, and faded from my world, leaving me only a bitter memory, a veiled picture and a quiet grave my feet never visited but once. Miss Eure loved me, sympathised in my aims, understood my tastes; she could give all I asked to complete the purpose of my life, and lift me at once and for ever from the hard lot I had struggled with for thirty years. One word would win the miracle, why should I hesitate to utter it?

I did not long—for three months from the day I first entered that shadowy room I stood there intent on asking her to be my wife. As I waited I lived again the strange hour once passed there, and felt as if it had been the beginning of another dream whose awakening was yet to come. I asked myself if the hard healthful reality was not better than such feverish visions, however brilliant, and the voice that is never silent when we interrogate it with sincerity answered, "Yes." "No matter, I choose to dream, so let the phantom of a wife come to me here as the phantom of a lover came to me so long ago." As I uttered these defiant words aloud, like a visible reply, Agatha appeared upon the threshold of the door. I knew she had heard me—for again I saw the soft-eyed, tender girl, and opened my arms to her without a word. She came at once, and clinging to me with unwonted tears upon her cheek, unwonted fervor in her voice, touched my forehead, as she had done in that earlier dream, whispering like one still doubtful of her happiness—

"Oh, Max! be kind to me, for in all the world I have only you to love."

I promised, and broke that promise in less than a year.

Part II

We were married quietly, went away till the nine days gossip was over, spent our honeymoon as that absurd month is usually spent, and came back to town with the first autumnal frosts; Agatha regretting that I was no longer entirely her own, I secretly thanking heaven that I might drop the lover, and begin my work again, for I was as an imprisoned creature in that atmosphere of "love in idleness," though my bonds were only a pair of loving arms. Madame Snow and son departed, we settled ourselves in the fine house and then endowed with every worldly blessing, I looked about me, believing myself master of my fate, but found I was its slave.

If Agatha could have joined me in my work we might have been happy; if she could have solaced herself with other pleasures and left me to my own, we might have been content; if she had loved me less, we might have gone our separate ways, and yet been friends like many another pair; but I soon found that her affection was of that exacting nature which promises but little peace unless met by one as warm. I had nothing but regard to give her, for it was not in her power to stir a deeper passion in me; I told her this before our marriage, told her I was a cold, hard man, wrapt in a single purpose; but what woman believes such confessions while her heart still beats fast with the memory of her betrothal? She said everything was possible to love, and prophesied a speedy change; I knew it would not come, but having given my warning left the rest to time. I hoped to lead a quiet life and prove that adverse circumstances, not the want of power, had kept me from excelling in the profession I had chosen; but to my infinite discomfort Agatha turned jealous of my art, for finding the mistress dearer than the wife, she tried to wean me from it, and seemed to feel that having given me love, wealth and ease, I should ask no more, but play the obedient subject to a generous queen. I rebelled against this, told her that one-half my time should be hers, the other belonged to me, and I would so employ it that it should bring honor to the name I had given her. But, Agatha was not used to seeing her will thwarted or her pleasure sacrificed to another, and soon felt that though I scrupulously fulfilled my promise, the one task was irksome, the other all absorbing; that though she had her husband at her side his heart was in his studio, and the hours spent with her were often the most listless in his day. Then began that sorrowful experience old as Adam's reproaches to Eve; we both did wrong, and neither repented; both were self-willed, sharp tongued and proud, and before six months of wedded life had passed we had known many of those scenes which so belittle character and lessen self-respect.

Agatha's love lived through all, and had I answered its appeals by patience, self-denial and genial friendship, if no warmer tie could exist, I might have spared her an early death, and myself from years of bitterest remorse; but I did not. Then her forbearance ended and my subtle punishment began.

"Away again to-night, Max? You have been shut up all day, and I hoped to have you to myself this evening. Hear how the storm rages without, see how cheery I have made all within for you, so put your hat away and stay, for this hour belongs to me, and I claim it."

Agatha took me prisoner as she spoke, and pointed to the cosy nest she had prepared for me. The room was bright and still; the lamp shone clear; the fire glowed; warm-hued curtains muffled the war of gust and sleet without; books, music, a wide-armed seat and a woman's wistful face invited me; but none of these things could satisfy me just then, and though I drew my wife nearer, smoothed her shining hair, and kissed the reproachful lips, I did not yield.

"You must let me go, Agatha, for the great German artist is here, I had rather give a year of life than miss this meeting with him. I have devoted many evenings to you, and though this hour is yours I shall venture to take it, and offer you a morning call instead. Here are novels, new songs, an instrument, embroidery and a dog, who can never offend by moody silence or unpalatable conversation—what more can a contented woman ask, surely not an absent-minded husband?"

"Yes, just that and nothing more, for she loves him, and he can supply a want that none of these things can. See how pretty I have tried to make myself for you alone; stay, Max, and make me happy."

"Dear, I shall find my pretty wife tomorrow, but the great painter will be gone; let me go, Agatha, and make me happy."

She drew herself from my arm, saying with a flash of the eye—"Max, you are a tyrant!"

"Am I? then you made me so with too much devotion."

"Ah, if you loved me as I loved there would be no selfishness on your part, no reproaches on mine. What shall I do to make myself dearer, Max?"

"Give me more liberty."

"Then I should lose you entirely, and lead the life of a widow. Oh, Max, this is hard, this is bitter, to give all and receive nothing in return."

She spoke passionately, and the truth of her reproach stung me, for I answered with that coldness that always wounded her:

"Do you count an honest name, sincere regard and much gratitude as nothing? I have given you these, and ask only peace and freedom in return. I desire to do justice to you and to myself, but I am not like you, never can be, and you must not hope it. You say love is allpowerful, prove it upon me, I am willing to be the fondest of husbands if I can; teach me, win me in spite of myself, and make me what you will; but leave me a little time to live and labor for that which is dearer to me than your faulty lord and master can ever be to you."

"Shall I do this?" and her face kindled as she put the question.

"Yes, here is an amusement for you, use what arts you will, make your love irresistible, soften my hard nature, convert me into your shadow, subdue me till I come at your call like a pet dog, and when you make your presence more powerful than painting I will own that you have won your will and made your theory good."

I was smiling as I spoke, for the twelve labors of Hercules seemed less impossible than this, but Agatha watched me with her glittering eyes; and answered slowly—

"I will do it. Now go, and enjoy your liberty while you may, but remember when I have conquered that you dared me to it, and keep your part of the compact. Promise this." She offered me her hand with a strange expression—I took it, said good-night, and hurried away, still smiling at the curious challenge given and accepted.

Agatha told me to enjoy my liberty, and I tried to do so that very night, but failed most signally, for I had not been an hour in the brilliant company gathered to meet the celebrated guest before I found it impossible to banish the thought of my solitary wife. I had left her often, yet never felt disturbed by more than a passing twinge of that uncomfortable bosom friend called conscience; but now the interest of the hour seemed lessened by regret, for through varying conversation held with those about me, mingling with the fine music that I heard, looking at me from every woman's face, and thrusting itself into my mind at every turn, came a vague, disturbing selfreproach, which slowly deepened to a strong anxiety. My attention wandered, words seemed to desert me, fancy to be frostbound, and even in the presence of the great man I had so ardently desired to see I could neither enjoy his society nor play my own part well. More than once I found myself listening for Agatha's voice; more than once I looked behind me expecting to see her figure, and more than once I resolved to go, with no desire to meet her.

"It is an acute fit of what women call nervousness; I will not yield to it," I thought, and plunged into the gayest group I saw, supped, talked, sang a song, and broke down; told a witty story, and spoiled it; laughed and tried to bear myself like the lightest-hearted guest in the rooms; but it would not do, for stronger and stronger grew the strange longing to go home, and soon it became uncontrollable. A foreboding fear that something had happened oppressed me, and suddenly leaving the festival at its height I drove home as if life and death depended on the saving of a second. Like one pursuing or pursued I rode, eager only to be there; yet when I stood on my own threshold I asked myself wonderingly, "Why such haste?" and stole in ashamed at my early return. The storm beat without, but within all was serene and still, and with noiseless steps I went up to the room where I had left my wife, pausing a moment at the half open door to collect myself, lest she should see the disorder of both mind and mien. Looking in I saw her sitting with neither book nor work beside her, and after a momentary glance began to think my anxiety had not been causeless, for she sat erect and motionless as an inanimate figure of intense thought; her eyes were fixed, face colorless, with an expression of iron determination, as if every energy of mind and body were wrought up to the achievement of a single purpose. There was something in the rigid attitude and stern aspect of this familiar shape that filled me with dismay, and found vent in the abrupt exclamation,

"Agatha, what is it?"

She sprang up like a steel spring when the pressure is removed, saw me, and struck her hands together with a wild gesture of surprise, alarm or pleasure, which I could not tell, for in the act she dropped into her seat white and breathless as if smitten with sudden death. Unspeakably shocked, I bestirred myself till she recovered, and though pale and spent, as if with some past exertion, soon seemed quite herself again.

"Agatha, what were you thinking of when I came in?" I asked, as she sat leaning against me with half closed eyes and a faint smile on her lips, as if the unwonted caresses I bestowed upon her were more soothing than any cordial I could give. Without stirring she replied,

"Of you, Max. I was longing for you, with heart and soul and will. You told me to win you in spite of yourself; and I was sending my love to find and bring you home. Did it reach you? did it lead you back and make you glad to come?"

A peculiar chill ran through me as I listened, though her voice was quieter, her manner gentler than usual as she spoke. She seemed to have such faith in her tender fancy, such assurance of its efficacy, and such a near approach to certain knowledge of its success, that I disliked the thought of continuing the topic, and answered cheerfully,

"My own conscience brought me home, dear; for, discovering that I had left my peace of mind behind me, I came back to find it. If your task is to cost a scene like this it will do more harm than good to both of us, so keep your love from such uncanny wanderings through time and space, and win me with less dangerous arts."

She smiled her strange smile, folded my

hand in her own, and answered, with soft exultation in her voice,

"It will not happen so again, Max; but I am glad, most glad you came, for it proves I have some power over this wayward heart of yours, where I shall knock until it opens wide and takes me in."

The events of that night made a deep impression on me, for from that night my life was changed. Agatha left me entirely free, never asked my presence, never upbraided me for long absences or silences when together. She seemed to find happiness in her belief that she should yet subdue me, and though I smiled at this in my indifference, there was something half pleasant, half pathetic in the thought of this proud woman leaving all warmer affections for my negligent friendship, the sight of this young wife laboring to win her husband's heart. At first I tried to be all she asked, but soon relapsed into my former life, and finding no reproaches followed, believed I should enjoy it as never before—but I did not. As weeks passed I slowly became conscious that some new power had taken possession of me, swaying my whole nature to its will; a power alien yet sovereign. Fitfully it worked, coming upon me when least desired, enforcing its commands regardless of time, place or mood; mysterious yet irresistible in its strength, this mental tyrant led me at all hours, in all stages of anxiety, repugnance and rebellion, from all pleasures or employments, straight to Agatha. If I sat at my easel the sudden summons came, and wondering at myself I obeyed it, to find her busied in some cheerful occupation, with apparently no thought or wish for me. If I left home I often paused abruptly in my walk or drive, turned and hurried back, simply because I could not resist the impulse that controlled me. If she went away I seldom failed to follow, and found no peace till I was at her side again. I grew moody and restless, slept ill, dreamed wild dreams, and often woke and wandered aimlessly, as if sent upon an unknown errand. I could not fix my mind upon my work; a spell seemed to have benumbed imagination and robbed both brain and hand of power to conceive and skill to execute.

At first I fancied this was only the reaction of entire freedom after long captivity, but I soon found I was bound to a more exacting mistress than my wife had ever been. Then I suspected that it was only the perversity of human nature, and that having gained my wish it grew valueless, and I longed for that which I had lost; but it was not this, for distasteful as my present life had become, the other seemed still more so when I recalled it. For a time I believed that Agatha might be right, that I was really learning to love her, and this unquiet mood was the awakening of that passion which comes swift and strong when it comes to such as I. If I had never loved I might have clung to this belief, but the memory of that earlier affection, so genial, entire and sweet, proved that the present fancy was only a delusion; for searching deeply into myself to discover the truth of this, I found that Agatha was no dearer, and to my own dismay detected a covert dread lurking there, harmless and vague, but threatening to deepen into aversion or resentment for some unknown offence; and while I accused myself of an unjust and ungenerous weakness, I shrank from the thought of her, even while I sought her with the assiduity but not the ardor of a lover.

Long I pondered over this inexplicable

state of mind, but found no solution of it; for I would not own, either to myself or Agatha, that the shadow of her prophecy had come to pass, though its substance was still wanting. She sometimes looked inquiringly into my face with those strange eyes of hers, sometimes chid me with a mocking smile when she found me sitting idly before my easel without a line or tint given though hours had passed; and often, when driven by that blind impulse I sought her anxiously among her friends, she would glance at those about her, saying, with a touch of triumph in her mien, "Am I not an enviable wife to have inspired such devotion in this grave husband?" Once, remembering her former words, I asked her playfully if she still "sent her love to find and bring me home?" but she only shook her head and answered, sadly,

"Oh, no; my love was burdensome to you, so I have rocked it to sleep and laid it where it will not trouble you again."

At last I decided that some undetected physical infirmity caused my disquiet, for years of labor and privation might well have worn the delicate machinery of heart or brain, and this warning suggested the wisdom of consulting medical skill in time. This thought grew as month after month increased my mental malady and began to tell upon my hitherto unbroken health. I wondered if Agatha knew how listless, hollow-eyed and wan I had grown; but she never spoke of it, and an unconquerable reserve kept me from uttering a complaint to her.

One day I resolved to bear it no longer, and hurried away to an old friend in whose skill and discretion I had entire faith. He was out, and while I waited I took up a book that lay among the medical works upon his table. I read a page, then a chapter, turning leaf after leaf with a rapid hand, devouring paragraph after paragraph with an eager eye. An hour passed, still I read on. Dr. L—— did not come, but I did not think of that, and when I laid down the book I no longer needed him, for in that hour I had discovered a new world, had seen the diagnosis of my symptoms set forth in unmistakable terms, and found the key to the mystery in the one word—Magnetism. This was years ago, before spirits had begun their labors for good or ill, before ether and hashish had gifted humanity with eternities of bliss in a second, and while Mesmer's mystical discoveries were studied only by the scientific or philosophical few. I knew nothing of these things, for my whole life had led another way, and no child could be more ignorant of the workings or extent of this wonderful power. There was Indian blood in my veins, and superstition lurked there still; consequently the knowledge that I was a victim of this occult magic came upon me like an awful revelation, and filled me with a storm of wrath, disgust and dread.

Like an enchanted spirit who has found the incantation that will free it from subjection, I rejoiced with a grim satisfaction even while I cursed myself for my long blindness, and with no thought for anything but instant accusation on my part, instant confession and atonement on hers, I went straight home, straight into Agatha's presence, and there, in words as brief as bitter, told her that her reign was over. All that was sternest, hottest and most unforgiving ruled me then, and like fire to fire roused a spirit equally strong and high. I might have subdued her by juster and more generous words, but remembering the humiliation of my secret slavery I forgot my own offence in hers, and set no curb on tongue or temper, letting the storm she had raised fall upon her with the suddenness of an unwonted, unexpected outburst.

As I spoke her face changed from its first dismay to a defiant calmness that made it hard as rock and cold as ice, while all expression seemed concentrated in her eye, which burned on me with an unwavering light. There was no excitement in her manner, no sign of fear, or shame, or grief in her mien, and when she answered me her voice was untremulous and clear as when I heard it first.

"Have you done? Then hear me: I knew you long before you dreamed that such a woman as Agatha Eure existed. I was solitary, and longed to be sincerely loved. I was rich, yet I could not buy what is unpurchasable; I was young, yet I could not make my youth sweet with affection; for nowhere did I see the friend whose nature was akin to mine until you passed before me, and I felt at once, 'There is the one I seek!' I never yet desired that I did not possess the coveted object, and believed I should not fail now. Years ago I learned the mysterious gift I was endowed with, and fostered it; for, unblessed with beauty, I hoped its silent magic might draw others near enough to see, under this cold exterior, the woman's nature waiting there. The first night you saw me I yielded to an irresistible longing to attract your eye, and for a moment see the face I had learned to love looking into mine. You know how well I succeeded—you know your own lips asked the favor I was so glad to give, and your own will led you to me. That day I made another trial of my skill and succeeded beyond my hopes, but dared not repeat it, for your strong nature was not easily subdued, it was too perilous a game for me to play, and I resolved that no delusion should make you mine. I would have a free gift or none. You offered me your hand, and believing that it held a loving heart, I took it, to find that heart barred against me, and another woman's name engraved upon its door. Was this a glad discovery for a wife to make? Do you wonder she reproached you when she saw her hopes turn to ashes, and could no longer conceal from herself that she was only a stepping-stone to lift an ambitious man to a position which she could not share? You think me weak and wicked; look back upon the year nearly done and ask yourself if many young wives have such a record of neglect, despised love, unavailing sacrifices, long suffering patience and deepening despair? I had been reading the tear-stained pages of this record when you bid me win you if I could; and with a bitter sense of the fitness of such a punishment, I resolved to do it, still cherishing a hope that some spark of affection might be found. I soon saw the vanity of such a hope, and this hard truth goaded me to redouble my efforts till I had entirely subjugated that arrogant spirit of yours, and made myself master where I would so gladly have been a loving subject. Do you think I have not suffered? have not wept bitter tears in secret, and been wrung by sharper anguish than you have ever known? If you had given any sign of affection, shown any wish to return to me, any shadow of regret for the wrong you had done me, I would have broken my wand like Prospero, and used no magic but the pardon of a faithful heart. You did not, and it has come to this. Before you condemn me, remember that you dared me to do it—that you bid me make my presence more powerful than Art—bid me convert you to my shadow, and subdue you till you came like a pet dog at my call. Have I not obeyed you? Have I not kept my part of the compact? Now keep yours."

There was something terrible in hearing words whose truth wounded while they fell, uttered in a voice whose concentrated passion made its tones distinct and deep, as if an accusing spirit read them from that book whose dread records never are effaced. My hot blood cooled, my harsh mood softened, and though it still burned, my resentment sank lower, for, remembering the little life to be, I wrestled with myself, and won humility enough to say, with regretful energy:

"Forgive me, Agatha, and let this sad past sleep. I have wronged you, but I believed I sinned no more than many another man who, finding love dead, hoped to feed his hunger with friendship and ambition. I never thought of such an act till I saw affection in your face; that tempted me, and I tried to repay all you gave me by the offer of the hand you mutely asked. It was a bargain often made in this strange world of ours, often repented as we repent now. Shall we abide by it, and by mutual forbearance recover mutual peace? or shall I leave you free, to make life sweeter with a better man, and find myself poor and honest as when we met?"

Something in my words stung her; and regarding me with the same baleful aspect, she lifted her slender hand, so wasted since I made it mine, that the single ornament it wore dropped into her palm, and holding it up, she said, as if prompted by the evil genius that lies hidden in every heart:

"I will do neither. I have outlived my love, but pride still remains; and I will not do as you have done, take cold friendship or selfish ambition to fill an empty heart; I will not be pitied as an injured woman, or pointed at as one who staked all on a man's faith and lost; I will have atonement for my long-suffering—you owe me this, and I claim it. Henceforth you are the slave of the ring, and when I command you must obey, for I possess a charm you cannot defy. It is too late to ask for pity, pardon, liberty or happier life; law and gospel joined us, and as yet law and gospel cannot put us asunder. You have brought this fate upon yourself, accept it, submit to it, for I have bought you with my wealth, I hold you with my mystic art, and body and soul, Max Erdmann, you are mine!"

I knew it was all over then, for a woman never flings such taunts in her husband's teeth till patience, hope and love are gone. A desperate purpose sprung up within me as I listened, yet I delayed a moment before I uttered it, with a last desire to spare us both.

"Agatha, do you mean that I am to lead the life I have been leading for three months—a life of spiritual slavery worse than any torment of the flesh?"

"I do."

"Are you implacable? and will you rob me of all self-control, all peace, all energy, all hope of gaining that for which I have paid so costly a price?"

"I will."

"Take back all you have given me, take my good name, my few friends, my hard-earned success; leave me stripped of every earthly blessing, but free me from this unnatural subjection, which is more terrible to me than death!"

"I will not!"

"Then your own harsh decree drives me from you, for I will break the bond that holds me, I will go out of this house and never cross its threshold while I live—never look into the face which has wrought me all this ill. There is no law, human or divine, that can give you a right to usurp the mastery of another will, and if it costs life and reason I will not submit to it."

"Go when and where you choose, put land and sea between us, break what ties you may, there is one you cannot dissolve, and when I summon you, in spite of all resistance, you must come."

"I swear I will not!"

I spoke out of a blind and bitter passion, but I kept my oath. How her eyes glittered as she lifted up that small pale hand of hers, pointed with an ominous gesture to the ring, and answered:

"Try it."

As she spoke like a sullen echo came the crash of the heavy picture that hung before us. It bore Lady Macbeth's name, but it was a painted image of my wife. I shuddered as I saw it fall, for to my superstitious fancy it seemed a fateful incident; but Agatha laughed a low metallic laugh that made me cold to hear, and whispered like a sibyl:

"Accept the omen; that is a symbol of the Art you worship so idolatrously that a woman's heart was sacrificed for its sake. See where it lies in ruins at your feet, never to bring you honor, happiness or peace; for I speak the living truth when I tell you that your ambitious hopes will vanish the cloud now rising like a veil between us, and the memory of this year will haunt you day and night, till the remorse you painted shall be written upon heart, and face, and life. Now go!"

Her swift words and forceful gesture seemed to banish me for ever, and, like one walking in his sleep, I left her there, a stern, still figure, with its shattered image at its feet.

That instant I departed, but not far—for as yet I could not clearly see which way duty led me. I made no confidante, asked no sympathy or help, told no one of my purpose, but resolving to take no decisive step rashly, I went away to a country house of Agatha's, just beyond the city, as I had once done before when busied on a work that needed solitude and quiet, so that if gossip rose it might be harmless to us both. Then I sat down and thought. Submit I would not, desert her utterly I could not, but I dared defy her, and I did; for as if some viewless spirit whispered the suggestion in my ear, I determined to oppose my will to hers, to use her weapons if I could, and teach her to be merciful through suffering like my own. She had confessed my power to draw her to me, in spite of coldness, poverty and all lack of the attractive graces women love; that clue inspired me with hope. I got books and pored over them till their meaning grew clear to me; I sought out learned men and gathered help from their wisdom; I gave myself to the task with indomitable zeal, for I was struggling for the liberty that alone made life worth possessing. The world believed me painting mimic woes, but I was living through a fearfully real one; friends fancied me busied with the mechanism of material bodies, but I was prying into the mysteries of human souls; and many envied my luxurious leisure in that leafy nest, while I was leading the life of a doomed convict, for as I kept my sinful vow so Agatha kept hers.

She never wrote, or sent, or came, but day and night she called me—day and night I resisted, saved only by the desperate means I used—means that made my own servant think me mad. I bid him lock me in my chamber; I dashed out at all hours to walk fast and far away into the lonely forest; I drowned consciousness in wine; I drugged myself with opiates, and when the crisis had passed, woke spent but victorious. All arts I tried, and slowly found that in this conflict of opposing wills my own grew stronger with each success, the other lost power with each defeat. I never wished to harm my wife, never called her, never sent a baneful thought or desire along that mental telegraph which stretched and thrilled between us; I only longed to free myself, and in this struggle weeks passed, yet neither won a signal victory, for neither proud heart knew the beauty of self-conquest and the power of submission.

One night I went up to the lonely tower that crowned the house, to watch the equinoctial storm that made a Pandemonium of the elements without. Rain streamed as if a second deluge was at hand; whirlwinds tore down the valley; the river chafed and foamed with an angry dash, and the city lights shone dimly through the flying mist as I watched them from my lofty room. The tumult suited me, for my own mood was stormy, dark and bitter, and when the cheerful fire invited me to bask before it I sat there wrapped in reveries as gloomy as the night. Presently the well-known premonition came with its sudden thrill through blood and nerves, and with a revengeful strength never felt before I gathered up my energies for the trial, as I waited some more urgent summons. None came, but in its place a sense of power flashed over me, a swift exultation dilated within me, time seemed to pause, the present rolled away, and nothing but an isolated memory remained, for fixing my thoughts on Agatha, I gave myself up to the dominant spirit that possessed me. I sat motionless, yet I willed to see her. Vivid as the flames that framed it, a picture started from the red embers, and clearly as if my bodily eye rested on it, I saw the well-known room, I saw my wife lying in a deep chair, wan and wasted as if with suffering of soul and body. I saw her grope with outstretched hands, and turn her head with eyes whose long lashes never lifted from the cheek where they lay so dark and still, and through the veil that seemed to wrap my senses I heard my own voice, strange and broken, whispering:

"God forgive me, she is blind!"

For a moment, the vision wandered mistily before me, then grew steady, and I saw her steal like a wraith across the lighted room, so dark to her; saw her bend over a little white nest my own hands placed there, and lift some precious burden in her feeble arms; saw her grope painfully back again, and sitting by that other fire—not solitary like my own—lay her pale cheek to that baby cheek and seem to murmur some lullaby that mother-love had taught her. Over my heart strong and sudden gushed a warmth never known before, and again, strange and broken through the veil that wrapped my senses, came my own voice whispering:

"God be thanked, she is not utterly alone!"

As if my breath dissolved it, the picture faded; but I willed again and another rose—my studio, dim with dust, damp with long disuse, dark with evening gloom—for one flickering lamp made the white shapes ghostly, and the pictured faces smile or frown with fitful vividness. There was no semblance of my old self there, but in the heart of the desolation and the darkness Agatha stood alone, with outstretched arms and an imploring face, full of a love and longing so intense that with a welcoming gesture and a cry that echoed through the room, I answered that mute appeal:

"Come to me! come to me!"

A gust thundered at the window, and rain fell like stormy tears, but nothing else replied; as the bright brands dropped the flames died out, and with it that sad picture of my deserted home. I longed to stir but could not, for I had called up a power I could not lay, the servant ruled the master now, and like one fastened by a spell I still sat leaning forward intent upon a single thought. Slowly from the gray embers smouldering on the hearth a third scene rose behind the smoke wreaths, changeful, dim and strange. Again my former home, again my wife, but this time standing on the threshold of the door I had sworn never to cross again. I saw the wafture of the cloak gathered about her, saw the rain beat on her shelterless head, and followed that slight figure through the deserted streets, over the long bridge where the lamps flickered in the wind, along the leafy road, up the wide steps and in at the door whose closing echo startled me to consciousness that my pulses were beating with a mad rapidity, that a cold dew stood upon my forehead, that every sense was supernaturally alert, and that all were fixed upon one point with a breathless intensity that made that little span of time as fearful as the moment when one hangs poised in air above a chasm in the grasp of nightmare. Suddenly I sprang erect, for through the uproar of the elements without, the awesome hush within, I heard steps ascending, and stood waiting in a speechless agony to see what shape would enter there.

One by one the steady footfalls echoed on my ear, one by one they seemed to bring the climax of some blind conflict nearer, one by one they knelled a human life away, for as the door swung open Agatha fell down before me, storm-beaten, haggard, spent, but loving still, for with a faint attempt to fold her hands submissively, she whispered:

"You have conquered, I am here!" and with that act grew still for ever, as with a great shock I woke to see what I had done.

* * *

Ten years have passed since then. I sit on that same hearth a feeble, white-haired man, and beside me, the one companion I shall ever know, my little son—dumb, blind and imbecile. I lavish tender names upon him, but receive no sweet sound in reply; I gather him close to my desolate heart, but meet no answering caress; I look with yearning glance, but see only those haunting eyes, with no gleam of recognition to warm them, no ray of intellect to inspire them, no change to deepen their sightless beauty; and this fair body moulded with the Divine sculptor's gentlest grace is always here before me, an embodied grief that wrings my heart with its pathetic innocence, its dumb reproach. This is the visible punishment for my sin, but there is an unseen retribution heavier than human judgment could inflict, subtler than human malice could conceive, for with a power made more omnipotent by death Agatha still calls me. God knows I am willing now, that I long with all the passion of desire, the anguish of despair to go to her, and He knows that the one tie that holds me is this aimless little life, this duty that I dare not neglect, this long atonement that I make. Day and night I listen to the voice that whispers to me through the silence of these years; day and night I answer with a yearning cry from the depths of a contrite spirit; day and night I cherish the one sustaining hope that Death, the great consoler, will soon free both father and son from the inevitable doom a broken law has laid upon them; for then I know that somewhere in the long hereafter my remorseful soul will find her, and with its poor offering of penitence and love fall down before her, humbly saying:

"You have conquered, I am here!"

The Fate of the Forrests

Part I

A group of four, two ladies and two gentlemen, leaned or lounged together in the soft brilliance of mingled moonlight and lamplight, that filled the luxurious room. Through the open windows came balmy gusts of ocean air, up from below rose the murmurous plash of waves, breaking on a quiet shore, and frequent bursts of music lent another charm to place and hour. A pause in the gay conversation was broken by the younger lady's vivacious voice:

"Now if the day of witches and wizards, astrologers and fortune-tellers was not over, how I should enjoy looking into a magic mirror, having my horoscope cast, or hearing my fate read by a charming black-eyed gipsy."

"The age of enchantment is not yet past, as all who are permitted to enter this magic circle confess; and one need not go far for 'a charming black-eyed gipsy' to decide one's destiny."

And with a half-serious, half-playful gesture the gentleman offered his hand to the fair-faced girl, who shook her head and answered, smilingly:

"No, I'll not tell your fortune, Captain Hay; and all your compliments cannot comfort me for the loss of the delightful *diablerie* I love to read about and long to experience. Modern gipsies are commonplace. I want a genuine Cagliostro, supernaturally elegant, gifted and mysterious. I wish the fable of his eternal youth were true, so that he might visit us, for where would he find a fitter company? You gentlemen are perfect sceptics, and I am a firm believer, while Ursula would inspire the dullest wizard, because she looks like one born to live a romance."

She did indeed. The beautiful woman, sitting where the light showered down upon her, till every charm seemed doubled. The freshest bloom of early womanhood glowed in a face both sweet and spirited, eloquent eyes shone lustrous and large, the lips smiled as if blissful visions fed the fancy, and above the white forehead dark, abundant hair made a graceful crown for a head which bore itself with a certain gentle pride, as if the power of beauty, grace and intellect lent an unconscious queenliness to their possessor. In the personal atmosphere of strength, brilliancy and tenderness that surrounded her, an acute observer would detect the presence of a daring spirit, a rich nature, a deep heart; and, looking closer, might also discover, in the curves of that sensitive mouth, the depths of those thoughtful eyes, traces of some hidden care, some haunting memory, or, perhaps, only that vague yet melancholy prescience which often marks those foredoomed to tragic lives. As her companions chatted this fleeting expression touched her face like a passing shadow, and the gentleman who had not yet spoken leaned nearer, as if eager to catch that evanescent gloom. She met his wistful glance with one of perfect serenity, saying, as an enchanting smile broke over her whole face:

"Yes, my life has been a romance thus far; may it have a happy ending. Evan, you were born in a land of charms and spells, can you not play the part of a Hindoo conjuror, and satisfy Kate's longing?"

"I can only play the part of a Hindoo devotee, and exhaust myself with strivings after the unattainable, like this poor little fire-worshipper," replied the young man, watching, with suspicious interest, a moth circling round the globe of light above his head, as if he dared not look at the fair speaker, lest his traitorous eyes should say too much.

"You are both sadly unromantic and ungallant men not to make an effort in our favor," exclaimed the lively lady. "I am in just the mood for a ghostly tale, a scene of mystery, a startling revelation, and where shall I look for an obliging magician to gratify me?"

"Here!"

The voice, though scarcely lifted above a whisper, startled the group as much as if a spirit spoke, and all eyes were turned towards the window, where white draperies were swaying in the wind. No uncanny apparition appeared behind the tentlike aperture, but the composed figure of a small, fragile-looking man, reclining in a lounging-chair. Nothing could have been more unimpressive at first glance, but at a second the eye was arrested, the attention roused, for an indefinable influence held one captive against one's will. Beardless, thin lipped, sharply featured and colorless as ivory was the face. A few locks of blonde hair streaked the forehead, and underneath it shone the controlling feature of this singular countenance. The eyes, that should have been a steely blue to match the fair surroundings, were of the intensest black, varying in expression with a startling rapidity, unless mastered by an art stronger than nature; by turns stealthily soft, keenly piercing, fiercely fiery or utterly expressionless, these mysterious eyes both attracted and repelled, with a subtle magnetism which few wills could resist, and which gave to this otherwise insignificant man a weird charm, which native grace and the possession of rare accomplishments made alluring, even to those who understood the fateful laws of temperament and race.

Languidly leaning in his luxurious chair, while one pale hand gathered back the curtain from before him, the new comer eyed the group with a swift glance, which in an instant had caught the meaning of each face and transferred it to the keeping of a memory which nothing could escape. Annoyance was the record set down against Ursula Forrest's name; mingled joy and shame against the other lady's; for, with the perfect breeding which was one of the man's chief attractions, he gave the precedence to women even in this rapid mental process. Aversion was emphatically marked against Evan Forrest's name, simple amusement fell to his companion's share. Captain Hay was the first to break the sudden silence which followed that one softly spoken word:

"Beg pardon, but upon my life I forgot you, Stähl. I thought you went half an hour ago, in your usual noiseless style, for who would dream of your choosing to lounge in the strong draught of a seabreeze?"

"It is I who should beg pardon for forgetting myself in such society, and indulging in the reveries that will come unbidden to such poor shadows as I."

The voice that answered, though low-toned, was singularly persuasive, and the words were uttered with an expression more engaging than a smile.

"Magician, you bade me look to you. I take you at your word. I dare you to show your skill, and prove that yours is no empty boast," said Kate Heath, with evident satisfaction at the offer and interest in its maker.

Rising slowly, Felix Stähl advanced towards her, and, despite his want of stature and vigor, which are the manliest attributes of manhood, no one felt the lack of them, because an instantaneous impression of vitality and power was made in defiance of external seeming. With both hands loosely folded behind him, he paused before Miss Heath, asking, tranquilly:

"Which wish shall I grant? Will you permit me to read your palm? Shall I show you the image of your lover in yonder glass? or shall I whisper in your ear the most secret hope, fear or regret, which you cherish? Honor me by choosing, and any one of these feats I will perform."

Kate stole a covert glance at the tall mirror, saw that it reflected no figure but that of the speaker, and with an irrepressible smile she snatched her eyes away, content, saying hastily:

"As the hardest feat of the three, you shall tell me what I most ardently desire, if the rest will submit to a like test. Can you read their hearts as well as mine?"

His eye went slowly round the little circle, and from each face the smile faded, as that searching gaze explored it. Constrained by its fascination, more than by curiosity or inclination, each person bowed their acquiescence to Kate's desire, and as Stähl's eye came back to her, he answered briefly, like one well assured of his own power:

"I can read their hearts. Shall I begin with you?"

For a moment she fluttered like a bird caught in a fowler's net, then with an effort composed both attitude and aspect, and looked up half-proudly, half-pleadingly, into the colorless countenance that bent till the lips were at her ear. Only three words, and the observers saw the conscious blood flush scarlet to her forehead, burning hotter and deeper as eyes fell, lips quivered and head sank in her hands, leaving a shame-stricken culprit where but an instant ago a bright, happy-hearted woman sat.

Before Ursula could reach her friend, or either gentleman exclaim, Stähl's uplifted hand imposed passive silence and obtained it, for already the magnetism of his presence made itself felt, filling the room with a supernatural atmosphere, which touched the commonplace with mystery, and woke fantastic fears or fancies like a spell. Without a look, a word for the weeping girl before him, he turned sharply round on Evan Forrest, signified by an imperious gesture that he should bend his tall head nearer, and when he did so, seemed to stab him with a breath. Pale with indignation and surprise, the young man sprang erect, demanding in a smothered voice:

"Who will prevent me?"

"I will."

As the words left Stähl's lips, Evan stirred as if to take him by the throat, but that thin, womanish hand closed like a steel spring round his wrist and held the strong arm powerless, as, with a disdainful smile, and warning "Remember where you are!" the other moved on undisturbed. Evan flung himself into a seat, vainly attempting self-control, while Stähl passed to Captain Hay, who sat regarding him with undisguised interest and amazement, which latter sentiment reached its climax as the magic whisper came.

"How in Heaven's name did you know that?" he cried, starting like one stupefied; then overturning his chair in his haste, he dashed out of the room with every mark of uncontrollable excitement and alarm.

"Dare you let me try my power on you, Miss Forrest?" asked Stähl, pausing at her side, with the first trace of emotion visible in his inscrutable face.

"I dare everything!" and as she spoke, Ursula's proud head rose erect, Ursula's dauntless eyes looked full into his own.

"In truth you do dare everything," he murmured below his breath, with a glance of passionate admiration. But the soft ardor that made his eyes wonderfully lovely for an instant flamed as suddenly into a flash of anger, for there was a perceptible recoil of the white shoulder as his breath touched it in bending, and when he breathed a single word into her ear, his face wore the stealthy ferocity of a tiger in the act of springing upon his unsuspecting prey. Had she been actually confronted with the veritable beast, it could scarcely have wrought a swifter panic than that one word. Fixed in the same half-shrinking, half-haughty attitude, she sat as if changed suddenly to stone. Her eyes, dark and dilated with some unconquerable horror, never left his face while light, color, life itself seemed to ebb slowly from her own, leaving it as beautiful yet woful to look upon as some marble Medusa's countenance. So sudden, so entire was the change in that blooming face, that Kate forgot her own dismay, and cried:

"Ursula, what is it?" while Evan, turning on the worker of the miracle, demanded hotly:

"What right have you to terrify women and insult men by hissing in their ears secret information dishonorably obtained?"

Neither question received an answer, for Ursula and Stähl seemed unconscious of any presence but their own, as each silently regarded the other with a gaze full of mutual intelligence, yet opposing emotions of triumph and despair. At the sound of Evan's voice, a shudder shook Ursula from head to foot, but her eye never wavered, and the icy fixture of her features remained unchanged as she asked in a sharp, shrill whisper—

"Is it true?"

"Behold the sign!" and with a gesture, too swift and unsuspected for any but herself to see or understand the revelation made, Stähl bared his left arm, held it before her eyes, and dropped it in the drawing of a breath. Whatever Ursula saw confirmed her dread; she uttered neither cry nor exclamation, but wrung her hands together in dumb anguish, while her lips moved without uttering a sound.

Kate Heath's over-wrought nerves gave way, and weeping hysterically, she clung to Evan, imploring him to take her home. Instantly assuming his usual languid courtesy of mien and manners, Stähl murmured regretful apologies, rang the bell for Miss Heath's carriage, and bringing her veil and mantle from the ante-room, implored the privilege of shawling her with a penitent devotion wonderfully winning, yet which did not prevent her shrinking from him and accepting no services but such as Evan half-unconsciously bestowed.

"You are coming with me? You promised mama to bring me safely back. Mr. Forrest, take pity on me, for I dare not go alone."

She spoke tearfully, still agitated by the secret wound inflicted by a whisper.

"Hay will gladly protect you, Kate; I cannot leave Ursula," began Evan, but a smooth, imperious voice took the word from his lips.

"Hay is gone, I shall remain with Ursula, and you, Forrest, will not desert Miss Heath in the distress which I have unhappily caused by granting her wish. Forgive me, and good-night."

As Stähl spoke, he kissed the hand that trembled in his own, with a glance that lingered long in poor Kate's memory, and led her towards her friend. But Evan's dark face kindled with the passion that he had vainly striven to suppress, and though he tried to curb his tongue, his eye looked a defiance as he placed himself beside his cousin, saying doggedly:

"I shall not leave Ursula to the tender mercies of a charlatan unless she bids me go. Kate, stay with us and lend your carriage to this gentleman, as his own is not yet here."

Bowing with a face of imperturbable composure, Stähl answered in his softest tones, bending an inquiring glance on Ursula:

"Many thanks, but I prefer to receive my dismissal from the lady of the house, not from its would-be master. Miss Forrest, shall I leave you to begin the work marked out for me? or shall I remain to unfold certain matters which nearly concern yourself, and which, if neglected, may result in misfortune to more than one of us?"

As if not only the words but the emphasis

with which they were pronounced recalled some forgotten fact, woke some new fear, Ursula started from her stupor of surprise and mental suffering into sudden action. All that had passed while she sat dumb seemed to return to her, and a quick glance from face to face appeared to decide her in the course she must pursue.

Rising she went to Kate, touched her wet cheek with lips that chilled it, and turning to her companions regarded them with an eye that seemed to pierce to the heart's core of each. What she read there none knew, but some purpose strong enough to steady and support her with a marvellous composure seemed born of that long scrutiny, for motioning her cousin from her she said:

"Go, Evan, I desire it."

"Go! and leave you with that man? I cannot, Ursula!"

"You must, you will, if I command it. I wish to be alone with him; I fear nothing, not even this magician, who in an instant has changed my life by a single word. See! I trust myself to his protection; I throw myself upon his mercy, and implore you to have faith in me."

With an air of almost pathetic dignity, a

gesture of infinite grace, she stretched a hand to either man, and as each grasped the soft prize a defiant glance was exchanged between them, a daring one was fixed upon the beautiful woman for whom, like spirits of good and ill, they were henceforth to contend.

"I shall obey you, but may I come to-morrow?" Evan whispered, as he pressed the hand that in his own was tremulous and warm.

"Yes, come to me early, I shall need you then—if ever."

And as the words left her lips that other hand in Felix Stähl's firm hold grew white and cold as if carved in marble.

With Kate still trembling on his arm, Evan left them; his last glance showing him his rival regarding his departure with an air of tranquil triumph, and Ursula, his proud, high-hearted cousin, sinking slowly on her knees before this man, who in an hour seemed to have won the right to make or mar her happiness for ever.

How the night passed Evan Forrest never knew. He took Kate home, and then till day dawned haunted beach and cliff like a restless ghost, thinking only of Ursula, remembering only that she bade him come early, and chiding the tardy sun until it rose upon a day that darkened all his life. As the city bells chimed seven from the spires that shone across the little bay, Evan re-entered his cousin's door; but before he could pronounce her name the lady who for years had filled a mother's place to the motherless girl came hurrying to meet him, with every mark of sleepless agitation in her weary yet restless face and figure.

"Thank heaven, you are come!" she ejaculated, drawing him aside into the anteroom. "Oh, Mr. Forrest, such a night as I have passed, so strange, so unaccountable, I am half distracted."

"Where is Ursula?" demanded Evan.

"Just where you left her, sir; she has not stirred since that dreadful Mr. Stähl went away."

"When was that?"

"Past midnight. At eleven I went down to give him a hint, but the door was fast, and for another hour the same steady sound of voices came up to me as had been going on since you left. When he did go at last it was so quietly I only knew it by the glimpse I caught of him gliding down the walk, and vanishing like a spirit in the shadow of the great gate."

"Then you went to Ursula?"

"I did, sir; I did, and found her sitting as I saw her when I left the room in the evening."

"What did she say? what did she do?"

"She said nothing, and she looked like death itself, so white, so cold, so still; not a sigh, a tear, a motion; and when I implored her to speak she only broke my heart with the look she gave me, as she whispered, 'Leave me in peace till Evan comes.' "

With one stride he stood before the closed door, but when he tapped no voice bade him enter, and opening he noiselessly glided in. She was there, sitting as Mrs. Yorke described her, and looking more like a pale ghost than a living woman. Evan's eye wandered round the room, hungry to discover some clue to the mystery, but nothing was changed. The lamps burned dimly in the glare of early sunshine streaming through the room; the curtains were still wafted to and fro by balmy breezes; the seats still stood scattered here and there as they were quitted; Captain Hay's chair still lay overthrown; Kate's gloves had been trodden under foot, and round the deep chair in the window still glowed the scattered petals of the rose with which Felix Stähl had regaled himself while lying there.

"Ursula!"

No answer came to his low call, and drawing nearer, Evan whispered tenderly:

"My darling, speak to me! It breaks my heart to see you so, and have no power to help you."

The dark eyes fixed on vacancy relaxed in their strained gaze, the cold hands locked together in her lap loosened their painful pressure, and with a long sigh Ursula turned towards him, saying, like one wakened from a heavy dream:

"I am glad you are come;" then as if some fear stung her, added with startling abruptness, "Evan! what did he whisper in your ear last night?"

Amazed at such a question, yet not ill pleased to answer it even then, for his full heart was yearning to unburden itself, the young man instantly replied, while his face glowed with hope, and his voice grew tender with the untold love that had long hovered on his lips:

"He said, 'You will never win your cousin;' but, Ursula, he lied, for I will win you even if he bring the powers of darkness to confound me. He read in my face what you must have read there long ago, and did not rebuke by one cold look, one forbidding word. Let me tell my love now; let me give you the shelter of my heart if you need it, and whatever grief or shame or fear has come to you let me help you bear it if I cannot banish it."

She did not speak, till kneeling before her he said imploringly:

"Ursula, you bade me trust you; I do entirely. Can you not place a like confidence in me?"

"No, Evan."

"Then you do not love as I love," he cried, with a foreboding fear heavy at his heart.

"No, I do not love as you love." The answer came like a soft echo, and her whole frame trembled for an instant as if some captive emotion struggled for escape and an iron hand restrained it. Her cousin saw it, and seizing both her hands, looked deep into her eyes, demanding, sternly:

"Do you love this man?"

"I shall marry him."

Evan stared aghast at the hard, white resolution stamped upon her face, as she looked straight before her with a blank yet steady gaze, seeming to see and own allegiance to a master invisible to him. A moment he struggled with a chaos of conflicting passions, then fought his way to a brief calmness, intent on fathoming the mystery that had wrought such a sudden change in both their lives.

"Ursula, as the one living relative whom you possess, I have a right to question you. Answer me truly, I conjure you, and deal honestly with the heart that is entirely your own. I can forget myself, can put away my own love and longing, can devote my whole time, strength, life to your service, if you need me. Something has happened that affects you deeply, let me know it. No common event would move you so, for lovers do not woo in this strange fashion, nor betrothed brides wear their happiness with such a face as you now wear."

"Few women have such lovers as mine, or such betrothals to tell. Ask me nothing, Evan,

I have told you all I may; go now, and let me rest, if any rest remains for me."

"Not yet," he answered, with as indomitable a purpose in his face as that which seemed to have fixed and frozen hers. "I must know more of this man before I give you up. Who and what is he?"

"Study, question, watch and analyse him. You will find him what he seems—no more, no less. I leave you free to do what you will, and claim an equal liberty for myself," she said.

"I thought he was a stranger to you as to me and others. You must have known him elsewhere, Ursula?"

"I never saw or knew him till a month ago."

Evan struck his hands together with a gesture of despair, as he sprang up, saying:

"Ah! I see it now. A month ago I left you, and in that little time you learned to love."

"Yes, in that little time I did learn to love."

Again the soft echo came, again the sadder tremor shook her, but she neither smiled, nor wept, nor turned her steady eyes away from the unseen but controlling presence that for her still seemed to haunt the room.

Evan Forrest was no blind lover, and despite his own bitter loss he was keen-eyed enough to see that some emotion deeper than caprice, stronger than pity, sharper than regret, now held possession of his cousin's heart. He felt that some tie less tender than that which bound him to her bound her to this man, who exercised such power over her proud spirit and strong will. Bent on reading the riddle, he rapidly glanced through the happy past, so shared with Ursula that he believed no event in the life of either was unknown to the other; yet here was a secret lying dark between them, and only one little month of absence had sowed the seed that brought such a harvest of distrust and pain. Suddenly he spoke:

"Ursula, has this man acquired power over you through any weakness of your own?"

A haughty flash kindled in her eyes, and for an instant her white face glowed with womanly humiliation at the doubt implied.

"I am as innocent of any sin or shame, any weakness or wrong, as when I lay a baby in my mother's arms. Would to God I lay there now as tranquilly asleep as she!"

The words broke from her with a tearless sob, and spreading her hands before her face he heard her murmur like a broken-hearted child:

"How could he, oh, how could he wound me with a thought like that?"

"I will not! I do not! Hear me, Ursula, and forgive me, if I cannot submit to see you leave me for a man like this without one effort to fathom the inexplicable change I find in you. Only tell me that he is worthy of you, that you love him and are happy, and I will be dumb. Can you do this to ease my heart and conscience, Ursula?"

"Yes, I can do more than that. Rest tranquil, dearest Evan. I know what I do; I do it freely, and in time you will acknowledge that I did well in marrying Felix Stähl."

"You are betrothed to him?"

"I am; his kiss is on my cheek, his ring is on my hand; I accept both."

With a look and gesture which he never could forget she touched the cheek where one deep spot of color burned as if branded there, and held up the hand whose only ornament beside its beauty was a slender ring formed of two twisted serpents, whose diamond eyes glittered with an uncanny resemblance of life.

"And you will marry him?" repeated Evan, finding the hard fact impossible to accept.

"I will."

"Soon, Ursula?"

"Very soon."

"You wish it so?"

"I wish what he wishes."

"You will go away with him?"

"To the end of the earth if he desires it."

"My God! is this witchcraft or infatuation?"

"Neither, it is woman's love, which is quick and strong to dare and suffer all things for those who are dearer to her than her life."

He could not see her face, for she had turned it from him, but in her voice trembled a tender fervor which could not be mistaken, and with a pang that wrung his man's heart sorely he relinquished all hope, and bade farewell to love, believing that no mystery existed but that which is inexplicable, the workings of a woman's heart.

"I am going, Ursula," he said; "you no longer have any need of me, and I must fight out my fight alone. God bless you, and remember whatever befalls, while life lasts you have one unalterable friend and lover in me."

As he spoke with full eyes, broken voice

and face eloquent with love, regret and pity, Ursula rose suddenly and fell upon his bosom, clinging there with passionate despair that deepened his ever growing wonder.

"God help you, Evan! love me, trust me, pity me, and so good-bye! good-bye!" she cried, in that strange paroxysm of emotion, as tearless, breathless, trembling and wearied, yet still self-controlled, she kissed and blessed and led him to the door. No pause upon the threshold; as he lingered she put him from her, closed and bolted it: then as if with him the sustaining power of her darkened life departed, she fell down upon the spot where he had stood, and lay there, beautiful and pale and still as some fair image of eternal sleep.

Part II

The nine days' wonder at the sudden wedding which followed that strange betrothal had died away, the honeymoon was over, and the bridal pair were alone together in their new home. Ursula stood at the window looking out, with eyes as wistful as a caged bird's, upon the fading leaves that fluttered in the autumn wind. Her husband lay on his couch, apparently absorbed in a vellum-covered volume, the cabalistic characters of which were far easier to decipher than the sweet, wan face he was studying covertly. The silence which filled the room was broken by a long sigh of pain as the book fell from Stähl's hand, and his head leaned wearily upon the pillow. Ursula heard the sigh, and, like a softly moving shadow, glided to his side, poured wine from an antique flask, and kneeling, held it to his lips. He drank thirstily, but the cordial seemed to impart neither strength nor comfort, for he drew his wife's head down beside him, saying:

"Kiss me, Ursula; I am so faint and cold, nothing seems to warm my blood, and my body freezes, while my heart burns with a never-dying fire."

With a meek obedience that robbed the act of all tenderness, she touched her ruddy lips to the paler ones that ardently returned the pressure, yet found no satisfaction there. Leaning upon his arm, he held her to him with a fierce fondness, in strange contrast to his feeble frame, saying earnestly:

"Ursula, before I married you I found such strength and solace, such warmth and happiness in your presence, that I coveted you as a precious healing for my broken health. Then I loved you, forgetful of self—loved you as you never will be loved again, and thanked heaven that my fate was so interwoven with your own that the utterance of a word secured my life's desire. But now, when I have made you wholly mine, and hope to bask in the sunshine of your beauty, youth and womanhood, I find a cold, still creature in my arms, and no spark of the fire that consumes me ever warms the image of my love. Must it be so? Can I never see you what you were again?"

"Never!" she answered, leaning there as pale and passive as if she were in truth a marble woman. "I vowed obedience at the altar, nothing more. I did not love you; I could not honor you, but I felt that I might learn to obey. I have done so, be content."

"Not I! Colder women have been taught love as well as obedience; you, too, shall be a docile pupil, and one day give freely what I sue for now. Other men woo before they wed, my wooing and my winning will come later—if I live long enough."

He turned her face towards him as he spoke and scanned it closely; but no grateful sign of softness, pity or regret appeared, and, with a broken exclamation, he put her from him, locked both hands across his eyes and lay silent, till some uncontrollable paroxysm of emotion had passed by. Presently he spoke, and the words betrayed what the pain had been.

"My mother—heaven bless her for her tenderness!—used to pray that her boy's life might be a long and happy one; it is a bitter thing to feel that the only woman now left me to love prays for the shortening of that same life, and can bestow no look or word to make its failing hours happy."

The unwonted tone of filial affection, the keen sorrow and the mournful acknowledgment of an inevitable doom touched Ursula as no ardent demonstration or passionate reproach had ever done. She softly lifted up the folded hands, saw that those deep eyes were wet with tears, and in that pallid countenance read the melancholy record of a life burdened with a sad heritage of pain, thwarted by unhappy love and darkened by allegiance to a superstitious vow. Great as her sacrifice had been, deep as the wound still was, and heavily as her captivity weighed on her proud heart, it was still womanly, generous and gentle; and, despite all wrongs, all blemishes, all bitter memories, she felt the fascination of this wild and wayward nature, as she had never done before, and yielded to its persuasive potency. Laying her cool hand on his hot forehead, she leaned over him, saying, with an accent of compassion sweeter to his ear than her most perfect song:

"No, Felix, I pray no prayers that heaven would refuse to grant. I only ask patience for myself, a serener spirit for you, and God's blessing upon Evan, wherever he may be."

Before the words of tender satisfaction which rose to Stähl's lips could be uttered, a noiseless servant brought a black-edged card. Ursula read and handed it to her husband.

"Mrs. Heath. Shall we see her, love?" he asked.

"As you please," was the docile answer, though an expression of mingled pain and sorrow passed across her face in speaking.

He half frowned at her meekness, then smiled and bade the man deny them, adding, as he left the room,

"I am too well content with this first glimpse of the coming happiness to be saddened by the lamentations of that poor lady over her wilful daughter, who had the bad taste to drown herself upon our wedding-day."

"Felix, may I ask you a question?"

"Anything of me, Ursula."

"Tell me what you whispered in Kate's ear on the evening which both of us remember well."

Questions were so rare, and proving a sign of interest, that Stähl made haste to answer, with a curious blending of disdain and pity,

"She bade me tell her the most ardent desire of her life, and I dared to answer truly, 'To win my heart.' "

"A true answer, but a cruel one," Ursula said.

"That cruel truthfulness is one of the savage attributes which two generations of civilization cannot entirely subdue in my race. Those who tamely submit to me I despise, but those who oppose me I first conquer and then faithfully love."

"Had you made poor Kate happy, you would not now regret the possession of a cold, untender wife."

"Who would gather a gay tulip when they can reach a royal rose, though thorns tear the hand that seizes it? For even when it fades its perfume lingers, gifting it with an enduring charm. Love, I have found my rose, so let the tulip fade—"

There he paused abruptly in his flowery speech, for with the swift instinct of a temperament like his, he was instantly conscious of the fact when her thoughts wandered, and a glance showed him that, though her attitude was unaltered, she was listening intently. A far-off bell had rung, the tones of a man's voice sounded from below, and the footsteps of an approaching servant grew audible. Stähl recognised the voice, fancied that Ursula did also, and assured himself of it by an unsuspected test that took the form of a caress. Passing his arm about her waist, his hand lay lightly above her heart, and as her cousin's name was announced he felt the sudden bound that glad heart gave, and counted the rapid throbs that sent the color to her cheeks and made her lips tremble. A black frown lowered on his forehead, and his eyes glittered ominously for an instant, but both betrayals were unseen, and nothing marred the gracious sweetness of his voice.

"Of course you will see your cousin, Ursula. I shall greet him in passing, and return when you have enjoyed each other alone."

"Alone!" she echoed, with a distrustful look at him, an anxious one about the room, as if no place seemed safe or sacred in that house where she was both mistress and slave.

He understood the glance, and answered with one so reproachful that she blushed for the ungenerous suspicion, as he said, with haughty emphasis:

"Yes, Ursula, alone. Whatever evil names I may deserve, those of spy and eavesdropper cannot be applied to me; and though my wife can neither love nor honor me, I will prove that she may trust me."

With that he left her, and meeting Evan just without, offered his hand frankly, and gave his welcome with a cordial grace that was irresistible. Evan could not refuse the hand, for on it shone a little ring which Ursula once wore, and yielding to the impulse awakened by that mute reminder of her, he betrayed exactly what his host desired to know, for instantaneous as was both recognition and submission, Stähl's quick eye divined the cause.

"Come often to us, Evan; forget the past, and remember only that through Ursula we are kindred now. She is waiting for you; go to her and remain as long as you incline, sure of a hearty welcome from both host and hostess."

Then he passed on, and Evan hurried to his cousin; eager, yet reluctant to meet her, lest in her face he should read some deeper mystery or greater change than he last saw there. She came to meet him smiling and serene, for whatever gust of joy or sorrow had swept over her, no trace of it remained; yet, when he took her in his arms, there broke from him the involuntary exclamation:

"Is this my cousin Ursula?"

"Yes, truly. Am I then so altered?"

"This is a reflection of what you were; that of what you are. Look, and tell me if I have not cause for wonder."

She did look as he drew a miniature from his bosom and led her to the mirror. The contrast was startling even to herself, for the painted face glowed with rosy bloom, hope shone in the eyes, happiness smiled from the lips, while youthful purity and peace crowned the fair forehead with enchanting grace. The living face was already wan and thin, many tears had robbed the cheeks of color, sleepless nights had dimmed the lustre of the eyes, much secret suffering and strife had hardened the soft curves of the mouth and deepened the lines upon the brow. Even among the dark waves of her hair silver threads shone here and there, unbidden, perhaps unknown; and over the whole woman a subtle blight had fallen, more tragical than death. Silently she compared the two reflections, for the first time realising all that she had lost, yet as she returned the miniature she only said, with pathetic patience:

"I am not what I was, but my heart remains unchanged, believe that, Evan."

"I do. Tell me, Ursula, are you happy now?"

Her eyes rose to his, and over her whole face there shone the sudden magic of a glow warmer and brighter than a smile.

"I am supremely happy now."

It was impossible to doubt her truth, however past facts or present appearances might seem to belie it, and Evan was forced to believe, despite his disappointment.

"He is kind to you, Ursula? You suffer no neglect, no tyranny nor wrong from this strange man?" he asked, still haunted by vague doubts.

She waved her hand about the lovely room, delicately dainty as a bride's bower should be, and answered, with real feeling:

"Does this look as if I suffered any neglect or wrong? Every want and whim is seen and gratified before expressed; I go and come unwatched, unquestioned; the winds of heaven are not allowed to visit me too roughly, and as for kindness, look there and see a proof of it."

She pointed to the garden where her husband walked alone, never quitting the wide terrace just below her window, though the sunshine that he loved had faded from the spot, and the autumn winds he dreaded blew gustily about him. He never lifted up his eyes, nor paused, nor changed his thoughtful attitude, but patiently paced to and fro, a mute reproach for Ursula's unjust suspicion.

"How frail he looks; if life with you cannot revive him he must be past hope."

Evan spoke involuntarily, and Ursula's hand half checked the words upon his lips; but neither looked the other in the face, and neither owned, even to themselves, how strong a hidden wish had grown.

"He will live because he resolves to live, for that frail body holds the most indomitable spirit I have ever known. But let me tell you why he lingers where every breath brings pain," said Ursula, and having told him, she added:

"Is not that both a generous and a gentle rebuke for an unkind doubt?"

"It is either a most exquisite piece of lover-like devotion or of consummate art. I think it is the latter, for he knows you well, and repays great sacrifices by graceful small ones, which touch and charm your woman's heart."

"You wrong him, Evan, and aversion blinds you to the better traits I have learned to see. An all absorbing love ennobles the most sinful man, and makes it possible for some woman to forgive and cling to him."

"I have no right to ask, but the strange spirit that has taken possession of you baffles and disquiets me past endurance. Tell me, Ursula, what you would not tell before, do you truly, tenderly love this man whom you have married?"

The question was uttered with an earnestness so solemn that it forced a truthful answer, and she looked up at him with the old frankness unobscured by any cloud, as she replied:

"But for one thing I should long ago have learned to love him. I know this, because even now I cannot wholly close my heart against the ardent affection that patiently appeals to it."

"And that one thing, that cursed mystery which has wrecked two lives, when am I to know it, Ursula?"

"Never till I lie on my deathbed, and not even then, unless—"

She caught back the words hovering on her lips, but her eye glanced furtively upon the solitary figure pacing there below, and Evan impetuously finished the broken sentence:

"Unless he is already dead—let it be so; I shall wait and yet prove his prophecy a false one by winning and wearing you when his baleful love is powerless."

"He is my husband, Evan, remember that. Now come with me, I am going to him, for he must not shiver there when I can give him the warmth his tropical nature loves."

But Evan would not go, and soon left her plunged in a new sea of anxious conjectures, doubts and dreads. Stähl awaited his wife's approach, saying within himself as he watched her coming under the gold and scarlet arches of the leafy walk, with unwonted elasticity in her step, color on her cheeks and smiles upon her lips:

"Good! I have found the spell that turns my snow image into flesh and blood; I will use it and enjoy the summer of her presence while I may."

He did use it, but so warily and well that though Ursula and Evan were dimly conscious of some unseen yet controlling hand that ruled their intercourse and shaped events, they found it hard to believe that studious invalid possessed and used such power. Evan came daily, and daily Ursula regained some of her lost energy and bloom, till an almost preternatural beauty replaced the pale loveliness her face had worn, and she seemed to glow and brighten with an inward fire, like some brilliant flower that held the fervor of a summer in its heart and gave it out again in one fair, fragrant hour.

Like a watchful shadow Evan haunted his cousin, conscious that they were drifting down a troubled stream without a pilot, yet feeling powerless to guide or govern his own life, so inextricably was it bound up in Ursula's. He saw that the vigor and vitality his presence gave her was absorbed by her husband, to whom she was a more potent stimulant than rare winds, balmy airs or costly drugs. He knew that the stronger nature subdued the weaker, and the failing life sustained itself by draining the essence of that other life, which, but for some sinister cross of fate, would have been an ever springing fountain of joy to a more generous and healthful heart.

The blind world applauded Felix Stähl's success, and envied him the splendid wife in whose affluent gifts of fortune, mind and person he seemed to revel with luxurious delight. It could not see the secret bitterness that poisoned peace; could not guess the unavailing effort, unappeased desire and fading hope that each day brought him; nor fathom the despair that filled his soul as he saw and felt the unmistakable tokens of his coming fate in hollow temples, wasting flesh and a mortal weariness that knew no rest; a despair rendered doubly bitter by the knowledge of his impotence to prevent another from reaping what he had sown with painful care.

Ursula's hard won submission deserted her when Evan came, for in reanimating the statue Stähl soon felt that he had lost his slave and found a master. The heart which had seemed slowly yielding to his efforts closed against him in the very hour of fancied conquest. No more meek services, no more pity shown in spite of pride, no more docile obedience to commands that wore the guise of entreaties. The captive spirit woke and beat against its bars, passionately striving to be free, though not a cry escaped its lips. Very soon her recovered gaiety departed, and her life became a vain effort to forget, for like all impetuous natures she sought oblivion in excitement and hurried from one scene of pleasure to another, finding rest and happiness in none. Her husband went with her everywhere, recklessly squandering the strength she gave him in a like fruitless quest, till sharply checked by warnings which could no longer be neglected.

One night in early spring when winter gaieties were drawing to a close, Ursula came down to him shining in festival array, with the evening fever already burning in her cheeks, the expectant glitter already kindling in her eyes, and every charm heightened with that skill which in womanly women is second nature. Not for his pride or pleasure had she made herself so fair, he knew that well, and the thought lent its melancholy to the tone in which he said:

"Ursula, I am ready, but so unutterably weak and weary that I cannot go."

"I can go without you. Be so good," and quite unmoved by the suffering that rarely found expression, she held her hand to him that he might clasp her glove. He rose to perform the little service with that courtesy which never failed him, asking, as he bent above the hand with trembling fingers and painful breath,

"Does Evan go with you?"

"Yes, he never fails me, he has neither weakness nor weariness to mar my pleasure or to thwart my will."

"Truly a tender and a wifely answer."

"I am not tender nor wifely; why assume the virtues which I never shall possess? They were not set down in the bond; that I fulfilled to the letter when I married you, and beyond the wearing of your name and ring I owe you nothing. Do I?"

"Yes, a little gratitude for the sincerity that placed a doomed life in your keeping; a little respect for the faith I have kept unbroken through all temptations; a little compassion for a malady that but for you would make my life a burden I would gladly lay down."

Time was when words like these would have touched and softened her, but not now, for she had reached the climax of her suffering, the extent of her endurance, and turning on him she gave vent to the passionate emotion which could no longer be restrained:

"I should have given you much gratitude if in helping me to save one life you had not doomed another. I should honestly respect the faith you boast of if such costly sacrifices were not demanded for its keeping. I should deeply pity that mortal malady if you had bravely borne it alone instead of seeking a selfish solace in bequeathing it to another. I tell you, Felix, you are killing me swiftly and surely by this dreadful life. Better end me at once than drive me mad, or leave me a strong soul prisoned in a feeble body like yourself."

For the first time in his life Stähl felt the touch of fear, not for himself but for her, lest that terrible affliction which so baffles human skill and science should fall upon the woman whom he loved with a selfish intensity which had tangled two lives and brought them to this pass.

"Hush, Ursula," he said, soothingly, "have patience, I shall soon be gone, and then— what will you do then?"

The question leaped to his lips, for at the word "gone" he saw the gloom lift from her face, leaving an expression of relief that unmistakably betrayed how heavily her burden had oppressed her. Undaunted by the almost fierce inquiry she fixed her eyes upon him, and answered steadily:

"I shall put off my bridal white, wear widow's weeds for a single year, and then"— there she, too, paused abruptly; but words were needless, for as Evan's step sounded on the stair she turned and hurried towards him, as if love, liberty and life all lay waiting for her there. Stähl watched them with a jealous pang that pierced the deeper as, remembering Ursula's taunt, he compared the young man with himself; the one rich in the stature, vigor, comeliness that make a manly man; the other, in sad truth, a strong spirit imprisoned in a ruined body. As he looked he clenched his pale hand hard, and muttered low between his set teeth:

"He shall not have her, if I sell my soul to thwart him!"

To Ursula's intense surprise and Evan's annoyance Stähl followed them into the carriage, with a brief apology for his seeming caprice. No one spoke during the short drive, but as they came into the brilliant rooms Ursula's surprise deepened to alarm, for in the utter change of mien and manner which had befallen her husband she divined the presence of some newborn purpose, and trembled for the issue. Usually he played the distasteful part of invalid with a grace and skill which made the undisguisable fact a passport to the sympathy and admiration of both men and women. But that night no vigorous young man bore himself more debonnairly, danced more indefatigably, or devoted himself more charmingly to the service of matron, maid and grateful hostess. Lost in amazement, Ursula and Evan watched him, gliding to and fro, vivacious, blithe and bland, leaving a trail of witty, wise or honied words behind him, and causing many glances of approval to follow that singular countenance, for now its accustomed pallor was replaced by a color no art could counterfeit, and the mysterious eyes burned with a fire that fixed and fascinated other eyes.

"What does it mean, Evan?" whispered Ursula, standing apart with her faithful shadow.

"Mischief, if I read it rightly," was the anxious answer, and at that moment, just before them, the object of their thoughts was accosted by a jovial gentleman, who exclaimed:

"God bless me, Stähl! Rumor said you were dying, like a liar as she is, and here I find you looking more like a bridegroom than when I left you at the altar six months ago."

"For once rumor tells the truth, Coventry. I am dying, but one may make their exit gracefully and end their tragedy or comedy with a grateful bow! I have had a generous share of pleasure; I thank the world for it; I make my adieu to-night, and tranquilly go home to rest."

Spoken with an untroubled smile the words were both touching and impressive, and the friendly Coventry was obliged to clear his voice before he could answer with an assumption of cheery unbelief:

"Not yet, my dear fellow, not yet; we cannot spare you this forty years, and with such a wife what right have you to talk of ending the happy drama which all predict your life will be?" then glad to change the subject, he added: "Apropos of predictions, do take pity on my curiosity and tell me if it is true that you entertained a party with some very remarkable prophecies, or something of that sort, just before your marriage with Miss Forrest. Hay once spoke mysteriously of it, but he went to the bad so soon after that I never made him satisfy me."

"I did comply with a lady's wish, but entertainment was not the result. I told Hay, what all the world knew, the next day, that certain dishonorable transactions of his were discovered, and warrants out for his arrest, and they hurried home to find my warning true."

"Yes, no one dreamed of such an end for the gay captain. I don't ask how your discovery was made, but I do venture to inquire if Miss Heath's tragical death was foretold that night?"

"That which indirectly caused her death

was made known to her that night, but for her sake you will pardon me that I keep the secret."

"A thousand pardons for asking, and yet I am tempted to put one more question. You look propitious, so pray tell me if your other predictions were fulfilled with equal success?"

"Yes; sooner or later they always are."

"Upon my life, that's very singular! Just for the amusement of the thing make one now, and let me see if your skill remains undiminished. Nothing personal, you know, but some general prediction that any one may know and verify."

Stähl paused a moment, bending his eyes on Ursula, who stood unseen by his companion, then answered slowly with a memorable tone and aspect:

"I prophesy that before the month is out the city will be startled by a murder, and the culprit will elude justice by death."

Coventry's florid countenance paled visibly, and hastily returning thanks for the undesirable favor so complacently granted, he took himself away to whisper the evil portent in the ears of all he met. As he disappeared

Stähl advanced to his wife, asking with an air of soft solicitude:

"Are you weary, love? or will you dance? Your cousin is negligent to-night."

"Oh, no, I have not wished to dance. Let us go now, and Evan, come to me to-morrow evening, when you will find a few friends and much music," she answered, with an unquiet glance at her husband, a significant one at her cousin, who obeyed it by leaving them with a silent bow.

The homeward drive was as quiet as the other had been, and when they alighted Stähl followed his wife into the drawing-room; there, dropping wearily into a seat, he removed the handkerchief which had been pressed to his lips, and she saw that it was steeped in blood.

"Pardon me—it was unavoidable. Please ring for Marjory," he said, feebly.

Ursula neither spoke nor stirred, but stood regarding him with an expression which alarmed him, it was so full of a strange, stern triumph. It gave him strength to touch the bell, and when the faithful old woman who had nursed him from his babyhood came hurrying in, to say quietly:

"Take that ugly thing away, and bring my drops; also your mistress's vinaigrette, she needs it."

"Not she, the icicle," muttered Marjory, who adored her master, and heartily disliked her mistress because she did not do likewise.

When the momentary faintness had cleared away Stähl's quick eye at once took in the scene before him. Marjory was carefully preparing the draught, and Ursula stood watching her with curious intentness.

"What is that?" she asked, as the old woman put down the tiny vial, containing a colorless and scentless liquid.

"Poison, madam, one drop of which will restore life, while a dozen will bring a sure and sudden death."

Ursula took up the little vial, read the label containing both the medicine and its maker's name, and laid it back again with a slight motion of head and lips, as if she gave a mute assent to some secret suggestion. Marjory's lamentations as she moved about him drew the wife's eyes to her husband, and meeting his she asked coldly:

"Can I help you?"

"Thanks, Marjory will tend me. Good-night, you'll not be troubled with me long."

"No, I shall not; I have borne enough."

She spoke low to herself, but both listeners heard her, and the old woman sternly answered:

"May the Lord forgive you for that speech, madam."

"He will, for He sees the innocent and the guilty, and He knows my sore temptation."

Then without another look or word she left them with the aspect of one walking in an evil dream.

All night Marjory hovered about her master, and early in the morning his physician came. A few words assured Stähl that his hour was drawing very near, and that whatever work remained to be done must be accomplished speedily. He listened calmly to the truth which he had forced from the reluctant doctor, and when he paused made no lament, but said, with more than his accustomed gentleness:

"You will oblige me by concealing this fact from my wife. It is best to let it break upon her by merciful degrees."

"I understand, sir, I will be dumb; but I

must caution you not to exert or agitate yourself in the least, for any undue exertion or excitement would be fatal in your weak state."

The worthy doctor spoke earnestly, but to his infinite amazement and alarm his patient rose suddenly from the couch on which he lay half dressed, and standing erect before him, said forcibly, while his hollow cheeks burned crimson, and his commanding eye almost enforced belief in his assertion:

"You are mistaken; I am not weak, for I have done with fear as well as hope, and if I choose to barter my month of life for one hour, one moment of exertion or excitement, I have the right to do it."

He paused, took breath and added:

"My wife intended to receive her friends tonight; she must not be disappointed, therefore you will not only tell her I am in no danger, but add that an unexpected crisis in my malady has come, and that with care and a season at the South I shall yet be a hale and hearty man. Grant me this favor, I shall not forget it."

The doctor was both a poor and a timid man; his generous but eccentric patient was a fortune to him; the falsehood seemed a kind one; the hint of a rich remembrance was irresistible, and bowing his acquiescence, he departed to obey directions to the letter.

All that day Ursula sat in her room writing steadily, and all that day her husband watched and waited for her coming, but sent no invitation and received no message. At dusk she went out alone. Her departure was unheard and unseen by any but the invalid, whose every sense was alert; his quick ear caught the soft rustle of her dress as she passed his door, and dragging himself to the window he saw her glide away, wrapped in a shrouding cloak. At that sight Stähl's hand was lifted to the bell, but he dropped it, saying to himself:

"No, if she did not mean to return she would have taken care to tell me she was coming back; women always betray themselves by too much art. I have it! she has been writing, Marjory says; the letter is to Evan; she fears he may not come to-night, and trusts no one but herself to post it. I must assure myself of this."

Nerved with new strength, he went down into the dainty room so happily prepared and dedicated to Ursula's sole use. It was empty, but the charm of her presence lingered there, and every graceful object spoke of her. Lights burned upon the writing-table; the ink was still wet in the pen, and scattered papers confirmed the report of her day's employment; but no written word was visible, no note or packet anywhere appeared. A brief survey satisfied her husband, and assured him of the truth of his suspicion.

"Oh, for an hour of my old strength to end this entanglement like a man, instead of being forced to wait for time and chance to aid me like a timorous woman," he sighed, looking out into the wild March night, tormented by an impotent desire to follow his truant wife, yet conscious that it was impossible unless he left a greater work undone, for hourly he felt his power decline, and one dark purpose made him tenacious of the life fast slipping from his hold.

For many moments he stood thinking deeply, so deeply that the approach of a light, rapid step roused him too late for escape. It was his wife's step; why was she returning so soon? had her heart failed her? had some unforeseen occurrence thwarted her? She had not been absent long enough to post a letter to reach Evan's lodgings, or the house of any friend, then where had she been? An uncontrollable impulse caused Stähl to step noiselessly into the shadow of a curtained recess as these thoughts flashed through his mind, and hardly had he done so when Ursula hurried in wet, wild-eyed and breathless, but wearing a look of pale determination which gave place to an expression of keen anxiety as she glanced about the room as if in search of something. Presently she murmured half aloud, "He shall never say again that I do not trust his honor. Lie there in safety till I need you, little friend," and lifting the cover of a carved ivory casket that ornamented the low chimneypiece, she gave some treasure to its keeping, saying, as she turned away with an air of feverish excitement, "Now for Evan and—my liberty!"

Nothing stirred in the room but the flicker of the fire and the softly moving pendulum of the clock that pointed to the hour of seven, till the door of Ursula's distant dressing-room closed behind her and a bell had summoned her maid. Then, from the recess, Stähl went straight to the ivory ornament and laid his hand upon its lid, yet paused long before he lifted it. The simple fact of her entire trust in him at any other time would have been the earnest safeguard of her secret; even now it restrained him by appealing to that inconsistent code of honor which governs many a man who would shoot his dearest friend for a hot word, and yet shrink with punctilious pride from breaking the seal of any letter that did not bear his name. Stähl hesitated till her last words stung his memory, making his own perfidy seem slight compared to hers. "I have a right to know," he said, "for when she forgets her honor I must preserve mine at any cost." A rapid gesture uncovered the casket, and showed him nothing but a small, sealed bottle, lying alone upon the velvet lining. A harmless little thing it looked, yet Stähl's face whitened terribly, and he staggered to a seat, as if the glance he gave had shown him his own death-warrant. He believed it had, for in size, shape, label and colorless contents the little vial was the counterpart of another last seen in Ursula's hand, one difference only in the two—that had been nearly empty, this was full to the lip.

In an instant her look, tone, gesture of the preceding night returned to him, and with the vivid recollection came the firm conviction that Ursula had yielded to a black temptation, and in her husband's name had purchased her husband's death. Till now no feeling but the intensest love had filled his heart towards her; Evan he had learned to hate, himself to despise, but of his wife he had made an idol and worshipped her with a blind passion that would not see defects, own disloyalty or suspect deceit.

From any other human being the treachery would not have been so base, but from her it was doubly bitter, for she knew and owned her knowledge of his exceeding love. "Am I not dying fast enough for her impatience? Could she not wait a little, and let me go happy in my ignorance?" he cried within himself, forgetting in the anguish of that moment the falsehood told her at his bidding, for the furtherance of another purpose as sinful but less secret than her own. How time passed he no longer knew nor cared, as leaning his head upon his hands, he took counsel with his own unquiet heart, for all the evil passions, the savage impulses of his nature were aroused, and raged rebelliously in utter defiance of the feeble prison that confined them. Like all strong yet selfish souls, the wrongs he had committed looked to him very light compared with this, and seeing only his own devotion, faith and patience, no vengeance seemed too heavy for a crime that would defraud him of his poor remnant of unhappy life. Suddenly he lifted up his head, and on his face was stamped a ruthless, reckless purpose, which no earthly power could change or stay. An awesome smile touched his white lips, and the ominous fierceness glittered in his eye—for he was listening to a devil that sat whispering in his heart.

"I shall have my hour of excitement sooner than I thought," he said low to himself, as he left the room, carrying the vial with him. "My last prediction will be verified, although the victim and the culprit are one, and Evan shall live to wish that Ursula had died before me."

An hour later Ursula came to him as he sat gloomily before his chamber fire, while Marjory stood tempting him to taste the cordial she had brought. As if some impassable and unseen abyss already yawned between them, she gave him neither wifely caress nor evening greeting, but pausing opposite, said, with an inclination of her handsome head, which would have seemed a haughty courtesy but for the gentle coldness of her tone:

"I have obeyed the request you sent me, and made ready to receive the friends whose coming would else have been delayed. Is it your pleasure that I excuse you to them, or will you join us as you have often done when other invalids would fear to leave their beds?"

Her husband looked at her as she spoke, wondering what woman's whim had led her to assume a dress rich in itself, but lustreless and sombre as a mourning garb; its silken darkness relieved only by the gleam of fair arms through folds of costly lace, and a knot of roses, scarcely whiter than the bosom they adorned.

"Thanks for your compliance, Ursula. I will come down later in the evening for a moment to receive congratulations on the restoration promised me. Shall I receive yours then?"

"No, now, for now I can wish you a long and happy life, can rejoice that time is given you to learn a truer faith, and ask you to forgive me if in thought, or word, or deed I have wronged or wounded you."

Strangely sweet and solemn was her voice, and for the first time in many months her old smile shed its serenest sunshine on her face, touching it with a meeker beauty than that which it had lost. Her husband shot one glance at her as the last words left her lips, then veiled the eyes that blazed with sudden scorn and detestation. His voice was always under his control, and tranquilly it answered her, while his heart cried out within him:

"I forgive as I would be forgiven, and trust that the coming years will be to you all that I desire to have them. Go to your pleasures, Ursula, and let me hear you singing, whether I am there or here."

"Can I do nothing else for you, Felix, before I go?" she asked, pausing, as she turned away, as if some involuntary impulse ruled her.

Stähl smiled a strange smile as he said, pointing to the goblet and the minute bottle Marjory had just placed on the table at his side:

"You shall sweeten a bitter draught for me by mixing it, and I will drink to you when I take it by-and-by."

His eye was on her now, keen, cold and steadfast, as she drew near to serve him. He saw the troubled look she fixed upon the cup, he saw her hand tremble as she poured the one safe drop, and heard a double meaning in her words:

"This is the first, I hope it may be the last time that I shall need to pour this dangerous draught for you."

She laid down the nearly emptied vial, replaced the cup and turned to go. But, as if bent on trying her to the utmost, though each test tortured him, Stähl arrested her by saying, with an unwonted tremor in his voice, a rebellious tenderness in his eyes:

"Stay, Ursula, I may fall asleep and so not see you until—morning. Bid me good-night, my wife."

She went to him, as if drawn against her will, and for a moment they stood face to face, looking their last on one another in this life. Then Stähl snatched her to him with an embrace almost savage in its passionate fervor, and Ursula kissed him once with the cold lips, that said, without a smile, "Good-night, my husband, sleep in peace!"

"Judas!" he muttered, as she vanished,

leaving him spent with the controlled emotions of that brief interview. Old Marjory heard the word, and from that involuntary betrayal seemed to gather courage for a secret which had burned upon her tongue for two mortal hours. As Stähl sunk again into his cushioned seat, and seemed about to relapse into his moody reverie, she leaned towards him, saying in a whisper:

"May I tell you something, sir?"

"Concerning what or whom, my old gossip?" he answered, listlessly, yet with even more than usual kindliness, for now this humble, faithful creature seemed his only friend.

"My mistress, sir," she said, nodding significantly.

His face woke then, he sat erect, and with an eager gesture bade her speak.

"I've long mistrusted her; for ever since her cousin came she has not been the woman or the wife she was at first. It's not for me to meddle, but it's clear to see that if you were gone there'd be a wedding soon."

Stähl frowned, eyed her keenly, seemed to catch some helpful hint from her indignant countenance, and answered, with a pensive smile:

"I know it, I forgive it; and am sure that, for my sake, you will be less frank to others. Is this what you wished to tell me, Marjory?"

"Bless your unsuspecting heart, I wish it was, sir. I heard her words last night, I watched her all to-day, and when she went out at dusk I followed her, and saw her buy it."

Stähl started, as if about to give vent to some sudden passion, but repressed it, and with a look of well-feigned wonder, asked:

"Buy what?"

Marjory pointed silently to the table, upon which lay three objects, the cup, the little vial and a rose that had fallen from Ursula's bosom as she bent to render her husband the small service he had asked of her. There was no time to feign horror, grief or doubt, for a paroxysm of real pain seized him in its gripe, and served him better than any counterfeit of mental suffering could have done. He conquered it by the power of an inflexible spirit that would not yield yet, and laying his thin hand on Marjory's arm, he whispered, hastily:

"Hush! Never hint that again, I charge you. I bade her get it, my store was nearly gone, and I feared I should need it in the night."

The old woman read his answer as he meant she should, and laid her withered cheek down on his hand, saying, with the tearless grief of age:

"Always so loving, generous and faithful! You may forgive her, but I never can."

Neither spoke for several minutes, then Stähl said:

"I will lie down and try to rest a little before I go—"

The sentence remained unfinished, as, with a weary yet wistful air, he glanced about the shadowy room, asking, dumbly, "Where?" Then he shook off the sudden influence of some deeper sentiment than fear that for an instant thrilled and startled him.

"Leave me, Marjory, set the door ajar, and let me be alone until I ring."

She went, and for an hour he lay listening to the steps of gathering guests, the sound of music, the soft murmur of conversation, and the pleasant stir of life that filled the house with its social charm, making his solitude doubly deep, his mood doubly bitter. Once

Ursula stole in, and finding him apparently asleep, paused for a moment studying the wan face, with its stirless lids, its damp forehead and its pale lips, scarcely parted by the fitful breath, then, like a sombre shadow, flitted from the room again, unconscious that the closed eyes flashed wide to watch her go.

Presently there came a sudden hush, and borne on the wings of an entrancing air Ursula's voice came floating up to him, like the sweet, soft whisper of some better angel, imploring him to make a sad life noble by one just and generous action at its close. No look, no tone, no deed of patience, tenderness or self-sacrifice of hers but rose before him now, and pleaded for her with the magic of that unconscious lay. No ardent hope, no fair ambition, no high purpose of his youth, but came again to show the utter failure of his manhood, and in the hour darkened by a last temptation his benighted soul groped blindly for a firmer faith than that which superstition had defrauded of its virtue. Like many another man, for one short hour Felix Stähl wavered between good and evil, and like so many a man in whom passion outweighs principle, evil won. As the magical music ceased, a man's voice took up the strain, a voice mellow, strong and clear, singing as if the exultant song were but the outpouring of a hopeful, happy heart. Like some wild creature wounded suddenly, Stähl leaped from his couch and stood listening with an aspect which would have appalled the fair musician and struck the singer dumb.

"She might have spared me that!" he panted, as through the heavy beating of his heart he heard the voice he hated lending music to the song he loved, a song of lovers parting in the summer night, whose dawn would break upon their wedding-day. Whatever hope of merciful relenting might have been kindled by one redeeming power was for ever quenched by that ill-timed air, for with a gesture of defiant daring, Stähl drew the full vial from his breast, dashed its contents into the cup, and drained it to the dregs.

A long shudder crept over him as he set it down, then a pale peace dawned upon his face, as, laying his weary head upon the pillow it would never find sleepless any more, he pressed the rose against his lips, saying, with a bitter smile that never left his face again:

"I won my rose, and her thorns have pierced me to the heart; but my blight is on her, and no other man will wear her in his bosom when I am gone."

Part III

"Stay, Evan, when the others go; I have much to say to you, and a packet of valuable papers to entrust to you. Do not forget."

"You regard me with a strange look, Ursula, you speak in a strange tone. What has happened?"

"They tell me that Felix will live, with care and a journey to the South."

"I catch your meaning now. You will go with him."

"No, my journey will be made alone."

She looked beyond him as she spoke, with a rapt yet tranquil glance, and such a sudden brightness shone upon her face that her cousin watched her half bewildered for a moment; then caught at a hope that filled him with a troubled joy, and whispered with beating heart and lowered voice:

"Shall I not follow you, Ursula?"

Her eye came back to him, clear and calm, yet very tender in its wistfulness, and though her words sounded propitious his hope died suddenly.

"I think you will follow soon, and I shall wait for you in the safe refuge I am seeking."

They stood silent for many minutes, thinking thoughts for which they had no words, then as a pause fell after music, Ursula said:

"Now I must sing again. Give me a draught of water, my throat is parched."

Her cousin served her, but before the water touched her lips the glass fell shattered at her feet, for a wild, shrill cry rang through the house silencing the gay sounds below, and rudely breaking the long hush that had reigned above. For one breathless instant all stood like living images of wonder, fear and fright, all waited for what should follow that dread cry. An agitated servant appeared upon the threshold seeking his mistress. She saw him, yet stood as if incapable of motion, as he made his way to her through a crowd of pale, expectant faces.

"What is it?" she asked, with lips that could hardly syllable the words.

"My master, madam—dead in his bed—old Marjory has just found him. I've sent for Doctor Keen," began the man, but Ursula only seemed to hear and understand one word:

"Dead!" she echoed—"so suddenly, so soon—it cannot be true. Evan, take me to him."

She stretched out her hands as if she had gone blind, and led by her cousin, left the room, followed by several guests, in whom curiosity or sympathy was stronger than etiquette or fear. Up they went, a strange procession, and entering the dusky room, lighted only by a single shaded lamp, found Marjory lamenting over her dead master in a paroxysm of the wildest grief. Evan passed in before his cousin, bent hastily and listened at the breathless lips, touched the chill forehead, and bared the wrist to feel if any flutter lingered in the pulse. But as he pushed back the loose sleeve of the wrapper, upon the wasted arm appeared a strange device. Two slender serpents twined together like the ring, and in the circle several Hindoo characters traced in the same deep red lines. At that sight the arm dropped from his hold, and he fell back daunted by a nameless fear which he could neither master nor divine.

As Ursula appeared the old woman's grief

changed to an almost fierce excitement, for rising she pointed from the dead husband to the living wife, crying shrilly:

"Come; come and see your work, fair-faced devil that you are! Here he lies, safe in the deadly sleep you gave him. Look at him and deny it if you dare!"

Ursula did look, and through the horror that blanched her face many eyes saw the shadow of remorse, the semblance of guilt. Stähl lay as she left him, his head pillowed on his arm with the easy grace habitual to him, but the pallor of that sleeping face was now changed to the awful grayness that living countenances never wear. A bitter smile still lingered on the white lips, and those mysterious eyes were wide open, full of a gloomy intelligence that appalled the beholder with the scornful triumph which still lurked there unconquered even by death. These defiant eyes appeared fixed on Ursula alone; she could not look away, nor break the spell that held her own, and through the hurried scene that followed she seemed to address her dead husband, not her living accuser.

"My work? the sleep I gave? what dare I

not deny?" she said, below her breath, like one bewildered.

"See her feign innocence with guilt stamped on her face!" cried Marjory, in a passion of indignant sorrow. "You killed him, that is your work. You drugged that cup with the poison I saw you buy to-day—that is the sleep you gave him—and you dare not deny that you hated him, wished him dead, and said last night you'd not be troubled long, for you had borne enough."

"I did not kill him! You saw me prepare his evening draught, and what proof have you that he did not pass away in sleep?" demanded Ursula, more firmly, yet with an awestruck gaze still fixed upon her husband's face.

"This is my proof!" and Marjory held up the empty counterpart of the little vial that lay on the table.

"That here! I left it in my—"

A hand at Ursula's lips cut short the perilous admission, as Evan whispered:

"Hush! for God's sake, own nothing yet."

"Too late for that," screamed Marjory, more and more excited by each word. "I found it in the ashes where she flung it in her haste, believing it was destroyed. I saw it glitter when I went to mend the fire before I woke my master. I knew it by the freshness of the label, and in a moment felt that my poor master was past all waking of mine, and found it so. I saw her buy it, I told him of it, but he loved her still and tried to deceive me with the kind lie that he bade her do it. I showed him that I knew the truth, and he only said, 'I know it, I forgive her, keep the secret for my sake,' and trusting her to the last, paid for his blind faith with his life."

"No, no, I never murdered him! I found him sleeping like a child an hour ago, and in that sleep he died," said Ursula, wringing her hands like one well nigh distraught.

"An hour ago! hear that and mark it all of you," cried Marjory. "Two hours ago she bade him good night before me, and he called her 'Judas,' as she kissed him and went. Now she owns that she returned and found him safely sleeping—God forgive me that I ever left him! for then she must have remixed the draught in which he drank his death. Oh, madam! could you have no pity, could you not remember how he loved you? see your rose fast shut in his poor dead hand—could you not leave him the one little month of life he had to live before you were set free?"

"One month!" said Ursula, with a startled look. "They told me he would live to be a hale, old man. Why was I so deceived?"

"Because he would not mar your pleasure even for a single night. He meant to tell you the sad truth gently, for he thought you had a woman's heart, and would mourn him a little though you could not love."

Paler Ursula could not become, but as mesh after mesh of the net in which she had unconsciously helped to snare herself appeared, her husband's purpose flashed upon her, yet seemed too horrible for belief, till the discovery of that last deceit was made; then like one crushed by an overwhelming blow, she covered up her face and sunk down at Evan's feet. He did not raise her up, and though a gust of eager, agitated voices went whispering through the room, no one spoke to her, no one offered comfort to the widow, counsel to the woman, pity to the culprit. They listened only to old Marjory, who poured forth her story with such genuine grief, such perfect sincerity, that all felt its pathos and few doubted its entire truth. Evan alone believed in Ursula's denial, even while to himself he owned that she had borne enough to make any means of liberation tempting. He saw more clearly than the rest how every act, look and word of hers condemned her; and felt with a bitter pang that such an accusation, even if proved false, must cast a shadow on her name and darken all her life.

Suddenly, when the stir was at its height, Ursula rose, calm, cold and steady; yet few who saw her then ever forgot the desolate despair which made that beautiful face a far more piteous sight than the dead one. Turning with all her wonted dignity, she confronted the excited group, and without a tear in her eye, a falter in her voice, a trace of shame, guilt or fear in mien or manner, she said clearly, solemnly,

"I am guilty of murder in my heart, for I did wish that man dead; but I did not kill him. The words I spoke that night were the expression of a resolve made in a moment of despair, a resolve to end my own life, when I could bear no more. To-day I was told that he would live; then my time seemed come, and believing this to be my last night on earth, I bade my husband farewell as we parted, and in a few hours hoped to lay down the burden he had made heavier than I could bear. That poison was purchased for myself, not him; he discovered it, believed I meant his death, and with a black art, which none can fathom but myself, so distorted my acts and words, before a witness, that the deed committed by himself should doom me to ignominy and avenge his wrong. I have no hope that any one will credit so wild a tale, and therein his safety lies; but God knows I speak the truth, and He will judge between us at a more righteous bar than any I can stand at here. Now do with me as you will, I am done."

Through all the bitter scenes of public accusation, trial and condemnation Ursula preserved the same mournful composure, as if having relinquished both hope and fear, no emotion remained to disturb the spirit of entire self-abnegation which had taken possession of her. All her cousin's entreaties, commands and prayers failed to draw from her the key to the mystery of her strange marriage; even when, after many merciful delays, sentence was at length pronounced upon her, and captivity for life was known to be her doom, she still refused to confess, saying:

"This fate is worse than death; but till I lie on my deathbed I will prove faithful to the promise made that man, traitorous as he was to me. I have done with the world, so leave me to such peace as I can know, and go your way, dear Evan, to forget that such a mournful creature lives."

But when all others fell away, when so-called friends proved timid, when enemies grew insolent and the whole world seemed to cast her off, one man was true to her, one man still loved, believed and honored her, still labored to save her when all others gave her up as lost, still stood between her and the curious, sharp-tongued, heavy-handed world, earning a great compassion for himself, and, in time, a juster, gentler sentiment in favor of the woman whose sin and shame he had so nobly helped to bear.

Weeks and months went heavily by, the city wearied itself with excited conjectures, conflicting rumors, varying opinions, and slowly came to look with more lenient eyes upon the beautiful culprit, whose tragic fate, with its unexplained mystery, began to plead for her more eloquently than the most gifted advocate. Few doubted her guilt, and, as she feared, few believed the accusations she brought against her dead husband; but the plea of temporary insanity had been made by her counsel, and though she strenuously denied its truth, there were daily growing hopes of pardon for an offense which, thanks to Evan's tireless appeals, now wore a far less heinous aspect than at first.

All the long summer days Ursula sat alone in her guarded room, tranquilly enjoying the sunshine that flickered through the leaves with which Evan had tried to mask the bars that shut out liberty but not heaven's light. All the balmy summer nights she lay on her narrow bed, haunted by dreams that made sleep a penance and not a pleasure, or watched, with wakeful eyes, the black shadow of a cross the moon cast upon her breast as it peered through the barred window like a ghostly face. To no one did she reveal the thoughts that burdened her, whitening her hair, furrowing her face and leaving on her forehead the impress of a great grief which no human joy could ever efface.

One autumn day Evan came hastening in full of a glad excitement, which for the moment seemed to give him back the cheery youthfulness he was fast losing. He found his cousin lying on the couch he had provided for her, for even the prison officers respected that faithful love, and granted every favor in their power. She, too, seemed to be blessed with a happy mood, for the gloom had left her eyes, a peaceful smile sat on her lips, and when she spoke her voice was musical, with an undertone of deep emotion.

"Bless your tranquil face, Ursula! One would think you guessed my tidings without telling. Yes, it is almost certain that the pardon will be granted, in answer to my prayers. One more touch will win the men who hold your fate in their hands, and that touch you can give by clearing up the mystery of Stähl's strange power over you. For your own sake and for mine do not deny me now."

"I will not."

The joy, surprise and satisfaction of the moment caused Evan to forget the sad condition upon which this confidence could be accorded. He thought only of all they had suffered, all they might yet enjoy if the pardon could be gained, and holding that thin hand fast in both his own, he listened, with absorbing interest, to the beloved voice that unfolded to him the romance within a romance, which had made a tragedy of three lives.

"I must take you far back into the past, Evan, for my secret is but the sequel of one begun long before our birth. Our grandfather, as you know, was made governor of an Indian province while still a young and comely man. One of the native princes, though a conquered subject, remained his friend, and the sole daughter of this prince loved the handsome Englishman with the despotic fervor of her race. The prince offered the hand of the fair Naya to his friend, but being already betrothed to an English girl, he courteously declined the alliance. That insult, as she thought it, never was forgiven or forgotten by the haughty princess; but, with the subtle craft of her half-savage nature, she devised a vengeance which should not only fall upon the offender, but pursue his descendants to the very last. No apparent breach was made in the friendship of the prince and governor, even when the latter brought his young wife to the residence. But from that hour Naya's curse was on his house, unsuspected and unsleeping, and as years went by the Fate of the Forrests became a tragical story throughout British India, for the brothers, nephews and sons of Roger Forrest all died violent or sudden deaths, and the old man himself was found murdered in the jungle when at the height of fame and favor.

"Two twin lads alone remained of all who had borne the name, and for a time the fatal doom seemed averted, as they grew to manhood, married and seemed born to know all the blessings which virtue and valor could deserve. But though the princess and her father were dead, the curse was still relentlessly executed by some of her kindred, for in the year of your birth your father vanished suddenly, utterly, in broad day, yet left no trace behind, and from that hour to this no clue to the lost man was ever found beyond a strong suspicion, which was never confirmed. In that same year a horrible discovery was made, which shocked and dismayed all Christian India, and was found hard of belief across the sea. Among the tribes that infested certain provinces, intent on mischief and difficult to subdue, was one class of assassins unknown even to the native governments of the country, and entirely unsuspected by the English. This society was as widely spread and carefully organized as it was secret, powerful and fanatical. Its members worshipped a gloomy divinity called Bohwanie, who, according to their heathen belief, was best propitiated by human sacrifices. The name of these devotees was Phansegars, or Brothers of the Good Work; and he who offered up the greatest number of victims was most favored by the goddess, and received a high place in the Hindoo heaven. All India was filled with amazement and affright at this discovery, and mysteries, till then deemed unfathomable, became as clear as day. Among others the Fate of the Forrests was revealed; for by the confession of the one traitor who betrayed the society, it appeared that the old prince and his sons had been members of the brotherhood, which had its higher and its lower grades, and when the young governor drew down upon himself the wrath of Naya, her kindred avenged her by propitiating Bohwanie with victim after victim from our fated family, always working so secretly that no trace of their art remained but the seal of death.

"This terrible discovery so dismayed my father that, taking you, an orphan then, and my mother, he fled to England, hoping to banish the dreadful past from his mind. But he never could, and it preyed upon him night and day. No male Forrest had escaped the doom since the curse was spoken, and an unconquerable foreboding haunted him that sooner or later he too should be sacrificed, though continents and oceans lay between him and the avengers. The fact that the black brotherhood was discovered and destroyed weighed little with him, for still a fear pursued him that Naya's kindred would hand down the curse from generation to generation, and execute with that tenacity of purpose which in that climate of the passions makes the humblest foe worthy of fear. He doubted all men, confided his secret to none, not even to his wife, and led a wandering life with us until my mother died. You remember, Evan, that the same malady that destroyed her fell likewise upon you, and that my father was forced to leave us in Paris, that he might comply with my mother's last desire and lay her in English ground. Before he went he took me apart and told me the dark history of our unfortunate family, that I might be duly impressed with the necessity of guarding you with a sleepless vigilance; for even then he could not free himself from that ominous foreboding, soon, alas! to be confirmed. It was a strange confidence to place in a girl of seventeen, but he had no friend at hand, and knowing how wholly I loved you, how safe I was from the Fate of the Forrests, he gave you to my charge and left us for a week. You know he never came again, but found his ghostly fear a sad reality in England, and on the day that was to give my mother's body to the earth he was discovered dead in his bed, with the marks of fingers at his throat, yet no other trace of his murderer ever appeared, and another dark secret was buried in the grave. You remember the horror and the grief that nearly killed me when the tidings came, and how from that hour there was a little cloud between us, a cloud I could not lift because I had solemnly promised my father that I would watch over you, yet conceal the fate that menaced you, lest it should mar your peace as it had done his own. Evan, I have kept my word till the danger is for ever past."

She paused there, but for a moment her cousin could only gaze at her, bewildered by the sudden light let in by the gloomy past. Presently he said, impetuously:

"You have, my faithful Ursula, and I will prove that I am grateful by watching over you with a vigilance as sleepless and devoted as your own. But tell me, was there nowhere in the world justice, power or wit enough to stay that savage curse? Why did not my father, or yours, appeal to the laws of either country and obtain redress?"

"They did, and, like others, appealed in vain; for, till the Phansegars were discovered, they knew not whom to accuse. After that, as Naya's kindred were all gone but a few newly-converted women and harmless children, no magistrate in India would condemn the innocent for the crimes of their race, and my father had no proofs to bring against them. Few in England believed the seemingly incredible story when it was related to them in the Indian reports. No, Evan, the wily princess entrusted her revenge to able hands, and well they did the work to the very last, as we have bitter cause to know. Every member of the brotherhood, and every helper of the curse, bore on his left arm the word 'Bohwanie!' in Hindoo characters. You saw the sign on that dead arm. Do you understand the secret now?"

"Great heavens, Ursula! Do you mean that Stähl, a Christian man, belonged to this heathen league? Surely you wrong him there."

"You will not think so when I have told all. It seemed as horrible, as incredible to me as now to you, when I first saw and comprehended on the night that changed both our lives. Stähl suspected, from many unconscious betrayals of mine (my dislike of India, my anxiety for you, then absent, and a hundred indications unseen by other eyes) that I knew the secret of the curse; he proved it by whispering the hated name of Bohwanie in my ear, and showing me the fatal sign—I knew it, for my father had told me that also. Need I tell you what recollections rushed upon me when I saw it, what visions of blood rose red before my panic-stricken eyes, how instantly I felt the truth of my instinctive aversion to him, despite his charms of mind and manner, and, above all, how utterly I was overpowered by a sense of your peril in the presence of your unknown enemy? A single thought, hope, purpose ruled me, to save you at any cost, and guard the secret still; for I felt that I possessed some power over that dread man, and resolved to use it to the uttermost. You left us, and then I learned at what a costly price I could purchase the life so dear to me. Stähl briefly told me that his mother and one old woman were the last of Naya's race, and when his grandfather, who belonged to the brotherhood, suffered death with them, he charged her to perpetuate the curse, as all the members of the family had pledged themselves to do. She promised, and when my father left India she followed, but could not discover his hiding-place, and with a blind faith in destiny, as native to her as her superstition, she left time to bring her victim to her. While resting from her quest in Germany she met and married Felix Stähl, the elder, a learned man, fond of the mysticism and wisdom of the East, who found an irresistible charm in the dark-eyed woman, who, for his sake, became a Christian in name, though she still clung to her Pagan gods in secret. With such parents what wonder that the son was the man we found him? for his father bequeathed him his features, feeble health, rare learning and accomplishments; his mother those Indian eyes that I never can forget, his fiery yet subtle nature, the superstitious temperament and the fatal vow.

"While the father lived she kept her secret hidden; when he died, Felix, then a man, was told it, and having been carefully prepared by every art, every appeal to the pride and passion of his race, every shadow years of hatred could bring to blacken the memory of the first Forrest and the wrong he was believed to have done their ancestors, Felix was induced to take upon himself the fulfilment of the family vow. Yet living in a Christian community, and having been bred up by a virtuous father, it was a hard task to assume, and only the commands of the mother whom he adored would have won compliance. He was told that but two Forrests now remained, one a girl who was to go scatheless, the other a boy, who, sooner or later, was to fall by his hand, for he was now the last male of his race as you of ours. How his mother discovered these facts he never knew, unless from the old woman who came to them from England to die near her kin. I suspect that she was the cause of my poor father's death, though Stähl swore that he never knew of it until I told him.

"After much urging, many commands, he gave the promise, asking only freedom to do the work as he would, for though the savage spirit of his Hindoo ancestors lived again in him, the influence of civilization made the savage modes of vengeance abhorrent to him. His mother soon followed the good professor, then leaving our meeting still to chance, Felix went roaming up and down the world a solitary, studious man, for ever haunted by the sinful deed he had promised to perform, and which grew ever more and more repugnant to him.

"In an evil hour we met; my name first arrested him; my beauty (I may speak of it now for it is gone) attracted him; my evident aversion piqued his pride and roused his will to overcome it; and then the knowledge of my love for you fanned his smouldering passion to a blaze and confirmed his wavering purpose. You asked on that sad night if I had learned to love while you were gone? I spoke truly when I answered yes, for absence proved how dear you had become to me, and I only waited your return to gratefully accept the love with which I knew your heart was overflowing. You came, and seeing Stähl's devotion, doubted the affection I never had confessed. He saw it plainly, he divined your passion, and in an hour decided upon gratifying his own desire, keeping the promise he made his mother, yet sparing himself the crime of murder, well knowing that for you life without me would be a fate more dark than any death he could devise. I pleaded, prayed and wept, but he was inexorable. To tell you was to destroy you, for he feared nothing; to keep the secret was to forfeit your love and sacrifice myself. One hope alone remained to me, a sinful yet a pardonable one in such a strait as mine; Felix could not live long; I might support life for a time by the thought that I had saved you, by the hope that I might soon undeceive and recompense you for the loss you had sustained. Evan, it was a natural yet unrighteous act, for I did evil that good might come of it, and such deeds never prosper. Better have left you in God's hand, better even have seen you dead and at peace than have condemned you to the life you have led and still must lead for years perhaps. I was a weak, loving, terror-stricken woman, and in that dreadful hour one fear overwhelmed all other passions, principles and thoughts. I could save you, and to accomplish that I would so gladly have suffered death in any shape. Believe that, dearest Evan, and forgive me for the fate to which I have condemned the man I love, truly, tenderly even to the end."

Her voice died in a broken sob as Evan gathered her close to his sore heart, and she clung there spent and speechless, as if the pain of parting were for ever over and her refuge found at last. Evan spoke first, happily and hopefully for, the future opened clearly, and the long twilight seemed about to break into a blissful dawn.

"You shall be repaid for your exceeding love, Ursula, with a devotion such as man never gave to woman until now. There is no longer any cloud between us, nor shall there be between you and the world. Justice shall be done, and then we will leave this city of bitter memories behind us, and go away together to begin the new life that lies before us."

"We shall begin a new life, but not together, Evan," was the low answer, as she tenderly laid her pale cheek to his, as if to soften the hard truth.

"But, love, you will be free at once; there can be no doubt of the pardon now."

"Yes, I shall soon be free, but human hands will not open my prison doors, and I humbly trust that I may receive pardon, but not from human lips. Evan, I told you I would never tell my secret till I lay on my deathbed; I lie there now."

If she had stabbed him with the hand folded about his neck, the act would not have shocked and startled him like those last words. They pierced him to the heart, and as if in truth he had received a mortal wound, he could only gaze at her in dumb dismay, with eyes full of anguish, incredulity and grief.

"Let me seem cruel that I may be merciful, and end both suspense and fear by telling all at once. There is no hope for me. I have prayed to live, but it cannot be, for slowly yet surely Felix has killed me. I said I would gladly die for you, God takes me at my word, and now I am content. Let me make my sacrifice cheerfully, and let the suffering I have known be my atonement for the wrong I did myself and you."

As she spoke so tranquilly, so tenderly, a veil seemed to fall from before her cousin's eyes. He looked into the face that smiled at him, saw there the shadow which no human love can banish, read perfect peace in its pale serenity, felt that life was a poor boon to ask for her, and with a pang that rent that faithful heart of his, silently relinquished the one sustaining hope which had upheld him through that gloomy year. Calm with a grief too deep for tears, he drew the wan and wasted creature who had given herself for him closer to the shelter of his arms, and changed her last fear to loving pride by saying, with a manful courage, a meek resignation that ennobled him by its sincerity:

"Rest here in peace, my Ursula. No selfish grief shall cloud your sunset or rob you of one hour of happy love. I can bear the parting, for I shall follow soon; and thank God that after the long bewilderment of this sad world we may enjoy together the new life which has no end."

Behind a Mask
or
A Woman's Power

By A. M. Barnard

CHAPTER I
Jean Muir

"Has she come?"

"No, Mamma, not yet."

"I wish it were well over. The thought of it worries and excites me. A cushion for my back, Bella."

And poor, peevish Mrs. Coventry sank into an easy chair with a nervous sigh and the air of a martyr, while her pretty daughter hovered about her with affectionate solicitude.

"Who are they talking of, Lucia?" asked the languid young man lounging on a couch near his cousin, who bent over her tapestry work with a happy smile on her usually haughty face.

"The new governess, Miss Muir. Shall I tell you about her?"

"No, thank you. I have an inveterate aversion to the whole tribe. I've often thanked heaven that I had but one sister, and she a spoiled child, so that I have escaped the infliction of a governess so long."

"How will you bear it now?" asked Lucia.

"Leave the house while she is in it."

"No, you won't. You're too lazy, Gerald," called out a younger and more energetic man, from the recess where he stood teasing his dogs.

"I'll give her a three days' trial; if she proves endurable I shall not disturb myself; if, as I am sure, she is a bore, I'm off anywhere, anywhere out of her way."

"I beg you won't talk in that depressing manner, boys. I dread the coming of a stranger more than you possibly can, but Bella *must* not be neglected; so I have nerved myself to endure this woman, and Lucia is good enough to say she will attend to her after tonight."

"Don't be troubled, Mamma. She is a nice person, I dare say, and when once we are used to her, I've no doubt we shall be glad to have her, it's so dull here just now. Lady Sydney said she was a quiet, accomplished, amiable girl, who needed a home, and would be a help to poor stupid me, so try to like her for my sake."

"I will, dear, but isn't it getting late? I do hope nothing has happened. Did you tell them to send a carriage to the station for her, Gerald?"

"I forgot it. But it's not far, it won't hurt her to walk" was the languid reply.

"It was indolence, not forgetfulness, I know. I'm very sorry; she will think it so rude to leave her to find her way so late. Do go and see to it, Ned."

"Too late, Bella, the train was in some time ago. Give your orders to me next time. Mother and I'll see that they are obeyed," said Edward.

"Ned is just at an age to make a fool of himself for any girl who comes in his way. Have a care of the governess, Lucia, or she will bewitch him."

Gerald spoke in a satirical whisper, but his brother heard him and answered with a good-humored laugh.

"I wish there was any hope of your making a fool of yourself in that way, old fellow. Set me a good example, and I promise to follow it. As for the governess, she is a woman, and should be treated with common civility. I should say a little extra kindness wouldn't be amiss, either, because she is poor, and a stranger."

"That is my dear, good-hearted Ned! We'll stand by poor little Muir, won't we?" And running to her brother, Bella stood on tiptoe to offer him a kiss which he could not refuse, for the rosy lips were pursed up invitingly, and the bright eyes full of sisterly affection.

"I do hope she has come, for, when I make an effort to see anyone, I hate to make it in vain. Punctuality is *such* a virtue, and I know this woman hasn't got it, for she promised to be here at seven, and now it is long after," began Mrs. Coventry, in an injured tone.

Before she could get breath for another complaint, the clock struck seven and the doorbell rang.

"There she is!" cried Bella, and turned toward the door as if to go and meet the newcomer.

But Lucia arrested her, saying authoritatively, "Stay here, child. It is her place to come to you, not yours to go to her."

"Miss Muir," announced a servant, and a little black-robed figure stood in the doorway. For an instant no one stirred, and the governess had time to see and be seen before a word was uttered. All looked at her, and she cast on the household group a keen glance that impressed them curiously; then her eyes fell, and bowing slightly she walked in. Edward came forward and received her with the frank cordiality which nothing could daunt or chill.

"Mother, this is the lady whom you expected. Miss Muir, allow me to apologize for our apparent neglect in not sending for you. There was a mistake about the carriage, or, rather, the lazy fellow to whom the order was given forgot it. Bella, come here."

"Thank you, no apology is needed. I did not expect to be sent for." And the governess meekly sat down without lifting her eyes.

"I am glad to see you. Let me take your things," said Bella, rather shyly, for Gerald, still lounging, watched the fireside group with languid interest, and Lucia never stirred. Mrs. Coventry took a second survey and began:

"You were punctual, Miss Muir, which pleases me. I'm a sad invalid, as Lady Sydney told you, I hope; so that Miss Coventry's lessons will be directed by my niece, and you will go to her for directions, as she knows what I wish. You will excuse me if I ask you a few questions, for Lady Sydney's note was very brief, and I left everything to her judgment."

"Ask anything you like, madam," answered the soft, sad voice.

"You are Scotch, I believe."

"Yes, madam."

"Are your parents living?"

"I have not a relation in the world."

"Dear me, how sad! Do you mind telling me your age?"

"Nineteen." And a smile passed over Miss Muir's lips, as she folded her hands with an air of resignation, for the catechism was evidently to be a long one.

"So young! Lady Sydney mentioned five-and-twenty, I think, didn't she, Bella?"

"No, Mamma, she only said she thought so. Don't ask such questions. It's not pleasant before us all," whispered Bella.

A quick, grateful glance shone on her from the suddenly lifted eyes of Miss Muir, as she said quietly, "I wish I was thirty, but, as I am not, I do my best to look and seem old."

Of course, every one looked at her then, and all felt a touch of pity at the sight of the pale-faced girl in her plain black dress, with no ornament but a little silver cross at her throat. Small, thin, and colorless she was, with yellow hair, gray eyes, and sharply cut, irregular, but very expressive features. Poverty seemed to have set its bond stamp upon her, and life to have had for her more frost than sunshine. But something in the lines of the mouth betrayed strength, and the clear, low voice had a curious mixture of command and entreaty in its varying tones. Not an attractive woman, yet not an ordinary one; and, as she sat there with her delicate hands lying in her lap, her head bent, and a bitter look on her thin face, she was more interesting than many a blithe and blooming girl. Bella's heart warmed to her at once, and she drew her seat nearer, while Edward went back to his dogs that his presence might not embarrass her.

"You have been ill, I think," continued Mrs. Coventry, who considered this fact the most interesting of all she had heard concerning the governess.

"Yes, madam, I left the hospital only a week ago."

"Are you quite sure it is safe to begin teaching so soon?"

"I have no time to lose, and shall soon gain

strength here in the country, if you care to keep me."

"And you are fitted to teach music, French, and drawing?"

"I shall endeavor to prove that I am."

"Be kind enough to go and play an air or two. I can judge by your touch; I used to play finely when a girl."

Miss Muir rose, looked about her for the instrument, and seeing it at the other end of the room went toward it, passing Gerald and Lucia as if she did not see them. Bella followed, and in a moment forgot everything in admiration. Miss Muir played like one who loved music and was perfect mistress of her art. She charmed them all by the magic of this spell; even indolent Gerald sat up to listen, and Lucia put down her needle, while Ned watched the slender white fingers as they flew, and wondered at the strength and skill which they possessed.

"Please sing," pleaded Bella, as a brilliant overture ended.

With the same meek obedience Miss Muir complied, and began a little Scotch melody, so sweet, so sad, that the girl's eyes filled, and Mrs. Coventry looked for one of her many pocket-handkerchiefs. But suddenly the music ceased, for, with a vain attempt to support herself, the singer slid from her seat and lay before the startled listeners, as white and rigid as if struck with death. Edward caught her up, and, ordering his brother off the couch, laid her there, while Bella chafed her hands, and her mother rang for her maid. Lucia bathed the poor girl's temples, and Gerald, with unwonted energy, brought a glass of wine. Soon Miss Muir's lips trembled, she sighed, then murmured, tenderly, with a pretty Scotch accent, as if wandering in the past, "Bide wi' me, Mither, I'm sae sick an sad here all alone."

"Take a sip of this, and it will do you good, my dear," said Mrs. Coventry, quite touched by the plaintive words.

The strange voice seemed to recall her. She sat up, looked about her, a little wildly, for a moment, then collected herself and said, with a pathetic look and tone, "Pardon me. I have been on my feet all day, and, in my eagerness to keep my appointment, I forgot to eat since morning. I'm better now; shall I finish the song?"

"By no means. Come and have some tea," said Bella, full of pity and remorse.

"Scene first, very well done," whispered Gerald to his cousin.

Miss Muir was just before them, apparently listening to Mrs. Coventry's remarks upon fainting fits; but she heard, and looked over her shoulders with a gesture like Rachel. Her eyes were gray, but at that instant they seemed black with some strong emotion of anger, pride, or defiance. A curious smile passed over her face as she bowed, and said in her penetrating voice, "Thanks. The last scene shall be still better."

Young Coventry was a cool, indolent man, seldom conscious of any emotion, any passion, pleasurable or otherwise; but at the look, the tone of the governess, he experienced a new sensation, indefinable, yet strong. He colored and, for the first time in his life, looked abashed. Lucia saw it, and hated Miss Muir with a sudden hatred; for, in all the years she had passed with her cousin, no look or word of hers had possessed such power. Coventry was himself again in an instant, with no trace of that passing change, but a look of interest in his usually dreamy eyes, and a touch of anger in his sarcastic voice.

"What a melodramatic young lady! I shall go tomorrow."

Lucia laughed, and was well pleased when he sauntered away to bring her a cup of tea from the table where a little scene was just taking place. Mrs. Coventry had sunk into her chair again, exhausted by the flurry of the fainting fit. Bella was busied about her; and Edward, eager to feed the pale governess, was awkwardly trying to make the tea, after a beseeching glance at his cousin which she did not choose to answer. As he upset the caddy and uttered a despairing exclamation, Miss Muir quietly took her place behind the urn, saying with a smile, and a shy glance at the young man, "Allow me to assume my duty at once, and serve you all. I understand the art of making people comfortable in this way. The scoop, please. I can gather this up quite well alone, if you will tell me how your mother likes her tea."

Edward pulled a chair to the table and made merry over his mishaps, while Miss Muir performed her little task with a skill and grace that made it pleasant to watch her.

Coventry lingered a moment after she had given him a steaming cup, to observe her more nearly, while he asked a question or two of his brother. She took no more notice of him than if he had been a statue, and in the middle of the one remark he addressed to her, she rose to take the sugar basin to Mrs. Coventry, who was quite won by the modest, domestic graces of the new governess.

"Really, my dear, you are a treasure; I haven't tasted such tea since my poor maid Ellis died. Bella never makes it good, and Miss Lucia always forgets the cream. Whatever you do you seem to do well, and that is *such* a comfort."

"Let me always do this for you, then. It will be a pleasure, madam." And Miss Muir came back to her seat with a faint color in her cheek which improved her much.

"My brother asked if young Sydney was at home when you left," said Edward, for Gerald would not take the trouble to repeat the question.

Miss Muir fixed her eyes on Coventry, and answered with a slight tremor of the lips, "No, he left home some weeks ago."

The young man went back to his cousin,

saying, as he threw himself down beside her, "I shall not go tomorrow, but wait till the three days are out."

"Why?" demanded Lucia.

Lowering his voice he said, with a significant nod toward the governess, "Because I have a fancy that she is at the bottom of Sydney's mystery. He's not been himself lately, and now he is gone without a word. I rather like romances in real life, if they are not too long, or difficult to read."

"Do you think her pretty?"

"Far from it, a most uncanny little specimen."

"Then why fancy Sydney loves her?"

"He is an oddity, and likes sensations and things of that sort."

"What do you mean, Gerald?"

"Get the Muir to look at you, as she did at me, and you will understand. Will you have another cup, Juno?"

"Yes, please." She liked to have him wait upon her, for he did it to no other woman except his mother.

Before he could slowly rise, Miss Muir glided to them with another cup on the salver; and, as Lucia took it with a cold nod, the girl said under her breath, "I think it honest to tell you that I possess a quick ear, and cannot help hearing what is said anywhere in the room. What you say of me is of no consequence, but you may speak of things which you prefer I should not hear; therefore, allow me to warn you." And she was gone again as noiselessly as she came.

"How do you like that?" whispered Coventry, as his cousin sat looking after the girl, with a disturbed expression.

"What an uncomfortable creature to have in the house! I am very sorry I urged her coming, for your mother has taken a fancy to her, and it will be hard to get rid of her," said Lucia, half angry, half amused.

"Hush, she hears every word you say. I know it by the expression of her face, for Ned is talking about horses, and she looks as haughty as ever you did, and that is saying much. Faith, this is getting interesting."

"Hark, she is speaking; I want to hear," and Lucia laid her hand on her cousin's lips. He kissed it, and then idly amused himself with turning the rings to and fro on the slender fingers.

"I have been in France several years,

madam, but my friend died and I came back to be with Lady Sydney, till—" Muir paused an instant, then added, slowly, "till I fell ill. It was a contagious fever, so I went of my own accord to the hospital, not wishing to endanger her."

"Very right, but are you sure there is no danger of infection now?" asked Mrs. Coventry anxiously.

"None, I assure you. I have been well for some time, but did not leave because I preferred to stay there, than to return to Lady Sydney."

"No quarrel, I hope? No trouble of any kind?"

"No quarrel, but—well, why not? You have a right to know, and I will not make a foolish mystery out of a very simple thing. As your family, only, is present, I may tell the truth. I did not go back on the young gentleman's account. Please ask no more."

"Ah, I see. Quite prudent and proper, Miss Muir. I shall never allude to it again. Thank you for your frankness. Bella, you will be careful not to mention this to your young friends; girls gossip sadly, and it would annoy Lady Sydney beyond everything to have this talked of."

"Very neighborly of Lady S. to send the dangerous young lady here, where there are *two* young gentlemen to be captivated. I wonder why she didn't keep Sydney after she had caught him," murmured Coventry to his cousin.

"Because she had the utmost contempt for a titled fool." Miss Muir dropped the words almost into his ear, as she bent to take her shawl from the sofa corner.

"How the deuce did she get there?" ejaculated Coventry, looking as if he had received another sensation. "She has spirit, though, and upon my word I pity Sydney, if he did try to dazzle her, for he must have got a splendid dismissal."

"Come and play billiards. You promised, and I hold you to your word," said Lucia, rising with decision, for Gerald was showing too much interest in another to suit Miss Beaufort.

"I am, as ever, your most devoted. My mother is a charming woman, but I find our evening parties slightly dull, when only my own family are present. Good night,

Mamma." He shook hands with his mother, whose pride and idol he was, and, with a comprehensive nod to the others, strolled after his cousin.

"Now they are gone we can be quite cozy, and talk over things, for I don't mind Ned any more than I do his dogs," said Bella, settling herself on her mother's footstool.

"I merely wish to say, Miss Muir, that my daughter has never had a governess and is sadly backward for a girl of sixteen. I want you to pass the mornings with her, and get her on as rapidly as possible. In the afternoon you will walk or drive with her, and in the evening sit with us here, if you like, or amuse yourself as you please. While in the country we are very quiet, for I cannot bear much company, and when my sons want gaiety, they go away for it. Miss Beaufort oversees the servants, and takes my place as far as possible. I am very delicate and keep my room till evening, except for an airing at noon. We will try each other for a month, and I hope we shall get on quite comfortably together."

"I shall do my best, madam."

One would not have believed that the

meek, spiritless voice which uttered these words was the same that had startled Coventry a few minutes before, nor that the pale, patient face could ever have kindled with such sudden fire as that which looked over Miss Muir's shoulder when she answered her young host's speech.

Edward thought within himself, Poor little woman! She has had a hard life. We will try and make it easier while she is here; and began his charitable work by suggesting that she might be tired. She acknowledged she was, and Bella led her away to a bright, cozy room, where with a pretty little speech and a good-night kiss she left her.

When alone Miss Muir's conduct was decidedly peculiar. Her first act was to clench her hands and mutter between her teeth, with passionate force, "I'll not fail again if there is power in a woman's wit and will!" She stood a moment motionless, with an expression of almost fierce disdain on her face, then shook her clenched hand as if menacing some unseen enemy. Next she laughed, and shrugged her shoulders with a true French shrug, saying low to herself, "Yes, the last scene *shall* be better than the first. *Mon dieu,* how tired and hungry I am!"

Kneeling before the one small trunk which held her worldly possessions, she opened it, drew out a flask, and mixed a glass of some ardent cordial, which she seemed to enjoy extremely as she sat on the carpet, musing, while her quick eyes examined every corner of the room.

"Not bad! It will be a good field for me to work in, and the harder the task the better I shall like it. *Merci,* old friend. You put heart and courage into me when nothing else will. Come, the curtain is down, so I may be myself for a few hours, if actresses ever are themselves."

Still sitting on the floor she unbound and removed the long abundant braids from her head, wiped the pink from her face, took out several pearly teeth, and slipping off her dress appeared herself indeed, a haggard, worn, and moody woman of thirty at least. The metamorphosis was wonderful, but the disguise was more in the expression she assumed than in any art of costume or false adornment. Now she was alone, and her mobile features settled into their natural expression, weary, hard, bitter. She had been lovely once, happy, innocent, and tender; but nothing of all this remained to the gloomy woman who leaned there brooding over some wrong, or loss, or disappointment which had darkened all her life. For an hour she sat so, sometimes playing absently with the scanty locks that hung about her face, sometimes lifting the glass to her lips as if the fiery draught warmed her cold blood; and once she half uncovered her breast to eye with a terrible glance the scar of a newly healed wound. At last she rose and crept to bed, like one worn out with weariness and mental pain.

CHAPTER II
A Good Beginning

Only the housemaids were astir when Miss Muir left her room next morning and quietly found her way into the garden. As she walked, apparently intent upon the flowers, her quick eye scrutinized the fine old house and its picturesque surroundings.

"Not bad," she said to herself, adding, as she passed into the adjoining park, "but the other may be better, and I will have the best."

Walking rapidly, she came out at length upon the wide green lawn which lay before the ancient hall where Sir John Coventry lived in solitary splendor. A stately old place, rich in oaks, well-kept shrubberies, gay gardens, sunny terraces, carved gables, spacious rooms, liveried servants, and every luxury befitting the ancestral home of a rich and honorable race. Miss Muir's eyes brightened as she looked, her step grew firmer, her carriage prouder, and a smile broke over her face; the smile of one well pleased at the prospect of the success of some cherished hope. Suddenly her whole air changed, she pushed back her hat, clasped her hands loosely before her, and seemed absorbed in girlish admiration of the fair scene that could not fail to charm any beauty-loving eye. The cause of this rapid change soon appeared. A hale, handsome man, between fifty and sixty, came through the little gate leading to the park, and, seeing the young stranger, paused to examine her. He had only time for a glance, however; she seemed conscious of his presence in a moment, turned with a startled look, uttered an exclamation of surprise, and looked as if hesitating whether to speak or run away. Gallant Sir John took off his hat and said, with the old-fashioned courtesy which became him well, "I beg your pardon for disturbing you, young lady. Allow me to atone for it by inviting you to walk where you will, and gather what flowers you like. I see you love them, so pray make free with those about you."

With a charming air of maidenly timidity and artlessness, Miss Muir replied, "Oh, thank you, sir! But it is I who should ask pardon for trespassing. I never should have dared if I had not known that Sir John was absent. I always wanted to see this fine old place, and ran over the first thing, to satisfy myself."

"And *are* you satisfied?" he asked, with a smile.

"More than satisfied—I'm charmed; for it is the most beautiful spot I ever saw, and I've seen many famous seats, both at home and abroad," she answered enthusiastically.

"The Hall is much flattered, and so would its master be if he heard you," began the gentleman, with an odd expression.

"I should not praise it to him—at least, not as freely as I have to you, sir," said the girl, with eyes still turned away.

"Why not?" asked her companion, looking much amused.

"I should be afraid. Not that I dread Sir John; but I've heard so many beautiful and noble things about him, and respect him so highly, that I should not dare to say much, lest he should see how I admire and—"

"And what, young lady? Finish, if you please."

"I was going to say, love him. I will say it, for he is an old man, and one cannot help loving virtue and bravery."

Miss Muir looked very earnest and pretty as she spoke, standing there with the sunshine glinting on her yellow hair, delicate face, and downcast eyes. Sir John was not a vain man, but he found it pleasant to hear himself commended by this unknown girl, and felt redoubled curiosity to learn who she was. Too well-bred to ask, or to abash her by avowing what she seemed unconscious of, he left both discoveries to chance; and when she turned, as if to retrace her steps, he offered her the handful of hothouse flowers which he held, saying, with a gallant bow, "In Sir John's name let me give you my little nosegay, with thanks for your good opinion, which, I assure you, is not entirely deserved, for I know him well."

Miss Muir looked up quickly, eyed him an instant, then dropped her eyes, and, coloring deeply, stammered out, "I did not know—I beg your pardon—you are too kind, Sir John."

He laughed like a boy, asking, mischievously, "Why call me Sir John? How do you know that I am not the gardener or the butler?"

"I did not see your face before, and no one

but yourself would say that any praise was undeserved," murmured Miss Muir, still overcome with girlish confusion.

"Well, well, we will let that pass, and the next time you come we will be properly introduced. Bella always brings her friends to the Hall, for I am fond of young people."

"I am not a friend. I am only Miss Coventry's governess." And Miss Muir dropped a meek curtsy. A slight change passed over Sir John's manner. Few would have perceived it, but Miss Muir felt it at once, and bit her lips with an angry feeling at her heart. With a curious air of pride, mingled with respect, she accepted the still offered bouquet, returned Sir John's parting bow, and tripped away, leaving the old gentleman to wonder where Mrs. Coventry found such a piquant little governess.

"That is done, and very well for a beginning," she said to herself as she approached the house.

In a green paddock close by fed a fine horse, who lifted up his head and eyed her inquiringly, like one who expected a greeting. Following a sudden impulse, she entered the paddock and, pulling a handful of clover, invited the creature to come and eat. This was evidently a new proceeding on the part of a lady, and the horse careered about as if bent on frightening the newcomer away.

"I see," she said aloud, laughing to herself. "I am not your master, and you rebel. Nevertheless, I'll conquer you, my fine brute."

Seating herself in the grass, she began to pull daisies, singing idly the while, as if unconscious of the spirited prancings of the horse. Presently he drew nearer, sniffing curiously and eyeing her with surprise. She took no notice, but plaited the daisies and sang on as if he was not there. This seemed to pique the petted creature, for, slowly approaching, he came at length so close that he could smell her little foot and nibble at her dress. Then she offered the clover, uttering caressing words and making soothing sounds, till by degrees and with much coquetting, the horse permitted her to stroke his glossy neck and smooth his mane.

It was a pretty sight—the slender figure in the grass, the high-spirited horse bending his proud head to her hand. Edward Coventry, who had watched the scene, found it impossible to restrain himself any longer and, leaping the wall, came to join the group, saying, with mingled admiration and wonder in countenance and voice, "Good morning, Miss Muir. If I had not seen your skill and courage proved before my eyes, I should be alarmed for your safety. Hector is a wild, wayward beast, and has damaged more than one groom who tried to conquer him."

"Good morning, Mr. Coventry. Don't tell tales of this noble creature, who has not deceived my faith in him. Your grooms did not know how to win his heart, and so subdue his spirit without breaking it."

Miss Muir rose as she spoke, and stood with her hand on Hector's neck while he ate the grass which she had gathered in the skirt of her dress.

"You have the secret, and Hector is your subject now, though heretofore he has rejected all friends but his master. Will you give him his morning feast? I always bring him bread and play with him before breakfast."

"Then you are not jealous?" And she looked up at him with eyes so bright and beautiful in expression that the young man wondered he had not observed them before.

"Not I. Pet him as much as you will; it will do him good. He is a solitary fellow, for he scorns his own kind and lives alone, like his master," he added, half to himself.

"Alone, with such a happy home, Mr. Coventry?" And a softly compassionate glance stole from the bright eyes.

"That was an ungrateful speech, and I retract it for Bella's sake. Younger sons have no position but such as they can make for themselves, you know, and I've had no chance yet."

"Younger sons! I thought—I beg pardon." And Miss Muir paused, as if remembering that she had no right to question.

Edward smiled and answered frankly, "Nay, don't mind me. You thought I was the heir, perhaps. Whom did you take my brother for last night?"

"For some guest who admired Miss Beaufort. I did not hear his name, nor observe him enough to discover who he was. I saw only your kind mother, your charming little sister, and—"

She stopped there, with a half-shy, half-grateful look at the young man which finished the sentence better than any words. He was still a boy, in spite of his one-and-twenty years, and a little color came into his brown cheek as the eloquent eyes met his and fell before them.

"Yes, Bella is a capital girl, and one can't help loving her. I know you'll get her on, for, really, she is the most delightful little dunce. My mother's ill health and Bella's devotion to her have prevented our attending to her education before. Next winter, when we go to town, she is to come out, and must be prepared for that great event, you know," he said, choosing a safe subject.

"I shall do my best. And that reminds me that I should report myself to her, instead of enjoying myself here. When one has been ill and shut up a long time, the country is so lovely one is apt to forget duty for pleasure. Please remind me if I am negligent, Mr. Coventry."

"That name belongs to Gerald. I'm only Mr. Ned here," he said as they walked toward the house, while Hector followed to the wall and sent a sonorous farewell after them.

Bella came running to meet them, and greeted Miss Muir as if she had made up her mind to like her heartily. "What a lovely bouquet you have got! I never can arrange flowers prettily, which vexes me, for Mamma is so fond of them and cannot go out herself. You have charming taste," she said, examining the graceful posy which Miss Muir had much improved by adding feathery grasses, delicate ferns, and fragrant wild flowers to Sir John's exotics.

Putting them into Bella's hand, she said, in a winning way, "Take them to your mother, then, and ask her if I may have the pleasure of making her a daily nosegay; for I should find real delight in doing it, if it would please her."

"How kind you are! Of course it would please her. I'll take them to her while the dew is still on them." And away flew Bella, eager to give both the flowers and the pretty message to the poor invalid.

Edward stopped to speak to the gardener, and Miss Muir went up the steps alone. The long hall was lined with portraits, and pacing slowly down it she examined them with interest. One caught her eye, and, pausing before it, she scrutinized it carefully. A young, beautiful, but very haughty female face. Miss Muir suspected at once who it was, and gave a decided nod, as if she saw and caught at some unexpected chance. A soft rustle behind her made her look around, and, seeing Lucia, she bowed, half turned, as if for another glance at the picture, and said, as if involuntarily, "How beautiful it is! May I ask if it is an ancestor, Miss Beaufort?"

"It is the likeness of my mother" was the reply, given with a softened voice and eyes that looked up tenderly.

"Ah, I might have known, from the resemblance, but I scarcely saw you last night. Excuse my freedom, but Lady Sydney treated me as a friend, and I forget my position. Allow me."

As she spoke, Miss Muir stooped to return the handkerchief which had fallen from Lucia's hand, and did so with a humble mien which touched the other's heart; for, though a proud, it was also a very generous one.

"Thank you. Are you better, this morning?" she said, graciously. And having received an affirmative reply, she added, as she walked on, "I will show you to the breakfast room, as Bella is not here. It is a very informal meal with us, for my aunt is never down and my cousins are very irregular in their hours. You can always have yours when you like, without waiting for us if you are an early riser."

Bella and Edward appeared before the others were seated, and Miss Muir quietly ate her breakfast, feeling well satisfied with her hour's work. Ned recounted her exploit with Hector, Bella delivered her mother's thanks for the flowers, and Lucia more than once recalled, with pardonable vanity, that the governess had compared her to her lovely mother, expressing by a look as much admiration for the living likeness as for the painted one. All kindly did their best to make the pale girl feel at home, and their cordial manner seemed to warm and draw her out; for soon she put off her sad, meek air and entertained them with gay anecdotes of her life in Paris, her travels in Russia when governess in Prince Jermadoff's family, and all manner of witty stories that kept them interested and merry long after the meal was over. In the middle of an absorbing adventure, Coventry came in, nodded lazily, lifted his brows, as if surprised at seeing the governess there, and began his breakfast as if the ennui of another day had already taken possession of him. Miss Muir stopped short, and no entreaties could induce her to go on.

"Another time I will finish it, if you like. Now Miss Bella and I should be at our books." And she left the room, followed by her pupil, taking no notice of the young master of the house, beyond a graceful bow in answer to his careless nod.

"Merciful creature! she goes when I come, and does not make life unendurable by moping about before my eyes. Does she belong to the moral, the melancholy, the romantic, or the dashing class, Ned?" said Gerald, lounging over his coffee as he did over everything he attempted.

"To none of them; she is a capital little woman. I wish you had seen her tame Hector this morning." And Edward repeated his story.

"Not a bad move on her part," said Coventry in reply. "She must be an observing as well as an energetic young person, to discover your chief weakness and attack it so soon. First tame the horse, and then the master. It will be amusing to watch the game, only I shall be under the painful necessity of checkmating you both, if it gets serious."

"You needn't exert yourself, old fellow, on my account. If I was not above thinking ill of an inoffensive girl, I should say you were the prize best worth winning, and advise you to take care of your own heart, if you've got one, which I rather doubt."

"I often doubt it, myself; but I fancy the little Scotchwoman will not be able to satisfy either of us upon that point. How does your highness like her?" asked Coventry of his cousin, who sat near him.

"Better than I thought I should. She is well-bred, unassuming, and very entertaining when she likes. She has told us some of the wittiest stories I've heard for a long time. Didn't our laughter wake you?" replied Lucia.

"Yes. Now atone for it by amusing me with a repetition of these witty tales."

"That is impossible; her accent and manner are half the charm," said Ned. "I wish you had kept away ten minutes longer, for your appearance spoilt the best story of all."

"Why didn't she go on?" asked Coventry, with a ray of curiosity.

"You forget that she overheard us last night, and must feel that you consider her a bore. She has pride, and no woman forgets speeches like those you made," answered Lucia.

"Or forgives them, either, I believe. Well, I must be resigned to languish under her displeasure then. On Sydney's account I take a slight interest in her; not that I expect to learn anything from her, for a woman with a mouth like that never confides or confesses anything. But I have a fancy to see what captivated him; for captivated he was, beyond a doubt, and by no lady whom he met in society. Did you ever hear anything of it, Ned?" asked Gerald.

"I'm not fond of scandal or gossip, and never listen to either." With which remark Edward left the room.

Lucia was called out by the housekeeper a moment after, and Coventry left to the society most wearisome to him, namely his own. As he entered, he had caught a part of the story which Miss Muir had been telling, and it had excited his curiosity so much that he found himself wondering what the end could be and wishing that he might hear it.

What the deuce did she run away for, when I came in? he thought. If she *is* amusing, she must make herself useful; for it's intensely dull, I own, here, in spite of Lucia. Hey, what's that?

It was a rich, sweet voice, singing a brilliant Italian air, and singing it with an expression that made the music doubly delicious. Stepping out of the French window, Coventry strolled along the sunny terrace, enjoying the song with the relish of a connoisseur. Others followed, and still he walked and listened, forgetful of weariness or time. As one exquisite air ended, he involuntarily applauded. Miss Muir's face appeared for an instant, then vanished, and no more music followed, though Coventry lingered, hoping to hear the voice again. For music was the one thing of which he never wearied, and neither Lucia nor Bella possessed skill enough to charm him. For an hour he loitered on the terrace or the lawn, basking in the sunshine, too indolent to seek occupation or society. At length Bella came out, hat in hand, and nearly stumbled over her brother, who lay on the grass.

"You lazy man, have you been dawdling here all this time?" she said, looking down at him.

"No, I've been very busy. Come and tell me how you've got on with the little dragon."

"Can't stop. She bade me take a run after my French, so that I might be ready for my drawing, and so I must."

"It's too warm to run. Sit down and amuse your deserted brother, who has had no society but bees and lizards for an hour."

He drew her down as he spoke, and Bella obeyed; for, in spite of his indolence, he was one to whom all submitted without dreaming of refusal.

"What have you been doing? Muddling your poor little brains with all manner of elegant rubbish?"

"No, I've been enjoying myself immensely. Jean is *so* interesting, so kind and clever. She didn't bore me with stupid grammar, but just talked to me in such pretty French that I got on capitally, and like it as I never expected to, after Lucia's dull way of teaching it."

"What did you talk about?"

"Oh, all manner of things. She asked questions, and I answered, and she corrected me."

"Questions about our affairs, I suppose?"

"Not one. She don't care two sous for us or our affairs. I thought she might like to know what sort of people we were, so I told her about Papa's sudden death, Uncle John, and you, and Ned; but in the midst of it she said, in her quiet way, 'You are getting too confidential, my dear. It is not best to talk too freely of one's affairs to strangers. Let us speak of something else.'"

"What were you talking of when she said that, Bell?"

"You."

"Ah, then no wonder she was bored."

"She was tired of my chatter, and didn't hear half I said; for she was busy sketching something for me to copy, and thinking of something more interesting than the Coventrys."

"How do you know?"

"By the expression of her face. Did you like her music, Gerald?"

"Yes. Was she angry when I clapped?"

"She looked surprised, then rather proud, and shut the piano at once, though I begged her to go on. Isn't Jean a pretty name?"

"Not bad; but why don't you call her Miss Muir?"

"She begged me not. She hates it, and loves to be called Jean, alone. I've imagined such a nice little romance about her, and someday I shall tell her, for I'm sure she has had a love trouble."

"Don't get such nonsense into your head, but follow Miss Muir's well-bred example and don't be curious about other people's affairs. Ask her to sing tonight; it amuses me."

"She won't come down, I think. We've planned to read and work in my boudoir, which is to be our study now. Mamma will stay in her room, so you and Lucia can have the drawing room all to yourselves."

"Thank you. What will Ned do?"

"He will amuse Mamma, he says. Dear old Ned! I wish you'd stir about and get him his commission. He is so impatient to be doing something and yet so proud he won't ask again, after you have neglected it so many times and refused Uncle's help."

"I'll attend to it very soon; don't worry me, child. He will do very well for a time, quietly here with us."

"You always say that, yet you know he chafes and is unhappy at being dependent on you. Mamma and I don't mind; but he is a man, and it frets him. He said he'd take matters into his own hands soon, and then you may be sorry you were so slow in helping him."

"Miss Muir is looking out of the window. You'd better go and take your run, else she will scold."

"Not she. I'm not a bit afraid of her, she's so gentle and sweet. I'm fond of her already. You'll get as brown as Ned, lying here in the sun. By the way, Miss Muir agrees with me in thinking him handsomer than you."

"I admire her taste and quite agree with her."

"She said he was manly, and that was more attractive than beauty in a man. She does express things so nicely. Now I'm off." And away danced Bella, humming the burden of Miss Muir's sweetest song.

" 'Energy is more attractive than beauty in a man.' She is right, but how the deuce *can* a man be energetic, with nothing to expend his energies upon?" mused Coventry, with his hat over his eyes.

A few moments later, the sweep of a dress caught his ear. Without stirring, a sidelong glance showed him Miss Muir coming across the terrace, as if to join Bella. Two stone steps led down to the lawn. He lay near them, and Miss Muir did not see him till close upon him. She started and slipped on the last step, recovered herself, and glided on, with a glance of unmistakable contempt as she passed the recumbent figure of the apparent sleeper. Several things in Bella's report had nettled him, but this look made him angry, though he would not own it, even to himself.

"Gerald, come here, quick!" presently called Bella, from the rustic seat where she stood beside her governess, who sat with her hand over her face as if in pain.

Gathering himself up, Coventry slowly obeyed, but involuntarily quickened his pace as he heard Miss Muir say, "Don't call him; *he* can do nothing"; for the emphasis on the word "he" was very significant.

"What is it, Bella?" he asked, looking rather wider awake than usual.

"You startled Miss Muir and made her turn her ankle. Now help her to the house, for she is in great pain; and don't lie there anymore to frighten people like a snake in the grass," said his sister petulantly.

"I beg your pardon. Will you allow me?" And Coventry offered his arm.

Miss Muir looked up with the expression

which annoyed him and answered coldly, "Thank you, Miss Bella will do as well."

"Permit me to doubt that." And with a gesture too decided to be resisted, Coventry drew her arm through his and led her into the house. She submitted quietly, said the pain would soon be over, and when settled on the couch in Bella's room dismissed him with the briefest thanks. Considering the unwonted exertion he had made, he thought she might have been a little more grateful, and went away to Lucia, who always brightened when he came.

No more was seen of Miss Muir till teatime; for now, while the family were in retirement, they dined early and saw no company. The governess had excused herself at dinner, but came down in the evening a little paler than usual and with a slight limp in her gait. Sir John was there, talking with his nephew, and they merely acknowledged her presence by the sort of bow which gentlemen bestow on governesses. As she slowly made her way to her place behind the urn, Coventry said to his brother, "Take her a footstool, and ask her how she is, Ned." Then, as if necessary to account for his politeness to his uncle, he explained how he was the cause of the accident.

"Yes, yes. I understand. Rather a nice little person, I fancy. Not exactly a beauty, but accomplished and well-bred, which is better for one of her class."

"Some tea, Sir John?" said a soft voice at his elbow, and there was Miss Muir, offering cups to the gentlemen.

"Thank you, thank you," said Sir John, sincerely hoping she had overheard him.

As Coventry took his, he said graciously, "You are very forgiving, Miss Muir, to wait upon me, after I have caused you so much pain."

"It is my duty, sir" was her reply, in a tone which plainly said, "but not my pleasure." And she returned to her place, to smile, and chat, and be charming, with Bella and her brother.

Lucia, hovering near her uncle and Gerald, kept them to herself, but was disturbed to find that their eyes often wandered to the cheerful group about the table, and that their attention seemed distracted by the frequent bursts of laughter and fragments of animated conversation which reached them. In the midst of an account of a tragic affair which she endeavored to make as interesting and pathetic as possible, Sir John burst into a hearty laugh, which betrayed that he had been listening to a livelier story than her own. Much annoyed, she said hastily, "I knew it would be so! Bella has no idea of the proper manner in which to treat a governess. She and Ned will forget the difference of rank and spoil that person for her work. She is inclined to be presumptuous already, and if my aunt won't trouble herself to give Miss Muir a hint in time, I shall."

"Wait till she has finished that story, I beg of you," said Coventry, for Sir John was already off.

"If you find that nonsense so entertaining, why don't you follow Uncle's example? I don't need you."

"Thank you. I will." And Lucia was deserted.

But Miss Muir had ended and, beckoning to Bella, left the room, as if quite unconscious of the honor conferred upon her or the dullness she left behind her. Ned went up to his mother, Gerald returned to make his peace with Lucia, and, bidding them good-night, Sir

John turned homeward. Strolling along the terrace, he came to the lighted window of Bella's study, and wishing to say a word to her, he half pushed aside the curtain and looked in. A pleasant little scene. Bella working busily, and near her in a low chair, with the light falling on her fair hair and delicate profile, sat Miss Muir, reading aloud. "Novels!" thought Sir John, and smiled at them for a pair of romantic girls. But pausing to listen a moment before he spoke, he found it was no novel, but history, read with a fluency which made every fact interesting, every sketch of character memorable, by the dramatic effect given to it. Sir John was fond of history, and failing eyesight often curtailed his favorite amusement. He had tried readers, but none suited him, and he had given up the plan. Now as he listened, he thought how pleasantly the smoothly flowing voice would wile away his evenings, and he envied Bella her new acquisition.

A bell rang, and Bella sprang up, saying, "Wait for me a minute. I must run to Mamma, and then we will go on with this charming prince."

Away she went, and Sir John was about to

retire as quietly as he came, when Miss Muir's peculiar behavior arrested him for an instant. Dropping the book, she threw her arms across the table, laid her head down upon them, and broke into a passion of tears, like one who could bear restraint no longer. Shocked and amazed, Sir John stole away; but all that night the kindhearted gentleman puzzled his brains with conjectures about his niece's interesting young governess, quite unconscious that she intended he should do so.

CHAPTER III
Passion and Pique

For several weeks the most monotonous tranquillity seemed to reign at Coventry House, and yet, unseen, unsuspected, a storm was gathering. The arrival of Miss Muir seemed to produce a change in everyone, though no one could have explained how or why. Nothing could be more unobtrusive and retiring than her manners. She was devoted to Bella, who soon adored her, and was only happy when in her society. She ministered in many ways to Mrs. Coventry's comfort, and that lady declared there never was such a nurse. She amused, interested and won Edward with her wit and womanly sympathy. She made Lucia respect and envy her for her accomplishments, and piqued indolent Gerald by her persistent avoidance of him, while Sir John was charmed with her respectful deference and the graceful little attentions she paid him in a frank and artless way, very winning to the lonely old man. The very servants liked her; and instead of being, what most governesses are, a forlorn creature hovering between superiors and inferiors, Jean Muir was the life of the house, and the friend of all but two.

Lucia disliked her, and Coventry distrusted her; neither could exactly say why, and neither owned the feeling, even to themselves. Both watched her covertly yet found no shortcoming anywhere. Meek, modest, faithful, and invariably sweet-tempered—they could complain of nothing and wondered at their own doubts, though they could not banish them.

It soon came to pass that the family was divided, or rather that two members were left very much to themselves. Pleading timidity, Jean Muir kept much in Bella's study and soon made it such a pleasant little nook that Ned and his mother, and often Sir John, came in to enjoy the music, reading, or cheerful chat which made the evenings so gay. Lucia at first was only too glad to have her cousin to herself, and he too lazy to care what went on about him. But presently he wearied of her society, for she was not a brilliant girl, and possessed few of those winning arts which charm a man and steal into his heart. Rumors of the merrymakings that went on reached him and made him curious to share them; echoes of fine music went sounding through the house, as he lounged about the empty drawing room; and peals of laughter reached him while listening to Lucia's grave discourse.

She soon discovered that her society had lost its charm, and the more eagerly she tried to please him, the more signally she failed. Before long Coventry fell into a habit of strolling out upon the terrace of an evening, and amusing himself by passing and repassing the window of Bella's room, catching glimpses of what was going on and reporting the result of his observations to Lucia, who was too proud to ask admission to the happy circle or to seem to desire it.

"I shall go to London tomorrow, Lucia," Gerald said one evening, as he came back from what he called "a survey," looking very much annoyed.

"To London?" exclaimed his cousin, surprised.

"Yes, I must bestir myself and get Ned his commission, or it will be all over with him."

"How do you mean?"

"He is falling in love as fast as it is possible for a boy to do it. That girl has bewitched him, and he will make a fool of himself very soon, unless I put a stop to it."

"I was afraid she would attempt a flirtation. These persons always do, they are such a mischief-making race."

"Ah, but there you are wrong, as far as little Muir is concerned. She does not flirt, and Ned has too much sense and spirit to be caught by a silly coquette. She treats him like an elder sister, and mingles the most attractive friendliness with a quiet dignity that captivates the boy. I've been watching them, and there he is, devouring her with his eyes, while she reads a fascinating novel in the most fascinating style. Bella and Mamma are absorbed in the tale, and see nothing; but Ned makes himself the hero, Miss Muir the heroine, and lives the love scene with all the ardor of a man whose heart has just waked up. Poor lad! Poor lad!"

Lucia looked at her cousin, amazed by the energy with which he spoke, the anxiety in his usually listless face. The change became him, for it showed what he might be, making one regret still more what he was. Before she could speak, he was gone again, to return presently, laughing, yet looking a little angry.

"What now?" she asked.

" 'Listeners never hear any good of themselves' is the truest of proverbs. I stopped a moment to look at Ned, and heard the following flattering remarks. Mamma is gone, and Ned was asking little Muir to sing that delicious barcarole she gave us the other evening.

" 'Not now, not here,' she said.

" 'Why not? You sang it in the drawing room readily enough,' said Ned, imploringly.

" 'That is a very different thing,' and she looked at him with a little shake of the head, for he was folding his hands and doing the passionate pathetic.

" 'Come and sing it there then,' said innocent Bella. 'Gerald likes your voice so much, and complains that you will never sing to him.'

" 'He never asks me,' said Muir, with an odd smile.

" 'He is too lazy, but he wants to hear you.'

" 'When he asks me, I will sing—if I feel like it.' And she shrugged her shoulders with a provoking gesture of indifference.

" 'But it amuses him, and he gets so bored down here,' began stupid little Bella. 'Don't be shy or proud, Jean, but come and entertain the poor old fellow.'

" 'No, thank you. I engaged to teach Miss Coventry, not to amuse Mr. Coventry' was all the answer she got.

" 'You amuse Ned, why not Gerald? Are you afraid of him?' asked Bella.

"Miss Muir laughed, such a scornful laugh, and said, in that peculiar tone of hers, 'I cannot fancy anyone being *afraid* of your elder brother.'

" 'I am, very often, and so would you be, if you ever saw him angry.' And Bella looked as if I'd beaten her.

" 'Does he ever wake up enough to be angry?' asked that girl, with an air of surprise. Here Ned broke into a fit of laughter, and they are at it now, I fancy, by the sound."

"Their foolish gossip is not worth getting excited about, but I certainly would send Ned away. It's no use trying to get rid of 'that girl,' as you say, for my aunt is as deluded about her as Ned and Bella, and she really does get the child along splendidly. Dispatch Ned, and then she can do no harm," said Lucia, watching Coventry's altered face as he stood in the moonlight, just outside the window where she sat.

"Have you no fears for me?" he asked smiling, as if ashamed of his momentary petulance.

"No, have you for yourself?" And a shade of anxiety passed over her face.

"I defy the Scotch witch to enchant me, except with her music," he added, moving down the terrace again, for Jean was singing like a nightingale.

As the song ended, he put aside the curtain, and said, abruptly, "Has anyone any commands for London? I am going there tomorrow."

"A pleasant trip to you," said Ned carelessly, though usually his brother's movements interested him extremely.

"I want quantities of things, but I must ask Mamma first." And Bella began to make a list.

"May I trouble you with a letter, Mr. Coventry?"

Jean Muir turned around on the music stool and looked at him with the cold keen glance which always puzzled him.

He bowed, saying, as if to them all, "I shall be off by the early train, so you must give me your orders tonight."

"Then come away, Ned, and leave Jean to write her letter."

And Bella took her reluctant brother from the room.

"I will give you the letter in the morning," said Miss Muir, with a curious quiver in her voice, and the look of one who forcibly suppressed some strong emotion.

"As you please." And Coventry went back to Lucia, wondering who Miss Muir was going to write to. He said nothing to his brother of the purpose which took him to town, lest a word should produce the catastrophe which he hoped to prevent; and Ned, who now lived in a sort of dream, seemed to forget Gerald's existence altogether.

With unwonted energy Coventry was astir seven next morning. Lucia gave him his breakfast, and as he left the room to order the carriage, Miss Muir came gliding downstairs, very pale and heavy-eyed (with a sleepless, tearful night, he thought) and, putting a delicate little letter into his hand, said hurriedly, "Please leave this at Lady Sydney's, and if you see her, say 'I have remembered.' "

Her peculiar manner and peculiar message struck him. His eye involuntarily glanced at the address of the letter and read young Sydney's name. Then, conscious of his mistake, he thrust it into his pocket with a hasty "Good morning," and left Miss Muir standing with one hand pressed on her heart, the other half extended as if to recall the letter.

All the way to London, Coventry found it impossible to forget the almost tragical expression of the girl's face, and it haunted him through the bustle of two busy days. Ned's affair was put in the way of being speedily accomplished, Bella's commissions were executed, his mother's pet delicacies provided for her, and a gift for Lucia, whom the family had given him for his future mate, as he was too lazy to choose for himself.

Jean Muir's letter he had not delivered, for Lady Sydney was in the country and her townhouse closed. Curious to see how she would receive his tidings, he went quietly in on his arrival at home. Everyone had dispersed to dress for dinner except Miss Muir, who was in the garden, the servant said.

"Very well, I have a message for her"; and, turning, the "young master," as they called him, went to seek her. In a remote corner he saw her sitting alone, buried in thought. As his step roused her, a look of surprise, followed by one of satisfaction, passed over her face, and, rising, she beckoned to him with an almost eager gesture. Much amazed, he went to her and offered the letter, saying kindly, "I regret that I could not deliver it. Lady Sydney is in the country, and I did not like to post it without your leave. Did I do right?"

"Quite right, thank you very much—it is better so." And with an air of relief, she tore the letter to atoms, and scattered them to the wind.

More amazed than ever, the young man was about to leave her when she said, with a mixture of entreaty and command, "Please stay a moment. I want to speak to you."

He paused, eyeing her with visible surprise, for a sudden color dyed her cheeks, and her lips trembled. Only for a moment, then she was quite self-possessed again.

Motioning him to the seat she had left, she remained standing while she said, in a low, rapid tone full of pain and of decision:

"Mr. Coventry, as the head of the house I want to speak to you, rather than to your mother, of a most unhappy affair which has occurred during your absence. My month of probation ends today; your mother wishes me to remain; I, too, wish it sincerely, for I am happy here, but I ought not. Read this, and you will see why."

She put a hastily written note into his hand and watched him intently while he read it. She saw him flush with anger, bite his lips, and knit his brows, then assume his haughtiest look, as he lifted his eyes and said in his most sarcastic tone, "Very well for a beginning. The boy has eloquence. Pity that it should be wasted. May I ask if you have replied to this rhapsody?"

"I have."

"And what follows? He begs you 'to fly with him, to share his fortunes, and be the good angel of his life.' Of course you consent?"

There was no answer, for, standing erect before him, Miss Muir regarded him with an expression of proud patience, like one who expected reproaches, yet was too generous to resent them. Her manner had its effect. Dropping his bitter tone, Coventry asked briefly, "Why do you show me this? What can I do?"

"I show it that you may see how much in earnest 'the boy' is, and how open I desire to be. You can control, advise, and comfort your brother, and help me to see what is my duty."

"You love him?" demanded Coventry bluntly.

"No!" was the quick, decided answer.

"Then why make him love you?"

"I never tried to do it. Your sister will testify that I have endeavored to avoid him as I—" And he finished the sentence with an unconscious tone of pique, "As you have avoided me."

She bowed silently, and he went on:

"I will do you the justice to say that nothing can be more blameless than your conduct toward myself; but why allow Ned to haunt you evening after evening? What could you expect of a romantic boy who had nothing to do but lose his heart to the first attractive woman he met?"

A momentary glisten shone in Jean Muir's steel-blue eyes as the last words left the young man's lips; but it was gone instantly, and her voice was full of reproach, as she said, steadily, impulsively, "If the 'romantic boy' had been allowed to lead the life of a man, as he longed to do, he would have had no time to lose his heart to the first sorrowful girl whom he pitied. Mr. Coventry, the fault is yours. Do not blame your brother, but generously own your mistake and retrieve it in the speediest, kindest manner."

For an instant Gerald sat dumb. Never since his father died had anyone reproved him; seldom in his life had he been blamed. It was a new experience, and the very novelty added to the effect. He saw his fault, regretted it, and admired the brave sincerity of the girl in telling him of it. But he did not know how to deal with the case, and was forced to confess not only past negligence but present incapacity. He was as honorable as he was proud, and with an effort he said frankly, "You are right, Miss Muir. I *am* to blame, yet as soon as I saw the danger, I tried to avert it. My visit to town was on Ned's account; he will have his commission very soon, and then he will be sent out of harm's way. Can I do more?"

"No, it is too late to send him away with a free and happy heart. He must bear his pain as he can, and it may help to make a man of him," she said sadly.

"He'll soon forget," began Coventry, who found the thought of gay Ned suffering an uncomfortable one.

"Yes, thank heaven, that is possible, for men."

Miss Muir pressed her hands together, with a dark expression on her half-averted face. Something in her tone, her manner, touched Coventry; he fancied that some old wound bled, some bitter memory awoke at the approach of a new lover. He was young, heart-whole, and romantic, under all his cool nonchalance of manner. This girl, who he fancied loved his friend and who was beloved by his brother, became an object of interest to him. He pitied her, desired to help her, and regretted his past distrust, as a chivalrous man always regrets injustice to a woman. She was happy here, poor, homeless soul, and she should stay. Bella loved her, his mother took comfort in her, and when

Ned was gone, no one's peace would be endangered by her winning ways, her rich accomplishments. These thoughts swept through his mind during a brief pause, and when he spoke, it was to say gently:

"Miss Muir, I thank you for the frankness which must have been painful to you, and I will do my best to be worthy of the confidence which you repose in me. You were both discreet and kind to speak only to me. This thing would have troubled my mother extremely, and have done no good. I shall see Ned, and try and repair my long neglect as promptly as possible. I know you will help me, and in return let me beg of you to remain, for he will soon be gone."

She looked at him with eyes full of tears, and there was no coolness in the voice that answered softly, "You are too kind, but I had better go; it is not wise to stay."

"Why not?"

She colored beautifully, hesitated, then spoke out in the clear, steady voice which was her greatest charm, "If I had known there were sons in this family, I never should have come. Lady Sydney spoke only of your sister, and when I found two gentlemen, I was troubled, because—I am so unfortunate—or rather, people are so kind as to like me more than I deserve. I thought I could stay a month, at least, as your brother spoke of going away, and you were already affianced, but—"

"I am not affianced."

Why he said that, Coventry could not tell, but the words passed his lips hastily and could not be recalled. Jean Muir took the announcement oddly enough. She shrugged her shoulders with an air of extreme annoyance, and said almost rudely, "Then you should be; you will be soon. But that is nothing to me. Miss Beaufort wishes me gone, and I am too proud to remain and become the cause of disunion in a happy family. No, I will go, and go at once."

She turned away impetuously, but Edward's arm detained her, and Edward's voice demanded, tenderly, "Where will you go, my Jean?"

The tender touch and name seemed to rob her of her courage and calmness, for, leaning on her lover, she hid her face and sobbed audibly.

"Now don't make a scene, for heaven's

sake," began Coventry impatiently, as his brother eyed him fiercely, divining at once what had passed, for his letter was still in Gerald's hand and Jean's last words had reached her lover's ear.

"Who gave you the right to read that, and to interfere in my affairs?" demanded Edward hotly.

"Miss Muir" was the reply, as Coventry threw away the paper.

"And you add to the insult by ordering her out of the house," cried Ned with increasing wrath.

"On the contrary, I beg her to remain."

"The deuce you do! And why?"

"Because she is useful and happy here, and I am unwilling that your folly should rob her of a home which she likes."

"You are very thoughtful and devoted all at once, but I beg you will not trouble yourself. Jean's happiness and home will be my care now."

"My dear boy, do be reasonable. The thing is impossible. Miss Muir sees it herself; she came to tell me, to ask how best to arrange matters without troubling my mother. I've been to town to attend to your affairs, and you may be off now very soon."

"I have no desire to go. Last month it was the wish of my heart. Now I'll accept nothing from you." And Edward turned moodily away from his brother.

"What folly! Ned, you *must* leave home. It is all arranged and cannot be given up now. A change is what you need, and it will make a man of you. We shall miss you, of course, but you will be where you'll see something of life, and that is better for you than getting into mischief here."

"Are you going away, Jean?" asked Edward, ignoring his brother entirely and bending over the girl, who still hid her face and wept. She did not speak, and Gerald answered for her.

"No, why should she if you are gone?"

"Do you mean to stay?" asked the lover eagerly of Jean.

"I wish to remain, but—" She paused and looked up. Her eyes went from one face to the other, and she added, decidedly, "Yes, I must go, it is not wise to stay even when you are gone."

Neither of the young men could have explained why that hurried glance affected them as it did, but each felt conscious of a willful desire to oppose the other. Edward suddenly felt that his brother loved Miss Muir, and was bent on removing her from his way. Gerald had a vague idea that Miss Muir feared to remain on his account, and he longed to show her that he was quite safe. Each felt angry, and each showed it in a different way, one being violent, the other satirical.

"You are right, Jean, this is not the place for you; and you must let me see you in a safer home before I go," said Ned, significantly.

"It strikes me that this will be a particularly safe home when your dangerous self is removed," began Coventry, with an aggravating smile of calm superiority.

"And *I* think that I leave a more dangerous person than myself behind me, as poor Lucia can testify."

"Be careful what you say, Ned, or I shall be forced to remind you that I am master here. Leave Lucia's name out of this disagreeable affair, if you please."

"You *are* master here, but not of me, or my

actions, and you have no right to expect obedience or respect, for you inspire neither. Jean, I asked you to go with me secretly; now I ask you openly to share my fortune. In my brother's presence I ask, and *will* have an answer."

He caught her hand impetuously, with a defiant look at Coventry, who still smiled, as if at boy's play, though his eyes were kindling and his face changing with the still, white wrath which is more terrible than any sudden outburst. Miss Muir looked frightened; she shrank away from her passionate young lover, cast an appealing glance at Gerald, and seemed as if she longed to claim his protection yet dared not.

"Speak!" cried Edward, desperately. "Don't look to him, tell me truly, with your own lips, do you, can you love me, Jean?"

"I have told you once. Why pain me by forcing another hard reply," she said pitifully, still shrinking from his grasp and seeming to appeal to his brother.

"You wrote a few lines, but I'll not be satisfied with that. You shall answer; I've seen love in your eyes, heard it in your voice, and I know it is hidden in your heart. You fear to own it; do not hesitate, no one can part us—speak, Jean, and satisfy me."

Drawing her hand decidedly away, she went a step nearer Coventry, and answered, slowly, distinctly, though her lips trembled, and she evidently dreaded the effect of her words, "I will speak, and speak truly. You have seen love in my face; it is in my heart, and I do not hesitate to own it, cruel as it is to force the truth from me, but this love is not for you. Are you satisfied?"

He looked at her with a despairing glance and stretched his hand toward her beseechingly. She seemed to fear a blow, for suddenly she clung to Gerald with a faint cry. The act, the look of fear, the protecting gesture Coventry involuntarily made were too much for Edward, already excited by conflicting passions. In a paroxysm of blind wrath, he caught up a large pruning knife left there by the gardener, and would have dealt his brother a fatal blow had he not warded it off with his arm. The stroke fell, and another might have followed had not Miss Muir with unexpected courage and strength wrested the knife from Edward and flung it into the little pond near by. Coventry dropped down upon the seat, for the blood poured from a deep wound in his arm, showing by its rapid flow that an artery had been severed. Edward stood aghast, for with the blow his fury passed, leaving him overwhelmed with remorse and shame.

Gerald looked up at him, smiled faintly, and said, with no sign of reproach or anger, "Never mind, Ned. Forgive and forget. Lend me a hand to the house, and don't disturb anyone. It's not much, I dare say." But his lips whitened as he spoke, and his strength failed him. Edward sprang to support him, and Miss Muir, forgetting her terrors, proved herself a girl of uncommon skill and courage.

"Quick! Lay him down. Give me your handkerchief, and bring some water," she said, in a tone of quiet command. Poor Ned obeyed and watched her with breathless suspense while she tied the handkerchief tightly around the arm, thrust the handle of his riding whip underneath, and pressed it firmly above the severed artery to stop the dangerous flow of blood.

"Dr. Scott is with your mother, I think. Go and bring him here" was the next order; and Edward darted away, thankful to do anything to ease the terror which possessed him. He was gone some minutes, and while they waited Coventry watched the girl as she knelt beside him, bathing his face with one hand while with the other she held the bandage firmly in its place. She was pale, but quite steady and self-possessed, and her eyes shone with a strange brilliancy as she looked down at him. Once, meeting his look of grateful wonder, she smiled a reassuring smile that made her lovely, and said, in a soft, sweet tone never used to him before, "Be quiet. There is no danger. I will stay by you till help comes."

Help did come speedily, and the doctor's first words were "Who improvised that tourniquet?"

"She did," murmured Coventry.

"Then you may thank her for saving your life. By Jove! It was capitally done"; and the old doctor looked at the girl with as much admiration as curiosity in his face.

"Never mind that. See to the wound, please, while I run for bandages, and salts, and wine."

Miss Muir was gone as she spoke, so fleetly that it was in vain to call her back or catch her. During her brief absence, the story was told by repentant Ned and the wound examined.

"Fortunately I have my case of instruments with me," said the doctor, spreading on the bench a long array of tiny, glittering implements of torture. "Now, Mr. Ned, come here, and hold the arm in that way, while I tie the artery. Hey! That will never do. Don't tremble so, man, look away and hold it steadily."

"I can't!" And poor Ned turned faint and white, not at the sight but with the bitter thought that he had longed to kill his brother.

"I will hold it," and a slender white hand lifted the bare and bloody arm so firmly, steadily, that Coventry sighed a sigh of relief, and Dr. Scott fell to work with an emphatic nod of approval.

It was soon over, and while Edward ran in to bid the servants beware of alarming their mistress, Dr. Scott put up his instruments and Miss Muir used salts, water, and wine so skillfully that Gerald was able to walk to his room, leaning on the old man, while the girl supported the wounded arm, as no sling could be made on the spot. As he entered the chamber, Coventry turned, put out his left hand, and with much feeling in his fine eyes said simply, "Miss Muir, I thank you."

The color came up beautifully in her pale cheeks as she pressed the hand and without a word vanished from the room. Lucia and the housekeeper came bustling in, and there was no lack of attendance on the invalid. He soon wearied of it, and sent them all away but Ned, who remorsefully haunted the chamber, looking like a comely young Cain and feeling like an outcast.

"Come here, lad, and tell me all about it. I was wrong to be domineering. Forgive me, and believe that I care for your happiness more sincerely than for my own."

These frank and friendly words healed the breach between the two brothers and completely conquered Ned. Gladly did he relate his love passages, for no young lover ever tires of that amusement if he has a sympathizing auditor, and Gerald *was* sympathetic now. For an hour did he lie listening patiently to the history of the growth of his brother's passion. Emotion gave the narrator eloquence, and Jean Muir's character was painted in glowing colors. All her unsuspected kindness to those about her was dwelt upon; all her faithful care, her sisterly interest in Bella, her gentle attentions to their mother, her sweet forbearance with Lucia, who plainly showed her dislike, and most of all, her friendly counsel, sympathy, and regard for Ned himself.

"She would make a man of me. She puts strength and courage into me as no one else can. She is unlike any girl I ever saw; there's no sentimentality about her; she is wise, and kind, and sweet. She says what she means, looks you straight in the eye, and is as true as steel. I've tried her, I know her, and—ah, Gerald, I love her so!"

Here the poor lad leaned his face into his hands and sighed a sigh that made his brother's heart ache.

"Upon my soul, Ned, I feel for you; and if there was no obstacle on her part, I'd do my best for you. She loves Sydney, and so there is nothing for it but to bear your fate like a man."

"Are you sure about Sydney? May it not be some one else?" and Ned eyed his brother with a suspicious look.

Coventry told him all he knew and surmised concerning his friend, not forgetting the letter. Edward mused a moment, then seemed relieved, and said frankly, "I'm glad it's Sydney and not you. I can bear it better."

"Me!" ejaculated Gerald, with a laugh.

"Yes, you; I've been tormented lately with a fear that you cared for her, or rather, she for you."

"You jealous young fool! We never see or speak to one another scarcely, so how could we get up a tender interest?"

"What do you lounge about on that terrace for every evening? And why does she get fluttered when your shadow begins to come and go?" demanded Edward.

"I like the music and don't care for the society of the singer, that's why I walk there. The fluttering is all your imagination; Miss Muir isn't a woman to be fluttered by a man's shadow." And Coventry glanced at his useless arm.

"Thank you for that, and for not saying 'little Muir,' as you generally do. Perhaps it was my imagination. But she never makes fun of you now, and so I fancied she might have lost her heart to the 'young master.' Women often do, you know."

"She used to ridicule me, did she?" asked Coventry, taking no notice of the latter part of his brother's speech, which was quite true nevertheless.

"Not exactly, she was too well-bred for that. But sometimes when Bella and I joked about you, she'd say something so odd or witty that it was irresistible. You're used to being laughed at, so you don't mind, I know, just among ourselves."

"Not I. Laugh away as much as you like," said Gerald. But he did mind, and wanted exceedingly to know what Miss Muir had said, yet was too proud to ask. He turned restlessly and uttered a sigh of pain.

"I'm talking too much; it's bad for you. Dr. Scott said you must be quiet. Now go to sleep, if you can."

Edward left the bedside but not the room, for he would let no one take his place. Coventry tried to sleep, found it impossible, and after a restless hour called his brother back.

"If the bandage was loosened a bit, it would ease my arm and then I could sleep. Can you do it, Ned?"

"I dare not touch it. The doctor gave orders

to leave it till he came in the morning, and I shall only do harm if I try."

"But I tell you it's too tight. My arm is swelling and the pain is intense. It can't be right to leave it so. Dr. Scott dressed it in a hurry and did it too tight. Common sense will tell you that," said Coventry impatiently.

"I'll call Mrs. Morris; she will understand what's best to be done." And Edward moved toward the door, looking anxious.

"Not she, she'll only make a stir and torment me with her chatter. I'll bear it as long as I can, and perhaps Dr. Scott will come tonight. He said he would if possible. Go to your dinner, Ned. I can ring for Neal if I need anything. I shall sleep if I'm alone, perhaps."

Edward reluctantly obeyed, and his brother was left to himself. Little rest did he find, however, for the pain of the wounded arm grew unbearable, and, taking a sudden resolution, he rang for his servant.

"Neal, go to Miss Coventry's study, and if Miss Muir is there, ask her to be kind enough to come to me. I'm in great pain, and she understands wounds better than anyone else in the house."

With much surprise in his face, the man

departed and a few moments after the door noiselessly opened and Miss Muir came in. It had been a very warm day, and for the first time she had left off her plain black dress. All in white, with no ornament but her fair hair, and a fragrant posy of violets in her belt, she looked a different woman from the meek, nunlike creature one usually saw about the house. Her face was as altered as her dress, for now a soft color glowed in her cheeks, her eyes smiled shyly, and her lips no longer wore the firm look of one who forcibly repressed every emotion. A fresh, gentle, and charming woman she seemed, and Coventry found the dull room suddenly brightened by her presence. Going straight to him, she said simply, and with a happy, helpful look very comforting to see, "I'm glad you sent for me. What can I do for you?"

He told her, and before the complaint was ended, she began loosening the bandages with the decision of one who understood what was to be done and had faith in herself.

"Ah, that's relief, that's comfort!" ejaculated Coventry, as the last tight fold fell away. "Ned was afraid I should bleed to death if he touched me. What will the doctor say to us?"

"I neither know nor care. I shall say to him that he is a bad surgeon to bind it so closely, and not leave orders to have it untied if necessary. Now I shall make it easy and put you to sleep, for that is what you need. Shall I? May I?"

"I wish you would, if you can."

And while she deftly rearranged the bandages, the young man watched her curiously. Presently he asked, "How came you to know so much about these things?"

"In the hospital where I was ill, I saw much that interested me, and when I got better, I used to sing to the patients sometimes."

"Do you mean to sing to me?" he asked, in the submissive tone men unconsciously adopt when ill and in a woman's care.

"If you like it better than reading aloud in a dreamy tone," she answered, as she tied the last knot.

"I do, much better," he said decidedly.

"You are feverish. I shall wet your forehead, and then you will be quite comfortable." She moved about the room in the quiet way which made it a pleasure to watch her, and, having mingled a little cologne with water, bathed his face as unconcernedly as if he had been a child. Her proceedings not only comforted but amused Coventry, who mentally contrasted her with the stout, beer-drinking matron who had ruled over him in his last illness.

"A clever, kindly little woman," he thought, and felt quite at his ease, she was so perfectly easy herself.

"There, now you look more like yourself," she said with an approving nod as she finished, and smoothed the dark locks off his forehead with a cool, soft hand. Then seating herself in a large chair near by, she began to sing, while tidily rolling up the fresh bandages which had been left for the morning. Coventry lay watching her by the dim light that burned in the room, and she sang on as easily as a bird, a dreamy, low-toned lullaby, which soothed the listener like a spell. Presently, looking up to see the effect of her song, she found the young man wide awake, and regarding her with a curious mixture of pleasure, interest, and admiration.

"Shut your eyes, Mr. Coventry," she said, with a reproving shake of the head, and an odd little smile.

He laughed and obeyed, but could not resist an occasional covert glance from under his lashes at the slender white figure in the great velvet chair. She saw him and frowned.

"You are very disobedient; why won't you sleep?"

"I can't, I want to listen. I'm fond of nightingales."

"Then I shall sing no more, but try something that has never failed yet. Give me your hand, please."

Much amazed, he gave it, and, taking it in both her small ones, she sat down behind the curtain and remained as mute and motionless as a statue. Coventry smiled to himself at first, and wondered which would tire first. But soon a subtle warmth seemed to steal from the soft palms that enclosed his own, his heart beat quicker, his breath grew unequal, and a thousand fancies danced through his brain. He sighed, and said dreamily, as he turned his face toward her, "I like this." And in the act of speaking, seemed to sink into a soft cloud which encompassed him about with an atmosphere of perfect repose. More than this he could not remember, for sleep, deep and dreamless, fell upon him, and when he woke, daylight was shining in between the curtains, his hand lay alone on the coverlet, and his fair-haired enchantress was gone.

CHAPTER IV
A Discovery

For several days Coventry was confined to his room, much against his will, though everyone did their best to lighten his irksome captivity. His mother petted him, Bella sang, Lucia read, Edward was devoted, and all the household, with one exception, were eager to serve the young master. Jean Muir never came near him, and Jean Muir alone seemed to possess the power of amusing him. He soon tired of the others, wanted something new; recalled the piquant character of the girl and took a fancy into his head that she would lighten his ennui. After some hesitation, he carelessly spoke of her to Bella, but nothing came of it, for Bella only said Jean was well, and very busy doing something lovely to surprise Mamma with. Edward complained that he never saw her, and Lucia ignored her existence altogether. The only intelligence the invalid received was from the gossip of two housemaids over their work in the next room.

From them he learned that the governess had been "scolded" by Miss Beaufort for going to Mr. Coventry's room; that she had taken it very sweetly and kept herself carefully out of the way of both young gentlemen, though it was plain to see that Mr. Ned was dying for her.

Mr. Gerald amused himself by thinking over this gossip, and quite annoyed his sister by his absence of mind.

"Gerald, do you know Ned's commission has come?"

"Very interesting. Read on, Bella."

"You stupid boy! You don't know a word I say," and she put down the book to repeat her news.

"I'm glad of it; now we must get him off as soon as possible—that is, I suppose he will want to be off as soon as possible." And Coventry woke up from his reverie.

"You needn't check yourself, I know all about it. I think Ned was very foolish, and that Miss Muir has behaved beautifully. It's quite impossible, of course, but I wish it wasn't, I do so like to watch lovers. You and Lucia are so cold you are not a bit interesting."

"You'll do me a favor if you'll stop all that

nonsense about Lucia and me. We are not lovers, and never shall be, I fancy. At all events, I'm tired of the thing, and wish you and Mamma would let it drop, for the present at least."

"Oh Gerald, you know Mamma has set her heart upon it, that Papa desired it, and poor Lucia loves you so much. How can you speak of dropping what will make us all so happy?"

"It won't make me happy, and I take the liberty of thinking that this is of some importance. I'm not bound in any way, and don't intend to be till I am ready. Now we'll talk about Ned."

Much grieved and surprised, Bella obeyed, and devoted herself to Edward, who very wisely submitted to his fate and prepared to leave home for some months. For a week the house was in a state of excitement about his departure, and everyone but Jean was busied for him. She was scarcely seen; every morning she gave Bella her lessons, every afternoon drove out with Mrs. Coventry, and nearly every evening went up to the Hall to read to Sir John, who found his wish granted without exactly knowing how it had been done.

The day Edward left, he came down from bidding his mother good-bye, looking very pale, for he had lingered in his sister's little room with Miss Muir as long as he dared.

"Good-bye, dear. Be kind to Jean," he whispered as he kissed his sister.

"I will, I will," returned Bella, with tearful eyes.

"Take care of Mamma, and remember Lucia," he said again, as he touched his cousin's beautiful cheek.

"Fear nothing. I will keep them apart," she whispered back, and Coventry heard it.

Edward offered his hand to his brother, saying, significantly, as he looked him in the eye, "I trust you, Gerald."

"You may, Ned."

Then he went, and Coventry tired himself with wondering what Lucia meant. A few days later he understood.

Now Ned is gone, little Muir will appear, I fancy, he said to himself; but "little Muir" did not appear, and seemed to shun him more carefully than she had done her lover. If he went to the drawing room in the evening hoping for music, Lucia alone was there. If he tapped at Bella's door, there was always a pause before she opened it, and no sign of Jean appeared though her voice had been audible when he knocked. If he went to the library, a hasty rustle and the sound of flying feet betrayed that the room was deserted at his approach. In the garden Miss Muir never failed to avoid him, and if by chance they met in hall or breakfast room, she passed him with downcast eyes and the briefest, coldest greeting. All this annoyed him intensely, and the more she eluded him, the more he desired to see her—from a spirit of opposition, he said, nothing more. It fretted and yet it entertained him, and he found a lazy sort of pleasure in thwarting the girl's little maneuvers. His patience gave out at last, and he resolved to know what was the meaning of this peculiar conduct. Having locked and taken away the key of one door in the library, he waited till Miss Muir went in to get a book for his uncle. He had heard her speak to Bella of it, knew that she believed him with his mother, and smiled to himself as he stole after her. She was standing in a chair, reaching up, and he had time to see a slender waist, a pretty foot, before he spoke.

"Can I help you, Miss Muir?"

She started, dropped several books, and turned scarlet, as she said hurriedly, "Thank you, no; I can get the steps."

"My long arm will be less trouble. I've got but one, and that is tired of being idle, so it is very much at your service. What will you have?"

"I—I—you startled me so I've forgotten." And Jean laughed, nervously, as she looked about her as if planning to escape.

"I beg your pardon, wait till you remember, and let me thank you for the enchanted sleep you gave me ten days ago. I've had no chance yet, you've shunned me so pertinaciously."

"Indeed I try not to be rude, but—" She checked herself, and turned her face away, adding, with an accent of pain in her voice, "It is not my fault, Mr. Coventry. I only obey orders."

"Whose orders?" he demanded, still standing so that she could not escape.

"Don't ask; it is one who has a right to command where you are concerned. Be sure that it is kindly meant, though it may seem folly to us. Nay, don't be angry, laugh at it, as I do, and let me run away, please."

She turned, and looked down at him with tears in her eyes, a smile on her lips, and an expression half sad, half arch, which was altogether charming. The frown passed from his face, but he still looked grave and said decidedly, "No one has a right to command in this house but my mother or myself. Was it she who bade you avoid me as if I was a madman or a pest?"

"Ah, don't ask. I promised not to tell, and you would not have me break my word, I know." And still smiling, she regarded him with a look of merry malice which made any other reply unnecessary. It was Lucia, he thought, and disliked his cousin intensely just then. Miss Muir moved as if to step down; he detained her, saying earnestly, yet with a smile, "Do you consider me the master here?"

"Yes," and to the word she gave a sweet, submissive intonation which made it expressive of the respect, regard, and confidence which men find pleasantest when women feel and show it. Unconsciously his face softened, and he looked up at her with a different glance from any he had ever given her before.

"Well, then, will you consent to obey me if I am not tyrannical or unreasonable in my demands?"

"I'll try."

"Good! Now frankly, I want to say that all this sort of thing is very disagreeable to me. It annoys me to be a restraint upon anyone's liberty or comfort, and I beg you will go and come as freely as you like, and not mind Lucia's absurdities. She means well, but hasn't a particle of penetration or tact. Will you promise this?"

"No."

"Why not?"

"It is better as it is, perhaps."

"But you called it folly just now."

"Yes, it seems so, and yet—" She paused, looking both confused and distressed.

Coventry lost patience, and said hastily, "You women are such enigmas I never expect to understand you! Well, I've done my best to make you comfortable, but if you prefer to lead this sort of life, I beg you will do so."

"I *don't* prefer it; it is hateful to me. I like to be myself, to have my liberty, and the confidence of those about me. But I cannot think it kind to disturb the peace of anyone, and so I try to obey. I've promised Bella to remain, but I will go rather than have another scene with Miss Beaufort or with you."

Miss Muir had burst out impetuously, and stood there with a sudden fire in her eyes, sudden warmth and spirit in her face and voice that amazed Coventry. She was angry, hurt, and haughty, and the change only made her more attractive, for not a trace of her former meek self remained. Coventry was electrified, and still more surprised when she added, imperiously, with a gesture as if to put him aside, "Hand me that book and move away. I wish to go."

He obeyed, even offered his hand, but she refused it, stepped lightly down, and went to the door. There she turned, and with the same indignant voice, the same kindling eyes and glowing cheeks, she said rapidly, "I know I have no right to speak in this way. I restrain myself as long as I can, but when I can bear no more, my true self breaks loose, and I defy everything. I am tired of being a cold, calm machine; it is impossible with an ardent nature like mine, and I shall try no longer. I cannot help it if people love me. I don't want their love. I only ask to be left in peace, and why I am tormented so I cannot see. I've neither beauty, money, nor rank, yet every foolish boy mistakes my frank interest for something warmer, and makes me miserable. It is my misfortune. Think of me what you will, but beware of me in time, for against my will I may do you harm."

Almost fiercely she had spoken, and with a warning gesture she hurried from the room, leaving the young man feeling as if a sudden thunder-gust had swept through the house. For several minutes he sat in the chair she left, thinking deeply. Suddenly he rose, went to his sister, and said, in his usual tone of indolent good nature, "Bella, didn't I hear Ned ask you to be kind to Miss Muir?"

"Yes, and I try to be, but she is so odd lately."

"Odd! How do you mean?"

"Why, she is either as calm and cold as a statue, or restless and queer; she cries at night, I know, and sighs sadly when she thinks I don't hear. Something is the matter."

"She frets for Ned perhaps," began Coventry.

"Oh dear, no; it's a great relief to her that he is gone. I'm afraid that she likes someone very much, and someone don't like her. Can it be Mr. Sydney?"

"She called him a 'titled fool' once, but perhaps that didn't mean anything. Did you ever ask her about him?" said Coventry, feeling rather ashamed of his curiosity, yet unable to resist the temptation of questioning unsuspecting Bella.

"Yes, but she only looked at me in her tragical way, and said, so pitifully, 'My little friend, I hope you will never have to pass through the scenes I've passed through, but keep your peace unbroken all your life.' After that I dared say no more. I'm very fond of her, I want to make her happy, but I don't know how. Can you propose anything?"

"I was going to propose that you make her come among us more, now Ned is gone. It must be dull for her, moping about alone. I'm sure it is for me. She is an entertaining little person, and I enjoy her music very much. It's good for Mamma to have gay evenings; so you bestir yourself, and see what you can do for the general good of the family."

"That's all very charming, and I've proposed it more than once, but Lucia spoils all my plans. She is afraid you'll follow Ned's example, and that is so silly."

"Lucia is a—no, I won't say fool, because she has sense enough when she chooses; but I wish you'd just settle things with Mamma, and then Lucia can do nothing but submit," said Gerald angrily.

"I'll try, but she goes up to read to Uncle, you know, and since he has had the gout, she stays later, so I see little of her in the evening. There she goes now. I think she will captivate the old one as well as the young one, she is so devoted."

Coventry looked after her slender black figure, just vanishing through the great gate, and an uncomfortable fancy took possession of him, born of Bella's careless words. He sauntered away, and after eluding his cousin, who seemed looking for him, he turned toward the Hall, saying to himself, I will see what is going on up here. Such things have happened. Uncle is the simplest soul alive, and if the girl is ambitious, she can do what she will with him.

Here a servant came running after him and gave him a letter, which he thrust into his pocket without examining it. When he reached the Hall, he went quietly to his uncle's study. The door was ajar, and looking in, he saw a scene of tranquil comfort, very pleasant to watch. Sir John leaned in his easy chair with one foot on a cushion. He was dressed with his usual care and, in spite of the gout, looked like a handsome, well-preserved old gentleman. He was smiling as he listened, and his eyes rested complacently on Jean Muir, who sat near him reading in her musical voice, while the sunshine glittered on her hair and the soft rose of her cheek. She read well, yet Coventry thought her heart was not in her task, for once when she paused, while Sir John spoke, her eyes had an absent expression, and she leaned her head upon her hand, with an air of patient weariness.

Poor girl! I did her great injustice; she has no thought of captivating the old man, but amuses him from simple kindness. She is tired. I'll put an end to her task; and Coventry entered without knocking.

Sir John received him with an air of polite resignation, Miss Muir with a perfectly expressionless face.

"Mother's love, and how are you today, sir?"

"Comfortable, but dull, so I want you to bring the girls over this evening, to amuse the old gentleman. Mrs. King has got out the antique costumes and trumpery, as I promised Bella she should have them, and tonight we are to have a merrymaking, as we used to do when Ned was here."

"Very well, sir, I'll bring them. We've all been out of sorts since the lad left, and a little jollity will do us good. Are you going back, Miss Muir?" asked Coventry.

"No, I shall keep her to give me my tea and get things ready. Don't read anymore, my dear, but go and amuse yourself with the pictures, or whatever you like," said Sir John; and like a dutiful daughter she obeyed, as if glad to get away.

"That's a very charming girl, Gerald," began Sir John as she left the room. "I'm much interested in her, both on her own account and on her mother's."

"Her mother's! What do you know of her mother?" asked Coventry, much surprised.

"Her mother was Lady Grace Howard, who ran away with a poor Scotch minister twenty years ago. The family cast her off, and she lived and died so obscurely that very little is known of her except that she left an orphan girl at some small French pension. This is the girl, and a fine girl, too. I'm surprised that you did not know this."

"So am I, but it is like her not to tell. She is a strange, proud creature. Lady Howard's daughter! Upon my word, that is a discovery," and Coventry felt his interest in his sister's governess much increased by this fact; for, like all wellborn Englishmen, he valued rank and gentle blood even more than he cared to own.

"She has had a hard life of it, this poor little girl, but she has a brave spirit, and will make her way anywhere," said Sir John admiringly.

"Did Ned know this?" asked Gerald suddenly.

"No, she only told me yesterday. I was

looking in the *Peerage* and chanced to speak of the Howards. She forgot herself and called Lady Grace her mother. Then I got the whole story, for the lonely little thing was glad to make a confidant of someone."

"That accounts for her rejection of Sydney and Ned: she knows she is their equal and will not snatch at the rank which is hers by right. No, she's not mercenary or ambitious."

"What do you say?" asked Sir John, for Coventry had spoken more to himself than to his uncle.

"I wonder if Lady Sydney was aware of this?" was all Gerald's answer.

"No, Jean said she did not wish to be pitied, and so told nothing to the mother. I think the son knew, but that was a delicate point, and I asked no questions."

"I shall write to him as soon as I discover his address. We have been so intimate I can venture to make a few inquiries about Miss Muir, and prove the truth of her story."

"Do you mean to say that you doubt it?" demanded Sir John angrily.

"I beg your pardon, Uncle, but I must confess I have an instinctive distrust of that young person. It is unjust, I dare say, yet I cannot banish it."

"Don't annoy me by expressing it, if you please. I have some penetration and experience, and I respect and pity Miss Muir heartily. This dislike of yours may be the cause of her late melancholy, hey, Gerald?" And Sir John looked suspiciously at his nephew.

Anxious to avert the rising storm, Coventry said hastily as he turned away, "I've neither time nor inclination to discuss the matter now, sir, but will be careful not to offend again. I'll take your message to Bella, so good-bye for an hour, Uncle."

And Coventry went his way through the park, thinking within himself, The dear old gentleman is getting fascinated, like poor Ned. How the deuce does the girl do it? Lady Howard's daughter, yet never told us; I don't understand that.

CHAPTER V

How the Girl Did It

At home he found a party of young friends, who hailed with delight the prospect of a revel at the Hall. An hour later, the blithe company trooped into the great saloon, where preparations had already been made for a dramatic evening.

Good Sir John was in his element, for he was never so happy as when his house was full of young people. Several persons were chosen, and in a few moments the curtains were withdrawn from the first of these impromptu tableaux. A swarthy, darkly bearded man lay asleep on a tiger skin, in the shadow of a tent. Oriental arms and drapery surrounded him; an antique silver lamp burned dimly on a table where fruit lay heaped in costly dishes, and wine shone readily in half-emptied goblets. Bending over the sleeper was a woman robed with barbaric splendor. One hand turned back the embroidered sleeve from the arm which held a scimitar; one slender foot in a scarlet sandal was visible under the white tunic; her purple mantle swept down from snowy shoulders; fillets of gold bound her hair, and jewels shone on neck and arms. She was looking over her shoulder toward the entrance of the tent, with a steady yet stealthy look, so effective that for a moment the spectators held their breath, as if they also heard a passing footstep.

"Who is it?" whispered Lucia, for the face was new to her.

"Jean Muir," answered Coventry, with an absorbed look.

"Impossible! She is small and fair," began Lucia, but a hasty "Hush, let me look!" from her cousin silenced her.

Impossible as it seemed, he was right nevertheless; for Jean Muir it was. She had darkened her skin, painted her eyebrows, disposed some wild black locks over her fair hair, and thrown such an intensity of expression into her eyes that they darkened and dilated till they were as fierce as any southern eyes that ever flashed. Hatred, the deepest and bitterest, was written on her sternly beautiful face, courage glowed in her glance, power spoke in the nervous grip of the slender hand that held the weapon, and the indomitable will of the woman was expressed—even the firm pressure of the little foot half hidden in the tiger skin.

"Oh, isn't she splendid?" cried Bella under her breath.

"She looks as if she'd use her sword well when the time comes," said someone admiringly.

"Good night to Holofernes; his fate is certain," added another.

"He is the image of Sydney, with that beard on."

"Doesn't she look as if she really hated him?"

"Perhaps she does."

Coventry uttered the last exclamation, for the two which preceded it suggested an explanation of the marvelous change in Jean. It was not all art: the intense detestation mingled with a savage joy that the object of her hatred was in her power was too perfect to be feigned; and having the key to a part of her story, Coventry felt as if he caught a glimpse of the truth. It was but a glimpse, however, for the curtain dropped before he had half analyzed the significance of that strange face.

"Horrible! I'm glad it's over," said Lucia coldly.

"Magnificent! Encore! Encore!" cried Gerald enthusiastically.

But the scene was over, and no applause could recall the actress. Two or three graceful or gay pictures followed, but Jean was in none, and each lacked the charm which real talent lends to the simplest part.

"Coventry, you are wanted," called a voice. And to everyone's surprise, Coventry went, though heretofore he had always refused to exert himself when handsome actors were in demand.

"What part am I to spoil?" he asked, as he entered the green room, where several excited young gentlemen were costuming and attitudinizing.

"A fugitive cavalier. Put yourself into this suit, and lose no time asking questions. Miss Muir will tell you what to do. She is in the tableau, so no one will mind you," said the manager pro tem, throwing a rich old suit toward Coventry and resuming the painting of a moustache on his own boyish face.

A gallant cavalier was the result of Gerald's hasty toilet, and when he appeared before the ladies a general glance of admiration was bestowed upon him.

"Come along and be placed; Jean is ready on the stage." And Bella ran before him, exclaiming to her governess, "Here he is, quite splendid. Wasn't he good to do it?"

Miss Muir, in the charmingly prim and puritanical dress of a Roundhead damsel, was arranging some shrubs, but turned suddenly and dropped the green branch she held, as her eye met the glittering figure advancing toward her.

"You!" she said with a troubled look, adding low to Bella, "Why did you ask *him?* I begged you not."

"He is the only handsome man here, and the best actor if he likes. He won't play usually, so make the most of him." And Bella was off to finish powdering her hair for "The Marriage à la Mode."

"I was sent for and I came. Do you prefer some other person?" asked Coventry, at a loss to understand the half-anxious, half-eager expression of the face under the little cap.

It changed to one of mingled annoyance and resignation as she said, "It is too late. Please kneel here, half behind the shrubs; put down your hat, and—allow me—you are too elegant for a fugitive."

As he knelt before her, she disheveled his hair, pulled his lace collar awry, threw away his gloves and sword, and half untied the cloak that hung about his shoulders.

"That is better; your paleness is excellent—nay, don't spoil it. We are to represent the picture which hangs in the Hall. I need tell you no more. Now, Roundheads, place yourselves, and then ring up the curtain."

With a smile, Coventry obeyed her; for the picture was of two lovers, the young cavalier kneeling, with his arm around the waist of the girl, who tries to hide him with her little mantle, and presses his head to her bosom in an ecstasy of fear, as she glances back at the approaching pursuers. Jean hesitated an instant and shrank a little as his hand touched her; she blushed deeply, and her eyes fell before his. Then, as the bell rang, she threw herself into her part with sudden spirit. One arm half covered him with her cloak, the other pillowed his head on the muslin kerchief folded over her bosom, and she looked backward with such terror in her eyes that more than one chivalrous young spectator longed to hurry to the rescue. It lasted but a moment; yet in that moment Coventry experienced another new sensation. Many women had smiled on him, but he had remained heart-whole, cool, and careless, quite unconscious of the power which a woman possesses and knows how to use, for the weal or woe of man. Now, as he knelt there with a soft arm about him, a slender waist yielding to his touch, and a maiden heart throbbing against his cheek, for the first time in his life he felt the indescribable spell of womanhood, and looked the ardent lover to perfection. Just as his face assumed this new and most becoming aspect, the curtain dropped, and clamorous encores recalled him to the fact that Miss Muir was trying to escape from his hold, which had grown painful in its unconscious pressure. He sprang up, half bewildered, and looking as he had never looked before.

"Again! Again!" called Sir John. And the young men who played the Roundheads, eager to share in the applause begged for a repetition in new attitudes.

"A rustle has betrayed you, we have fired and shot the brave girl, and she lies dying, you know. That will be effective; try it, Miss Muir," said one. And with a long breath, Jean complied.

The curtain went up, showing the lover still on his knees, unmindful of the captors who clutched him by the shoulder, for at his feet the girl lay dying. Her head was on his breast, now, her eyes looked full into his, no longer wild with fear, but eloquent with the love which even death could not conquer. The power of those tender eyes thrilled Coventry with a strange delight, and set his heart beating as rapidly as hers had done. She felt his hands tremble, saw the color flash into his cheek, knew that she had touched him at last, and when she rose it was with a sense of triumph which she found it hard to conceal. Others thought it fine acting; Coventry tried to believe so; but Lucia set her teeth, and, as the curtain fell on that second picture, she left her place to hurry behind the scenes, bent on putting an end to such dangerous play. Several actors were complimenting the mimic lovers. Jean took it merrily, but Coventry, in spite of himself, betrayed that he was excited by something deeper than mere gratified vanity.

As Lucia appeared, his manner changed to its usual indifference; but he could not quench the unwonted fire of his eyes, or keep all trace of emotion out of his face, and she saw this with a sharp pang.

"I have come to offer my help. You must be tired, Miss Muir. Can I relieve you?" said Lucia hastily.

"Yes, thank you. I shall be very glad to leave the rest to you, and enjoy them from the front."

So with a sweet smile Jean tripped away, and to Lucia's dismay Coventry followed.

"I want you, Gerald; please stay," she cried.

"I've done my part—no more tragedy for me tonight." And he was gone before she could entreat or command.

There was no help for it; she must stay and do her duty, or expose her jealousy to the quick eyes about her. For a time she bore it; but the sight of her cousin leaning over the chair she had left and chatting with the governess, who now filled it, grew unbearable, and she dispatched a little girl with a message to Miss Muir.

"Please, Miss Beaufort wants you for Queen Bess, as you are the only lady with red hair. Will you come?" whispered the child, quite unconscious of any hidden sting in her words.

"Yes, dear, willingly though I'm not stately enough for Her Majesty, nor handsome enough," said Jean, rising with an untroubled face, though she resented the feminine insult.

"Do you want an Essex? I'm all dressed for it," said Coventry, following to the door with a wistful look.

"No, Miss Beaufort said *you* were not to come. She doesn't want you both together," said the child decidedly.

Jean gave him a significant look, shrugged her shoulders, and went away smiling her odd smile, while Coventry paced up and down the hall in a curious state of unrest, which made him forgetful of everything till the young people came gaily out to supper.

"Come, bonny Prince Charlie, take me down, and play the lover as charmingly as you did an hour ago. I never thought you had so much warmth in you," said Bella, taking his arm and drawing him on against his will.

"Don't be foolish, child. Where is—Lucia?"

Why he checked Jean's name on his lips and substituted another's, he could not tell; but a sudden shyness in speaking of her possessed him, and though he saw her nowhere, he would not ask for her. His cousin came down looking lovely in a classical costume; but Gerald scarcely saw her, and, when the merriment was at its height, he slipped away to discover what had become of Miss Muir.

Alone in the deserted drawing room he found her, and paused to watch her a moment before he spoke; for something in her attitude and face struck him. She was leaning wearily back in the great chair which had served for a throne. Her royal robes were still unchanged, though the crown was off and all her fair hair hung about her shoulders. Excitement and exertion made her brilliant, the rich dress became her wonderfully, and an air of luxurious indolence changed the meek governess into a charming woman. She leaned on the velvet cushions as if she were used to such support; she played with the jewels which had crowned her as carelessly as if she were born to wear them; her attitude was full of negligent grace, and the expression of her face half proud, half pensive, as if her thoughts were bittersweet.

One would know she was wellborn to see her now. Poor girl, what a burden a life of dependence must be to a spirit like hers! I wonder what she is thinking of so intently. And Coventry indulged in another look before he spoke.

"Shall I bring you some supper, Miss Muir?"

"Supper!" she ejaculated, with a start. "Who thinks of one's body when one's soul is—" She stopped there, knit her brows, and laughed faintly as she added, "No, thank you. I want nothing but advice, and that I dare not ask of anyone."

"Why not?"

"Because I have no right."

"Everyone has a right to ask help, especially the weak of the strong. Can I help you? Believe me, I most heartily offer my poor services."

"Ah, you forget! This dress, the borrowed

splendor of these jewels, the freedom of this gay evening, the romance of the part you played, all blind you to the reality. For a moment I cease to be a servant, and for a moment you treat me as an equal."

It was true; he *had* forgotten. That soft, reproachful glance touched him, his distrust melted under the new charm, and he answered with real feeling in voice and face, "I treat you as an equal because you *are* one; and when I offer help, it is not to my sister's governess alone, but to Lady Howard's daughter."

"Who told you that?" she demanded, sitting erect.

"My uncle. Do not reproach him. It shall go no further, if you forbid it. Are you sorry that I know it?"

"Yes."

"Why?"

"Because I will not be pitied!" And her eyes flashed as she made a half-defiant gesture.

"Then, if I may not pity the hard fate which has befallen an innocent life, may I admire the courage which meets adverse fortune so bravely, and conquers the world by winning the respect and regard of all who see and honor it?"

Miss Muir averted her face, put up her hand, and answered hastily, "No, no, not that! Do not be kind; it destroys the only barrier now left between us. Be cold to me as before, forget what I am, and let me go on my way, unknown, unpitied, and unloved!"

Her voice faltered and failed as the last word was uttered, and she bent her face upon her hand. Something jarred upon Coventry in this speech, and moved him to say, almost rudely, "You need have no fears for me. Lucia will tell you what an iceberg I am."

"Then Lucia would tell me wrong. I have the fatal power of reading character; I know you better than she does, and I see—" There she stopped abruptly.

"What? Tell me and prove your skill," he said eagerly.

Turning, she fixed her eyes on him with a penetrating power that made him shrink as she said slowly, "Under the ice I see fire, and warn you to beware lest it prove a volcano."

For a moment he sat dumb, wondering at the insight of the girl; for she was the first to discover the hidden warmth of a nature too proud to confess its tender impulses, or the ambitions that slept till some potent voice awoke them. The blunt, almost stern manner in which she warned him away from her only made her more attractive; for there was no conceit or arrogance in it, only a foreboding fear emboldened by past suffering to be frank. Suddenly he spoke impetuously:

"You are right! I am not what I seem, and my indolent indifference is but the mask under which I conceal my real self. I could be as passionate, as energetic and aspiring as Ned, if I had any aim in life. I have none, and so I am what you once called me, a thing to pity and despise."

"I never said that!" cried Jean indignantly.

"Not in those words, perhaps; but you looked it and thought it, though you phrased it more mildly. I deserved it, but I shall deserve it no longer. I am beginning to wake from my disgraceful idleness, and long for some work that shall make a man of me. Why do you go? I annoy you with my confessions. Pardon me. They are the first I ever made; they shall be the last."

"No, oh no! I am too much honored by your confidence; but is it wise, is it loyal to tell *me* your hopes and aims? Has not Miss Beaufort the first right to be your confidante?"

Coventry drew back, looking intensely annoyed, for the name recalled much that he would gladly have forgotten in the novel excitement of the hour. Lucia's love, Edward's parting words, his own reserve so strangely thrown aside, so difficult to resume. What he would have said was checked by the sight of a half-open letter which fell from Jean's dress as she moved away. Mechanically he took it up to return it, and, as he did so, he recognized Sydney's handwriting. Jean snatched it from him, turning pale to the lips as she cried, "Did you read it? What did you see? Tell me, tell me, on your honor!"

"On my honor, I saw nothing but this single sentence, 'By the love I bear you, believe what I say.' No more, as I am a gentleman. I know the hand, I guess the purport of the letter, and as a friend of Sydney, I earnestly desire to help you, if I can. Is this the matter upon which you want advice?"

"Yes."

"Then let me give it?"

"You cannot, without knowing all, and it is so hard to tell!"

"Let me guess it, and spare you the pain of telling. May I?" And Coventry waited eagerly for her reply, for the spell was still upon him.

Holding the letter fast, she beckoned him to follow, and glided before him to a secluded little nook, half boudoir, half conservatory. There she paused, stood an instant as if in doubt, then looked up at him with confiding eyes and said decidedly, "I will do it; for, strange as it may seem, you are the only person to whom I *can* speak. You know Sydney, you have discovered that I am an equal, you have offered your help. I accept it; but oh, do not think me unwomanly! Remember how alone I am, how young, and how much I rely upon your sincerity, your sympathy!"

"Speak freely. I am indeed your friend." And Coventry sat down beside her, forgetful of everything but the soft-eyed girl who confided in him so entirely.

Speaking rapidly, Jean went on, "You know that Sydney loved me, that I refused him and went away. But you do not know that his importunities nearly drove me wild, that he threatened to rob me of my only treasure, my good name, and that, in desperation, I tried to kill myself. Yes, mad, wicked as it was, I did long to end the life which was, at best, a burden, and under his persecution had become a torment. You are shocked, yet what I say is the living truth. Lady Sydney will confirm it, the nurses at the hospital will confess that it was not a fever which brought me there; and here, though the external wound is healed, my heart still aches and burns with the shame and indignation which only a proud woman can feel."

She paused and sat with kindling eyes, glowing cheeks, and both hands pressed to her heaving bosom, as if the old insult roused her spirit anew. Coventry said not a word, for surprise, anger, incredulity, and admiration mingled so confusedly in his mind that he forgot to speak, and Jean went on, "That wild act of mine convinced him of my indomitable dislike. He went away, and I believed that this stormy love of his would be cured by absence. It is not, and I live in daily fear of fresh entreaties, renewed persecution. His mother promised not to betray where I had gone, but he found me out and wrote to me. The letter I asked you to take to Lady Sydney was a reply to his, imploring him to leave me in peace. You failed to deliver it, and I was glad, for I thought silence might quench hope. All in vain; this is a more passionate appeal than ever, and he vows he will never desist from his endeavors till I give another man the right to protect me. I *can* do this—I am sorely tempted to do it, but I rebel against the cruelty. I love my freedom, I have no wish to marry at this man's bidding. What can I do? How can I free myself? Be my friend, and help me!"

Tears streamed down her cheeks, sobs choked her words, and she clasped her hands imploringly as she turned toward the young man in all the abandonment of sorrow, fear, and supplication. Coventry found it hard to meet those eloquent eyes and answer calmly, for he had no experience in such scenes and knew not how to play his part. It is this absurd dress and that romantic nonsense which makes me feel so unlike myself, he thought, quite unconscious of the dangerous power which the dusky room, the midsummer warmth and fragrance, the memory of the "romantic nonsense," and, most of all, the presence of a beautiful, afflicted woman had over him. His usual self-possession deserted him, and he could only echo the words which had made the strongest impression upon him:

"You *can* do this, you are tempted to do it. Is Ned the man who can protect you?"

"No" was the soft reply.

"Who then?"

"Do not ask me. A good and honorable man; one who loves me well, and would devote his life to me; one whom once it would have been happiness to marry, but now—"

There her voice ended in a sigh, and all her fair hair fell down about her face, hiding it in a shining veil.

"Why not now? This is a sure and speedy way of ending your distress. Is it impossible?"

In spite of himself, Gerald leaned nearer, took one of the little hands in his, and pressed it as he spoke, urgently, compassionately, nay, almost tenderly. From behind the veil came a heavy sigh, and the brief answer, "It is impossible."

"Why, Jean?"

She flung her hair back with a sudden gesture, drew away her hand, and answered, almost fiercely, "Because I do not love him! Why do you torment me with such questions? I tell you I am in a sore strait and cannot see my way. Shall I deceive the good man, and secure peace at the price of liberty and truth? Or shall I defy Sydney and lead a life of dread? If he menaced my life, I should not fear; but he menaces that which is dearer than life—my good name. A look, a word can tarnish it; a scornful smile, a significant shrug can do me more harm than any blow; for I am a woman—friendless, poor, and at the mercy of his tongue. Ah, better to have died, and so have been saved the bitter pain that has come now!"

She sprang up, clasped her hands over her head, and paced despairingly through the little room, not weeping, but wearing an expression more tragical than tears. Still feeling as if he had suddenly stepped into a romance, yet finding a keen pleasure in the part assigned him, Coventry threw himself into it with spirit, and heartily did his best to console the poor girl who needed help so much. Going to her, he said as impetuously as Ned ever did, "Miss Muir—nay, I will say Jean, if that will comfort you—listen, and rest assured that no harm shall touch you if I can ward it off. You are needlessly alarmed. Indignant you may well be, but, upon my life, I think you wrong Sydney. He is violent, I know, but he is too honorable a man to injure you by a light word, an unjust act. He did but threaten, hoping to soften you. Let me see him, or write to him. He is my friend; he will listen to me. Of that I am sure."

"Be sure of nothing. When a man like Sydney loves and is thwarted in his love, nothing can control his headstrong will. Promise me you will not see or write to him. Much as I fear and despise him, I will submit, rather than any harm should befall you—or your brother. You promise me, Mr. Coventry?"

He hesitated. She clung to his arm with unfeigned solicitude in her eager, pleading face, and he could not resist it.

"I promise; but in return you must promise to let me give what help I can; and, Jean, never say again that you are friendless."

"You are so kind! God bless you for it. But I dare not accept your friendship; *she* will not permit it, and I have no right to mar her peace."

"Who will not permit it?" he demanded hotly.

"Miss Beaufort."

"Hang Miss Beaufort!" exclaimed Coventry, with such energy that Jean broke into a musical laugh, despite her trouble. He joined in it, and, for an instant they stood looking at one another as if the last barrier were down, and they were friends indeed. Jean paused suddenly, with the smile on her lips, the tears still on her cheek, and made a warning gesture. He listened: the sound of feet mingled with calls and laughter proved that they were missed and sought.

"That laugh betrayed us. Stay and meet them. I cannot." And Jean darted out upon the lawn. Coventry followed; for the thought of confronting so many eyes, so many questions, daunted him, and he fled like a coward. The sound of Jean's flying footsteps guided him, and he overtook her just as she paused behind a rose thicket to take breath.

"Fainthearted knight! You should have stayed and covered my retreat. Hark! they are coming! Hide! Hide!" she panted, half in fear, half in merriment, as the gay pursuers rapidly drew nearer.

"Kneel down; the moon is coming out and the glitter of your embroidery will betray you," whispered Jean, as they cowered behind the roses.

"Your arms and hair will betray you. 'Come under my plaiddie,' as the song says." And Coventry tried to make his velvet cloak cover the white shoulders and fair locks.

"We are acting our parts in reality now. How Bella will enjoy the thing when I tell her!" said Jean as the noises died away.

"Do not tell her," whispered Coventry.

"And why not?" she asked, looking up into the face so near her own, with an artless glance.

"Can you not guess why?"

"Ah, you are so proud you cannot bear to be laughed at."

"It is not that. It is because I do not want you to be annoyed by silly tongues; you have enough to pain you without that. I am your friend, now, and I do my best to prove it."

"So kind, so kind! How can I thank you?" murmured Jean. And she involuntarily nestled closer under the cloak that sheltered both.

Neither spoke for a moment, and in the silence the rapid beating of two hearts was heard. To drown the sound, Coventry said softly, "Are you frightened?"

"No, I like it," she answered, as softly, then added abruptly, "But why do we hide? There is nothing to fear. It is late. I must go. You are kneeling on my train. Please rise."

"Why in such haste? This flight and search only adds to the charm of the evening. I'll not get up yet. Will you have a rose, Jean?"

"No, I will not. Let me go, Mr. Coventry, I insist. There has been enough of this folly. You forget yourself."

She spoke imperiously, flung off the cloak, and put him from her. He rose at once, saying, like one waking suddenly from a pleasant dream, "I do indeed forget myself."

Here the sound of voices broke on them, nearer than before. Pointing to a covered walk that led to the house, he said, in his usually cool, calm tone, "Go in that way; I will cover your retreat." And turning, he went to meet the merry hunters.

Half an hour later, when the party broke up, Miss Muir joined them in her usual quiet dress, looking paler, meeker, and sadder than usual. Coventry saw this, though he neither looked at her nor addressed her. Lucia saw it also, and was glad that the dangerous girl had fallen back into her proper place again, for she had suffered much that night. She appropriated her cousin's arm as they went through the park, but he was in one of his taciturn moods, and all her attempts at conversation were in vain. Miss Muir walked alone, singing softly to herself as she followed in the dusk. Was Gerald so silent because he listened to that fitful song? Lucia thought so, and felt her dislike rapidly deepening to hatred.

When the young friends were gone, and the family were exchanging good-nights among themselves, Jean was surprised by Coventry's offering his hand, for he had never done it before, and whispering, as he held it, though Lucia watched him all the while, "I have not given my advice, yet."

"Thanks, I no longer need it. I have decided for myself."

"May I ask how?"

"To brave my enemy."

"Good! But what decided you so suddenly?"

"The finding of a friend." And with a grateful glance she was gone.

CHAPTER VI
On the Watch

"If you please, Mr. Coventry, did you get the letter last night?" were the first words that greeted the "young master" as he left his room next morning.

"What letter, Dean? I don't remember any," he answered, pausing, for something in the maid's manner struck him as peculiar.

"It came just as you left for the Hall, sir. Benson ran after you with it, as it was marked 'Haste.' Didn't you get it, sir?" asked the woman, anxiously.

"Yes, but upon my life, I forgot all about it till this minute. It's in my other coat, I suppose, if I've not lost it. That absurd masquerading put everything else out of my head." And speaking more to himself than to the maid, Coventry turned back to look for the missing letter.

Dean remained where she was, apparently busy about the arrangement of the curtains at the hall window, but furtively watching meanwhile with a most unwonted air of curiosity.

"Not there, I thought so!" she muttered, as Coventry impatiently thrust his hand into one pocket after another. But as she spoke, an expression of amazement appeared in her face, for suddenly the letter was discovered.

"I'd have sworn it wasn't there! I don't understand it, but she's a deep one, or I'm much deceived." And Dean shook her head like one perplexed, but not convinced.

Coventry uttered an exclamation of satisfaction on glancing at the address and, standing where he was, tore open the letter.

> Dear C:
>
> I'm off to Baden. Come and join me, then you'll be out of harm's way; for if you fall in love with J. M. (and you can't escape if you stay where she is), you will incur the trifling inconvenience of having your brains blown out by
>
> Yours truly, F. R. Sydney

"The man is mad!" ejaculated Coventry, staring at the letter while an angry flush rose to his face. "What the deuce does he mean by writing to me in that style? Join him—not I! And as for the threat, I laugh at it. Poor Jean! This headstrong fool seems bent on tormenting her. Well, Dean, what are you waiting for?" he demanded, as if suddenly conscious of her presence.

"Nothing, sir; I only stopped to see if you found the letter. Beg pardon, sir."

And she was moving on when Coventry asked, with a suspicious look, "What made you think it was lost? You seem to take an uncommon interest in my affairs today."

"Oh dear, no, sir. I felt a bit anxious, Benson is so forgetful, and it was me who sent him after you, for I happened to see you go out, so I felt responsible. Being marked that way, I thought it might be important so I asked about it."

"Very well, you can go, Dean. It's all right, you see."

"I'm not so sure of that," muttered the woman, as she curtsied respectfully and went away, looking as if the letter had *not* been found.

Dean was Miss Beaufort's maid, a grave, middle-aged woman with keen eyes and a somewhat grim air. Having been long in the family, she enjoyed all the privileges of a faithful and favorite servant. She loved her young mistress with an almost jealous affection. She watched over her with the vigilant care of a mother and resented any attempt at interference on the part of others. At first she had pitied and liked Jean Muir, then distrusted her, and now heartily hated her, as the cause of the increased indifference of Coventry toward his cousin. Dean knew the depth of Lucia's love, and though no man, in her eyes, was worthy of her mistress, still, having honored him with her regard, Dean felt bound to like him, and the late change in his manner disturbed the maid almost as much as it did the mistress. She watched Jean narrowly, causing that amiable creature much amusement but little annoyance, as yet, for Dean's slow English wit was no match for the subtle mind of the governess. On the preceding night, Dean had been sent up to the Hall with costumes and had there seen something which much disturbed her. She began to speak of it while undressing her mistress, but Lucia, being in an unhappy mood, had so sternly ordered her not to gossip that the tale remained untold, and she was forced to bide her time.

Now I'll see how *she* looks after it; though there's not much to be got out of *her* face, the deceitful hussy, thought Dean, marching down the corridor and knitting her black brows as she went.

"Good morning, Mrs. Dean. I hope you are none the worse for last night's frolic. You had the work and we the play," said a blithe voice behind her; and turning sharply, she confronted Miss Muir. Fresh and smiling, the governess nodded with an air of cordiality which would have been irresistible with anyone but Dean.

"I'm quite well, thank you, miss," she returned coldly, as her keen eye fastened on the girl as if to watch the effect of her words. "I had a good rest when the young ladies and gentlemen were at supper, for while the maids cleared up, I sat in the 'little anteroom.' "

"Yes, I saw you, and feared you'd take cold. Very glad you didn't. How is Miss Beaufort? She seemed rather poorly last night" was the tranquil reply, as Jean settled the little frills about her delicate wrists. The cool question was a return shot for Dean's hint that she had been where she could oversee the interview between Coventry and Miss Muir.

"She is a bit tired, as any *lady* would be after such an evening. People who are *used* to *play-acting* wouldn't mind it, perhaps, but Miss Beaufort don't enjoy *romps* as much as *some* do."

The emphasis upon certain words made Dean's speech as impertinent as she desired. But Jean only laughed, and as Coventry's step was heard behind them, she ran downstairs, saying blandly, but with a wicked look, "I won't stop to thank you now, lest Mr. Coventry should bid me good-morning, and so increase Miss Beaufort's indisposition."

Dean's eyes flashed as she looked after the girl with a wrathful face, and went her way, saying grimly, "I'll bide my time, but I'll get the better of her yet."

Fancying himself quite removed from "last night's absurdity," yet curious to see how Jean would meet him, Coventry lounged into the breakfast room with his usual air of listless indifference. A languid nod and murmur was all the reply he vouchsafed to the greetings of cousin, sister, and governess as he sat down and took up his paper.

"Have you had a letter from Ned?" asked Bella, looking at the note which her brother still held.

"No" was the brief answer.

"Who then? You look as if you had received bad news."

There was no reply, and, peeping over his arm, Bella caught sight of the seal and exclaimed, in a disappointed tone, "It is the Sydney crest. I don't care about the note now. Men's letters to each other are not interesting."

Miss Muir had been quietly feeding one of Edward's dogs, but at the name she looked up and met Coventry's eyes, coloring so distressfully that he pitied her. Why he should take the trouble to cover her confusion, he did not stop to ask himself, but seeing the curl of Lucia's lip, he suddenly addressed her with an air of displeasure, "Do you know that Dean is getting impertinent? She presumes too much on her age and your indulgence, and forgets her place."

"What has she done?" asked Lucia coldly.

"She troubles herself about my affairs and

takes it upon herself to keep Benson in order."

Here Coventry told about the letter and the woman's evident curiosity.

"Poor Dean, she gets no thanks for reminding you of what you had forgotten. Next time she will leave your letters to their fate, and perhaps it will be as well, if they have such a bad effect upon your temper, Gerald."

Lucia spoke calmly, but there was an angry color in her cheek as she rose and left the room. Coventry looked much annoyed, for on Jean's face he detected a faint smile, half pitiful, half satirical, which disturbed him more than his cousin's insinuation. Bella broke the awkward silence by saying, with a sigh, "Poor Ned! I do so long to hear again from him. I thought a letter had come for some of us. Dean said she saw one bearing his writing on the hall table yesterday."

"She seems to have a mania for inspecting letters. I won't allow it. Who was the letter for, Bella?" said Coventry, putting down his paper.

"She wouldn't or couldn't tell, but looked very cross and told me to ask you."

"Very odd! I've had none," began Coventry.

"But I had one several days ago. Will you please read it, and my reply?" And as she spoke, Jean laid two letters before him.

"Certainly not. It would be dishonorable to read what Ned intended for no eyes but your own. You are too scrupulous in one way, and not enough so in another, Miss Muir." And Coventry offered both the letters with an air of grave decision, which could not conceal the interest and surprise he felt.

"You are right. Mr. Edward's note *should* be kept sacred, for in it the poor boy has laid bare his heart to me. But mine I beg you will read, that you may see how well I try to keep my word to you. Oblige me in this, Mr. Coventry; I have a right to ask it of you."

So urgently she spoke, so wistfully she looked, that he could not refuse and, going to the window, read the letter. It was evidently an answer to a passionate appeal from the young lover, and was written with consummate skill. As he read, Gerald could not help thinking, If this girl writes in this way to a man whom she does *not* love, with what a world of power and passion would she write to one whom she *did* love. And this thought kept returning to him as his eyes went over line after line of wise argument, gentle reproof, good counsel, and friendly regard. Here and there a word, a phrase, betrayed what she had already confessed, and Coventry forgot to return the letter, as he stood wondering who was the man whom Jean loved.

The sound of Bella's voice recalled him, for she was saying, half kindly, half petulantly, "Don't look so sad, Jean. Ned will outlive it, I dare say. You remember you said once men never died of love, though women might. In his one note to me, he spoke so beautifully of you, and begged me to be kind to you for his sake, that I try to be with all my heart, though if it was anyone but you, I really think I should hate them for making my dear boy so unhappy."

"You are too kind, Bella, and I often think I'll go away to relieve you of my presence; but unwise and dangerous as it is to stay, I haven't the courage to go. I've been so happy here." And as she spoke, Jean's head dropped lower over the dog as it nestled to her affectionately.

Before Bella could utter half the loving

words that sprang to her lips, Coventry came to them with all languor gone from face and mien, and laying Jean's letter before her, he said, with an undertone of deep feeling in his usually emotionless voice, "A right womanly and eloquent letter, but I fear it will only increase the fire it was meant to quench. I pity my brother more than ever now."

"Shall I send it?" asked Jean, looking straight up at him, like one who had entire reliance on his judgment.

"Yes, I have not the heart to rob him of such a sweet sermon upon self-sacrifice. Shall I post it for you?"

"Thank you; in a moment." And with a grateful look, Jean dropped her eyes. Producing her little purse, she selected a penny, folded it in a bit of paper, and then offered both letter and coin to Coventry, with such a pretty air of business, that he could not control a laugh.

"So you won't be indebted to me for a penny? What a proud woman you are, Miss Muir."

"I am; it's a family failing." And she gave him a significant glance, which recalled to him the memory of who she was. He understood her feeling, and liked her the better for it, knowing that he would have done the same had he been in her place. It was a little thing, but if done for effect, it answered admirably, for it showed a quick insight into his character on her part, and betrayed to him the existence of a pride in which he sympathized heartily. He stood by Jean a moment, watching her as she burnt Edward's letter in the blaze of the spirit lamp under the urn.

"Why do you do that?" he asked involuntarily.

"Because it is my duty to forget" was all her answer.

"Can you always forget when it becomes a duty?"

"I wish I could! I wish I could!"

She spoke passionately, as if the words broke from her against her will, and, rising hastily, she went into the garden, as if afraid to stay.

"Poor, dear Jean is very unhappy about something, but I can't discover what it is. Last night I found her crying over a rose, and now she runs away, looking as if her heart was broken. I'm glad I've got no lessons."

"What kind of a rose?" asked Coventry from behind his paper as Bella paused.

"A lovely white one. It must have come from the Hall; we have none like it. I wonder if Jean was ever going to be married, and lost her lover, and felt sad because the flower reminded her of bridal roses."

Coventry made no reply, but felt himself change countenance as he recalled the little scene behind the rose hedge, where he gave Jean the flower which she had refused yet taken. Presently, to Bella's surprise, he flung down the paper, tore Sydney's note to atoms, and rang for his horse with an energy which amazed her.

"Why, Gerald, what has come over you? One would think Ned's restless spirit had suddenly taken possession of you. What are you going to do?"

"I'm going to work" was the unexpected answer, as Coventry turned toward her with an expression so rarely seen on his fine face.

"What has waked you up all at once?" asked Bella, looking more and more amazed.

"You did," he said, drawing her toward him.

"I! When? How?"

"Do you remember saying once that energy was better than beauty in a man, and that no one could respect an idler?"

"I never said anything half so sensible as that. Jean said something like it once, I believe, but I forgot. Are you tired of doing nothing, at last, Gerald?"

"Yes, I neglected my duty to Ned, till he got into trouble, and now I reproach myself for it. It's not too late to do other neglected tasks, so I'm going at them with a will. Don't say anything about it to anyone, and don't laugh at me, for I'm in earnest, Bell."

"I know you are, and I admire and love you for it, my dear old boy," cried Bella enthusiastically, as she threw her arms about his neck and kissed him heartily. "What will you do first?" she asked, as he stood thoughtfully smoothing the bright head that leaned upon his shoulder, with that new expression still clear and steady in his face.

"I'm going to ride over the whole estate, and attend to things as a master should; not leave it all to Bent, of whom I've heard many complaints, but have been too idle to inquire about them. I shall consult Uncle, and endeavor to be all that my father was in his time. Is that a worthy ambition, dear?"

"Oh, Gerald, let me tell Mamma. It will make her so happy. You are her idol, and to hear you say these things, to see you look so like dear Papa, would do more for her spirits than all the doctors in England."

"Wait till I prove what my resolution is worth. When I have really done something, then I'll surprise Mamma with a sample of my work."

"Of course you'll tell Lucia?"

"Not on any account. It is a little secret between us, so keep it till I give you leave to tell it."

"But Jean will see it at once; she knows everything that happens, she is so quick and wise. Do you mind her knowing?"

"I don't see that I can help it if she is so wonderfully gifted. Let her see what she can, I don't mind her. Now I'm off." And with a kiss to his sister, a sudden smile on his face, Coventry sprang upon his horse and rode away at a pace which caused the groom to stare after him in blank amazement.

Nothing more was seen of him till dinnertime, when he came in so exhilarated by his brisk ride and busy morning that he found some difficulty in assuming his customary manner, and more than once astonished the family by talking animatedly on various subjects which till now had always seemed utterly uninteresting to him. Lucia was amazed, his mother delighted, and Bella could hardly control her desire to explain the mystery; but Jean took it very calmly and regarded him with the air of one who said, "I understand, but you will soon tire of it." This nettled him more than he would confess, and he exerted himself to silently contradict that prophecy.

"Have you answered Mr. Sydney's letter?" asked Bella, when they were all scattered about the drawing room after dinner.

"No," answered her brother, who was pacing up and down with restless steps, instead of lounging near his beautiful cousin.

"I ask because I remembered that Ned sent a message for him in my last note, as he thought you would know Sydney's address. Here it is, something about a horse. Please put it in when you write," and Bella laid the note on the writing table nearby.

"I'll send it at once and have done with it,"

muttered Coventry and, seating himself, he dashed off a few lines, sealed and sent the letter, and then resumed his march, eyeing the three young ladies with three different expressions, as he passed and repassed. Lucia sat apart, feigning to be intent upon a book, and her handsome face looked almost stern in its haughty composure, for though her heart ached, she was too proud to own it. Bella now lay on the sofa, half asleep, a rosy little creature, as unconsciously pretty as a child. Miss Muir sat in the recess of a deep window, in a low lounging chair, working at an embroidery frame with a graceful industry pleasant to see. Of late she had worn colors, for Bella had been generous in gifts, and the pale blue muslin which flowed in soft waves about her was very becoming to her fair skin and golden hair. The close braids were gone, and loose curls dropped here and there from the heavy coil wound around her well-shaped head. The tip of one dainty foot was visible, and a petulant litle gesture which now and then shook back the falling sleeve gave glimpses of a round white arm. Ned's great hound lay nearby, the sunshine flickered on her through the leaves, and as she sat smiling to herself, while the dexterous hands shaped leaf and flower, she made a charming picture of all that is most womanly and winning; a picture which few men's eyes would not have liked to rest upon.

Another chair stood near her, and as Coventry went up and down, a strong desire to take it possessed him. He was tired of his thoughts and wished to be amused by watching the changes of the girl's expressive face, listening to the varying tones of her voice, and trying to discover the spell which so strongly attracted him in spite of himself. More than once he swerved from his course to gratify his whim, but Lucia's presence always restrained him, and with a word to the dog, or a glance from the window, as pretext for a pause, he resumed his walk again. Something in his cousin's face reproached him, but her manner of late was so repellent that he felt no desire to resume their former familiarity, and, wishing to show that he did not consider himself bound, he kept aloof. It was a quiet test of the power of each woman over this man; they instinctively felt it, and both tried to conquer. Lucia spoke several times, and tried to speak frankly and affably;

but her manner was constrained, and Coventry, having answered politely, relapsed into silence. Jean said nothing, but silently appealed to eye and ear by the pretty picture she made of herself, the snatches of song she softly sang, as if forgetting that she was not alone, and a shy glance now and then, half wistful, half merry, which was more alluring than graceful figure or sweet voice. When she had tormented Lucia and tempted Coventry long enough, she quietly asserted her supremacy in a way which astonished her rival, who knew nothing of the secret of her birth, which knowledge did much to attract and charm the young man. Letting a ball of silk escape from her lap, she watched it roll toward the promenader, who caught and returned it with an alacrity which added grace to the trifling service. As she took it, she said, in the frank way that never failed to win him, "I think you must be tired; but if exercise is necessary, employ your energies to some purpose and put your mother's basket of silks in order. They are in a tangle, and it will please her to know that you did it, as your brother used to do."

"Hercules at the distaff," said Coventry

gaily, and down he sat in the long-desired seat. Jean put the basket on his knee, and as he surveyed it, as if daunted at his task, she leaned back, and indulged in a musical little peal of laughter charming to hear. Lucia sat dumb with surprise, to see her proud, indolent cousin obeying the commands of a governess, and looking as if he heartily enjoyed it. In ten minutes she was as entirely forgotten as if she had been miles away; for Jean seemed in her wittiest, gayest mood, and as she now treated the "young master" like an equal, there was none of the former meek timidity. Yet often her eyes fell, her color changed, and the piquant sallies faltered on her tongue, as Coventry involuntarily looked deep into the fine eyes which had once shone on him so tenderly in that mimic tragedy. He could not forget it, and though neither alluded to it, the memory of the previous evening seemed to haunt both and lend a secret charm to the present moment. Lucia bore this as long as she could, and then left the room with the air of an insulted princess; but Coventry did not, and Jean feigned not to see her go. Bella was fast asleep, and before he knew how it came to pass, the young man was listening to the story of his companion's life. A sad tale, told with wonderful skill, for soon he was absorbed in it. The basket slid unobserved from his knee, the dog was pushed away, and, leaning forward, he listened eagerly as the girl's low voice recounted all the hardships, loneliness, and grief of her short life. In the midst of a touching episode she started, stopped, and looked straight before her, with an intent expression which changed to one of intense contempt, and her eye turned to Coventry's, as she said, pointing to the window behind him, "We are watched."

"By whom?" he demanded, starting up angrily.

"Hush, say nothing, let it pass. I am used to it."

"But *I* am not, and I'll not submit to it. Who was it, Jean?" he answered hotly.

She smiled significantly at a knot of rose-colored ribbon, which a little gust was blowing toward them along the terrace. A black frown darkened the young man's face as he sprang out of the long window and went rapidly out of sight, scrutinizing each green nook as he passed. Jean laughed quietly as she watched him, and said softly to herself, with her eyes on the fluttering ribbon, "That was a fortunate accident, and a happy inspiration. Yes, my dear Mrs. Dean, you will find that playing the spy will only get your mistress as well as yourself into trouble. You would not be warned, and you must take the consequences, reluctant as I am to injure a worthy creature like yourself."

Soon Coventry was heard returning. Jean listened with suspended breath to catch his first words, for he was not alone.

"Since you insist that it was you and not your mistress, I let it pass, although I still have my suspicions. Tell Miss Beaufort I desire to see her for a few moments in the library. Now go, Dean, and be careful for the future, if you wish to stay in my house."

The maid retired, and the young man came in looking both ireful and stern.

"I wish I had said nothing, but I was startled, and spoke involuntarily. Now you are angry, and I have made fresh trouble for poor Miss Lucia. Forgive me as I forgive her, and let it pass. I have learned to bear this surveillance, and pity her causeless jealousy," said Jean, with a self-reproachful air.

"I will forgive the dishonorable act, but I cannot forget it, and I intend to put a stop to it. I am not betrothed to my cousin, as I told you once, but you, like all the rest, seem bent on believing that I am. Hitherto I have cared too little about the matter to settle it, but now I shall prove beyond all doubt that I am free."

As he uttered the last word, Coventry cast on Jean a look that affected her strangely. She grew pale, her work dropped on her lap, and her eyes rose to his, with an eager, questioning expression, which slowly changed to one of mingled pain and pity, as she turned her face away, murmuring in a tone of tender sorrow, "Poor Lucia, who will comfort her?"

For a moment Coventry stood silent, as if weighing some fateful purpose in his mind. As Jean's rapt sigh of compassion reached his ear, he had echoed it within himself, and half repented of his resolution; then his eye rested on the girl before him looking so lonely in her sweet sympathy for another that his heart yearned toward her. Sudden fire shot into his eye, sudden warmth replaced the cold sternness of his face, and his steady voice faltered suddenly, as he said, very low, yet very earnestly, "Jean, I have tried to love her, but I cannot. Ought I to deceive her, and make myself miserable to please my family?"

"She is beautiful and good, and loves you tenderly; is there no hope for her?" asked Jean, still pale, but very quiet, though she held one hand against her heart, as if to still or hide its rapid beating.

"None," answered Coventry.

"But can you not learn to love her? Your will is strong, and most men would not find it a hard task."

"I cannot, for something stronger than my own will controls me."

"What is that?" And Jean's dark eyes were fixed upon him, full of innocent wonder.

His fell, and he said hastily, "I dare not tell you yet."

"Pardon! I should not have asked. Do not consult me in this matter; I am not the person to advise you. I can only say that it seems to me as if any man with an empty heart would be glad to have so beautiful a woman as your cousin."

"My heart is not empty," began Coventry, drawing a step nearer, and speaking in a passionate voice. "Jean, I *must* speak; hear me. I cannot love my cousin, because I love you."

"Stop!" And Jean sprang up with a commanding gesture. "I will not hear you while any promise binds you to another. Remember your mother's wishes, Lucia's hopes, Edward's last words, your own pride, my humble lot. You forget yourself, Mr. Coventry. Think well before you speak, weight the cost of this act, and recollect who I am before you insult me by any transient passion, any false vows."

"I have thought, I do weigh the cost, and I swear that I desire to woo you as humbly, honestly as I would any lady in the land. You speak of my pride. Do I stoop in loving my equal in rank? You speak of your lowly lot, but poverty is no disgrace, and the courage with which you bear it makes it beautiful. I should have broken with Lucia before I spoke, but I could not control myself. My mother loves you, and will be happy in my happiness. Edward must forgive me, for I have tried to do my best, but love is irresistible. Tell me, Jean, is there any hope for me?"

He had seized her hand and was speaking impetuously, with ardent face and tender tone, but no answer came, for as Jean turned her eloquent countenance toward him, full of maiden shame and timid love, Dean's prim figure appeared at the door, and her harsh voice broke the momentary silence, saying, sternly, "Miss Beaufort is waiting for you, sir."

"Go, go at once, and be kind, for my sake, Gerald," whispered Jean, for he stood as if deaf and blind to everything but her voice, her face.

As she drew his head down to whisper, her cheek touched his, and regardless of Dean, he kissed it, passionately, whispering back, "My little Jean! For your sake I can be anything."

"Miss Beaufort is waiting. Shall I say you will come, sir?" demanded Dean, pale and grim with indignation.

"Yes, yes, I'll come. Wait for me in the garden, Jean." And Coventry hurried away, in no mood for the interview but anxious to have it over.

As the door closed behind him, Dean walked up to Miss Muir, trembling with anger, and laying a heavy hand on her arm, she said below her breath, "I've been expecting this, you artful creature. I saw your game and did my best to spoil it, but you are too quick for me. You think you've got him. There you are mistaken; for as sure as my name is Hester Dean, I'll prevent it, or Sir John shall."

"Take your hand away and treat me with proper respect, or you will be dismissed from this house. Do you know who I am?" And Jean drew herself up with a haughty air, which impressed the woman more deeply than her words. "I am the daughter of Lady Howard and, if I choose it, can be the wife of Mr. Coventry."

Dean drew back amazed, yet not convinced. Being a well-trained servant, as well as a prudent woman, she feared to overstep the bounds of respect, to go too far, and get her mistress as well as herself into trouble. So, though she still doubted Jean, and hated her more than ever, she controlled herself. Dropping a curtsy, she assumed her usual air of deference, and said, meekly, "I beg pardon, miss. If I'd known, I should have conducted myself differently, of course, but ordinary governesses make so much mischief in a house, one can't help mistrusting them. I don't wish to meddle or be overbold, but being fond of my dear young lady, I naturally take her part, and must say that Mr. Coventry has not acted like a gentleman."

"Think what you please, Dean, but I advise you to say as little as possible if you wish to remain. I have not accepted Mr. Coventry yet, and if he chooses to set aside the engagement his family made for him, I think he has a right to do so. Miss Beaufort would hardly care to marry him against his will, because he pities her for her unhappy love," and with a tranquil smile, Miss Muir walked away.

CHAPTER VII

The Last Chance

"She will tell Sir John, will she? Then I must be before her, and hasten events. It will be as well to have all sure before there can be any danger. My poor Dean, you are no match for me, but you may prove annoying, nevertheless."

These thoughts passed through Miss Muir's mind as she went down the hall, pausing an instant at the library door, for the murmur of voices was heard. She caught no word, and had only time for an instant's pause as Dean's heavy step followed her. Turning, Jean drew a chair before the door, and, beckoning to the woman, she said, smiling still, "Sit here and play watchdog. I am going to Miss Bella, so you can nod if you will."

"Thank you, miss. I will wait for my young lady. She may need me when this hard time is over." And Dean seated herself with a resolute face.

Jean laughed and went on; but her eyes

gleamed with sudden malice, and she glanced over her shoulder with an expression which boded ill for the faithful old servant.

"I've got a letter from Ned, and here is a tiny note for you," cried Bella as Jean entered the boudoir. "Mine is a very odd, hasty letter, with no news in it, but his meeting with Sydney. I hope yours is better, or it won't be very satisfactory."

As Sydney's name passed Bella's lips, all the color died out of Miss Muir's face, and the note shook with the tremor of her hand. Her very lips were white, but she said calmly, "Thank you. As you are busy, I'll go and read my letter on the lawn." And before Bella could speak, she was gone.

Hurrying to a quiet nook, Jean tore open the note and read the few blotted lines it contained.

> I have seen Sydney; he has told me all; and, hard as I found it to believe, it was impossible to doubt, for he has discovered proofs which cannot be denied. I make no reproaches, shall demand no confession or atonement, for I cannot forget that I once

loved you. I give you three days to find another home, before I return to tell the family who you are. Go at once, I beseech you, and spare me the pain of seeing your disgrace.

Slowly, steadily she read it twice over, then sat motionless, knitting her brows in deep thought. Presently she drew a long breath, tore up the note, and rising, went slowly toward the Hall, saying to herself, "Three days, only three days! Can it be accomplished in so short a time? It shall be, if wit and will can do it, for it is my last chance. If this fails, I'll not go back to my old life, but end all at once."

Setting her teeth and clenching her hands, as if some memory stung her, she went on through the twilight, to find Sir John waiting to give her a hearty welcome.

"You look tired, my dear. Never mind the reading tonight; rest yourself, and let the book go," he said kindly, observing her worn look.

"Thank you, sir. I am tired, but I'd rather read, else the book will not be finished before I go."

"Go, child! Where are you going?" demanded Sir John, looking anxiously at her as she sat down.

"I will tell you by-and-by, sir." And opening the book, Jean read for a little while.

But the usual charm was gone; there was no spirit in the voice of the reader, no interest in the face of the listener, and soon he said, abruptly, "My dear, pray stop! I cannot listen with a divided mind. What troubles you? Tell your friend, and let him comfort you."

As if the kind words overcame her, Jean dropped the book, covered up her face, and wept so bitterly that Sir John was much alarmed; for such a demonstration was doubly touching in one who usually was all gaiety and smiles. As he tried to soothe her, his words grew tender, his solicitude full of a more than paternal anxiety, and his kind heart overflowed with pity and affection for the weeping girl. As she grew calmer, he urged her to be frank, promising to help and counsel her, whatever the affliction or fault might be.

"Ah, you are too kind, too generous! How can I go away and leave my one friend?"

sighed Jean, wiping the tears away and looking up at him with grateful eyes.

"Then you do care a little for the old man?" said Sir John with an eager look, an involuntary pressure of the hand he held.

Jean turned her face away, and answered, very low, "No one ever was so kind to me as you have been. Can I help caring for you more than I can express?"

Sir John was a little deaf at times, but he heard that, and looked well pleased. He had been rather thoughtful of late, had dressed with unusual care, been particularly gallant and gay when the young ladies visited him, and more than once, when Jean paused in the reading to ask a question, he had been forced to confess that he had not been listening; though, as she well knew, his eyes had been fixed upon her. Since the discovery of her birth, his manner had been peculiarly benignant, and many little acts had proved his interest and goodwill. Now, when Jean spoke of going, a panic seized him, and desolation seemed about to fall upon the old Hall. Something in her unusual agitation struck him as peculiar and excited his curiosity. Never had she seemed so interesting as now, when she sat beside him with tearful eyes, and some soft trouble in her heart which she dared not confess.

"Tell me everything, child, and let your friend help you if he can." Formerly he said "father" or "the old man," but lately he always spoke of himself as her "friend."

"I will tell you, for I have no one else to turn to. I must go away because Mr. Coventry has been weak enough to love me."

"What, Gerald?" cried Sir John, amazed.

"Yes; today he told me this, and left me to break with Lucia; so I ran to you to help me prevent him from disappointing his mother's hopes and plans."

Sir John had started up and paced down the room, but as Jean paused he turned toward her, saying, with an altered face, "Then you do not love him? Is it possible?"

"No, I do not love him," she answered promptly.

"Yet he is all that women usually find attractive. How is it that you have escaped, Jean?"

"I love someone else" was the scarcely audible reply.

Sir John resumed his seat with the air of a

man bent on getting at a mystery, if possible.

"It will be unjust to let you suffer for the folly of these boys, my little girl. Ned is gone, and I was sure that Gerald was safe; but now that his turn has come, I am perplexed, for he cannot be sent away."

"No, it is I who must go; but it seems so hard to leave this safe and happy home, and wander away into the wide, cold world again. You have all been too kind to me, and now separation breaks my heart."

A sob ended the speech, and Jean's head went down upon her hands again. Sir John looked at her a moment, and his fine old face was full of genuine emotion, as he said slowly, "Jean, will you stay and be a daughter to the solitary old man?"

"No, sir" was the unexpected answer.

"And why not?" asked Sir John, looking surprised, but rather pleased than angry.

"Because I could not be a daughter to you; and even if I could, it would not be wise, for the gossips would say you were not old enough to be the adopted father of a girl like me. Sir John, young as I am, I know much of the world, and am sure that this kind plan is impractical; but I thank you from the bottom of my heart."

"Where will you go, Jean?" asked Sir John, after a pause.

"To London, and try to find another situation where I can do no harm."

"Will it be difficult to find another home?"

"Yes. I cannot ask Mrs. Coventry to recommend me, when I have innocently brought so much trouble into her family; and Lady Sydney is gone, so I have no friend."

"Except John Coventry. I will arrange all that. When will you go, Jean?"

"Tomorrow."

"So soon!" And the old man's voice betrayed the trouble he was trying to conceal.

Jean had grown very calm, but it was the calmness of desperation. She had hoped that the first tears would produce the avowal for which she waited. It had not, and she began to fear that her last chance was slipping from her. Did the old man love her? If so, why did he not speak? Eager to profit by each moment, she was on the alert for any hopeful hint, any propitious word, look, or act, and every nerve was strung to the utmost.

"Jean, may I ask one question?" said Sir John.

"Anything of me, sir."

"This man whom you love—can he not help you?"

"He could if he knew, but he must not."

"If he knew what? Your present trouble?"

"No. My love."

"He does know this, then?"

"No, thank heaven! And he never will."

"Why not?"

"Because I am too proud to own it."

"He loves you, my child?"

"I do not know—I dare not hope it," murmured Jean.

"Can I not help you here? Believe me, I desire to see you safe and happy. Is there nothing I can do?"

"Nothing, nothing."

"May I know the name?"

"No! No! Let me go; I cannot bear this questioning!" And Jean's distressful face warned him to ask no more.

"Forgive me, and let me do what I may. Rest here quietly. I'll write a letter to a good friend of mine, who will find you a home, if you leave us."

As Sir John passed into his inner study, Jean watched him with despairing eyes and wrung her hands, saying to herself, Has all my skill deserted me when I need it most? How can I make him understand, yet not overstep the bounds of maiden modesty? He is so blind, so timid, or so dull he will not see, and time is going fast. What shall I do to open his eyes?

Her own eyes roved about the room, seeking for some aid from inanimate things, and soon she found it. Close behind the couch where she sat hung a fine miniature of Sir John. At first her eye rested on it as she contrasted its placid comeliness with the unusual pallor and disquiet of the living face seen through the open door, as the old man sat at his desk trying to write and casting covert glances at the girlish figure he had left behind him. Affecting unconsciousness of this, Jean gazed on as if forgetful of everything but the picture, and suddenly, as if obeying an irresistible impulse, she took it down, looked long and fondly at it, then, shaking her curls about her face, as if to hide the act, pressed it to her lips and seemed to weep over it in an uncontrollable paroxysm of tender grief. A sound startled her, and like a guilty thing, she turned to replace the picture; but it dropped from her hand as she uttered a faint cry and hid her face, for Sir John stood before her, with an expression which she could not mistake.

"Jean, why did you do that?" he asked, in an eager, agitated voice.

No answer, as the girl sank lower, like one overwhelmed with shame. Laying his hand on the bent head, and bending his own, he whispered, "Tell me, is the name John Coventry?"

Still no answer, but a stifled sound betrayed that his words had gone home.

"Jean, shall I go back and write the letter, or may I stay and tell you that the old man loves you better than a daughter?"

She did not speak, but a little hand stole out from under the falling hair, as if to keep him. With a broken exclamation he seized it, drew her up into his arms, and laid his gray head on her fair one, too happy for words. For a moment Jean Muir enjoyed her success; then, fearing lest some sudden mishap should destroy it, she hastened to make all secure. Looking up with well-feigned timidity and half-confessed affection, she said softly, "Forgive me that I could not hide this better. I meant to go away and never tell it, but you were so kind it made the parting doubly hard. Why did you ask such dangerous questions? Why did you look, when you should have been writing my dismissal?"

"How could I dream that you loved me, Jean, when you refused the only offer I dared make? Could I be presumptuous enough to fancy you would reject young lovers for an old man like me?" asked Sir John, caressing her.

"You are not old, to me, but everything I love and honor!" interrupted Jean, with a touch of genuine remorse, as this generous, honorable gentleman gave her both heart and home, unconscious of deceit. "It is I who am presumptuous, to dare to love one so far above me. But I did not know how dear you were to me till I felt that I must go. I ought not to accept this happiness. I am not worthy of it; and you will regret your kindness when the world blames you for giving a home to one so poor, and plain, and humble as I."

"Hush, my darling. I care nothing for the idle gossip of the world. If you are happy here, let tongues wag as they will. I shall be too busy enjoying the sunshine of your presence to heed anything that goes on about me. But, Jean, you are sure you love me? It seems incredible that I should win the heart that has been so cold to younger, better men than I."

"Dear Sir John, be sure of this, I love you truly. I will do my best to be a good wife to you, and prove that, in spite of my many faults, I possess the virtue of gratitude."

If he had known the strait she was in, he would have understood the cause of the sudden fervor of her words, the intense thankfulness that shone in her face, the real humility that made her stoop and kiss the generous hand that gave so much. For a few moments she enjoyed and let him enjoy the happy present, undisturbed. But the anxiety which devoured her, the danger which menaced her, soon recalled her, and forced her to wring yet more from the unsuspicious heart she had conquered.

"No need of letters now," said Sir John, as they sat side by side, with the summer moonlight glorifying all the room. "You have found a home for life; may it prove a happy one."

"It is not mine yet, and I have a strange foreboding that it never will be," she answered sadly.

"Why, my child?"

"Because I have an enemy who will try to destroy my peace, to poison your mind against me, and to drive me out from my paradise, to suffer again all I have suffered this last year."

"You mean that mad Sydney of whom you told me?"

"Yes. As soon as he hears of this good fortune to poor little Jean, he will hasten to mar it. He is my fate; I cannot escape him, and wherever he goes my friends desert me; for he has the power and uses it for my destruction. Let me go away and hide before he comes, for, having shared your confidence, it will break my heart to see you distrust and turn from me, instead of loving and protecting."

"My poor child, you are superstitious. Be easy. No one can harm you now, no one would dare attempt it. And as for my deserting you, that will soon be out of my power, if I have my way."

"How, dear Sir John?" asked Jean, with a

flutter of intense relief at her heart, for the way seemed smoothing before her.

"I will make you my wife at once, if I may. This will free you from Gerald's love, protect you from Sydney's persecution, give you a safe home, and me the right to cherish and defend with heart and hand. Shall it be so, my child?"

"Yes; but oh, remember that I have no friend but you! Promise me to be faithful to the last—to believe in me, to trust me, protect and love me, in spite of all misfortunes, faults, and follies. I will be true as steel to you, and make your life as happy as it deserves to be. Let us promise these things now, and keep the promises unbroken to the end."

Her solemn air touched Sir John. Too honorable and upright himself to suspect falsehood in others, he saw only the natural impulse of a lovely girl in Jean's words, and, taking the hand she gave him in both of his, he promised all she asked, and kept that promise to the end. She paused an instant, with a pale, absent expression, as if she searched herself, then looked up clearly in the confiding face above her, and promised what she faithfully performed in afteryears.

"When shall it be, little sweetheart? I leave all to you, only let it be soon, else some gay young lover will appear, and take you from me," said Sir John, playfully, anxious to chase away the dark expression which had stolen over Jean's face.

"Can you keep a secret?" asked the girl, smiling up at him, all her charming self again.

"Try me."

"I will. Edward is coming home in three days. I must be gone before he comes. Tell no one of this; he wishes to surprise them. And if you love me, tell nobody of your approaching marriage. Do not betray that you care for me until I am really yours. There will be such a stir, such remonstrances, explanations, and reproaches that I shall be worn out, and run away from you all to escape the trial. If I could have my wish, I would go to some quiet place tomorrow and wait till you come for me. I know so little of such things, I cannot tell how soon we may be married; not for some weeks, I think."

"Tomorrow, if we like. A special license permits people to marry when and where they please. My plan is better than yours. Listen, and tell me if it can be carried out. I will go to town tomorrow, get the license, invite my friend, the Reverend Paul Fairfax, to return with me, and tomorrow evening you come at your usual time, and, in the presence of my discreet old servants, make me the happiest man in England. How does this suit you, my little Lady Coventry?"

The plan which seemed made to meet her ends, the name which was the height of her ambition, and the blessed sense of safety which came to her filled Jean Muir with such intense satisfaction that tears of real feeling stood in her eyes, and the glad assent she gave was the truest word that had passed her lips for months.

"We will go abroad or to Scotland for our honeymoon, till the storm blows over," said Sir John, well knowing that this hasty marriage would surprise or offend all his relations, and feeling as glad as Jean to escape the first excitement.

"To Scotland, please. I long to see my father's home," said Jean, who dreaded to meet Sydney on the continent.

They talked a little longer, arranging all

things, Sir John so intent on hurrying the event that Jean had nothing to do but give a ready assent to all his suggestions. One fear alone disturbed her. If Sir John went to town, he might meet Edward, might hear and believe his statements. Then all would be lost. Yet this risk must be incurred, if the marriage was to be speedily and safely accomplished; and to guard against the meeting was Jean's sole care. As they went through the park—for Sir John insisted upon taking her home—she said, clinging to his arm:

"Dear friend, bear one thing in mind, else we shall be much annoyed, and all our plans disarranged. Avoid your nephews; you are so frank your face will betray you. They both love me, are both hot-tempered, and in the first excitement of the discovery might be violent. You must incur no danger, no disrespect for my sake; so shun them both till we are safe—particularly Edward. He will feel that his brother has wronged him, and that you have succeeded where he failed. This will irritate him, and I fear a stormy scene. Promise to avoid both for a day or two; do not listen to them, do not see them, do not write to or receive letters from them. It is foolish, I know; but you are all I have, and I am haunted by a strange foreboding that I am to lose you."

Touched and flattered by her tender solicitude, Sir John promised everything, even while he laughed at her fears. Love blinded the good gentleman to the peculiarity of the request; the novelty, romance, and secrecy of the affair rather bewildered though it charmed him; and the knowledge that he had outrivaled three young and ardent lovers gratified his vanity more than he would confess. Parting from the girl at the garden gate, he turned homeward, feeling like a boy again, and loitered back, humming a love lay, quite forgetful of evening damps, gout, and the five-and-fifty years which lay so lightly on his shoulders since Jean's arms had rested there. She hurried toward the house, anxious to escape Coventry; but he was waiting for her, and she was forced to meet him.

"How could you linger so long, and keep me in suspense?" he said reproachfully, as he took her hand and tried to catch a glimpse of her face in the shadow of her hat brim.

"Come and rest in the grotto. I have so much to say, to hear and enjoy."

"Not now; I am too tired. Let me go in and sleep. Tomorrow we will talk. It is damp and chilly, and my head aches with all this worry." Jean spoke wearily, yet with a touch of petulance, and Coventry, fancying that she was piqued at his not coming for her, hastened to explain with eager tenderness.

"My poor little Jean, you do need rest. We wear you out, among us, and you never complain. I should have come to bring you home, but Lucia detained me, and when I got away I saw my uncle had forestalled me. I shall be jealous of the old gentleman, if he is so devoted. Jean, tell me one thing before we part; I am free as air, now, and have a right to speak. Do you love me? Am I the happy man who has won your heart? I dare to think so, to believe that this telltale face of yours has betrayed you, and to hope that I have gained what poor Ned and wild Sydney have lost."

"Before I answer, tell me of your interview with Lucia. I have a right to know," said Jean.

Coventry hesitated, for pity and remorse were busy at his heart when he recalled poor Lucia's grief. Jean was bent on hearing the humiliation of her rival. As the young man paused, she frowned, then lifted up her face wreathed in softest smiles, and laying her hand on his arm, she said, with most effective emphasis, half shy, half fond, upon his name, "Please tell me, Gerald!"

He could not resist the look, the touch, the tone, and taking the little hand in his, he said rapidly, as if the task was distasteful to him, "I told her that I did not, could not love her; that I had submitted to my mother's wish, and, for a time, had felt tacitly bound to her, though no words had passed between us. But now I demanded my liberty, regretting that the separation was not mutually desired."

"And she—what did she say? How did she bear it?" asked Jean, feeling in her own woman's heart how deeply Lucia's must have been wounded by that avowal.

"Poor girl! It was hard to bear, but her pride sustained her to the end. She owned that no pledge tied me, fully relinquished any claim my past behavior had seemed to have given her, and prayed that I might find another woman to love me as truly, tenderly as she had done. Jean, I felt like a villain; and yet I never plighted my word to her, never really loved her, and had a perfect right to leave her, if I would."

"Did she speak of me?"

"Yes."

"What did she say?"

"Must I tell you?"

"Yes, tell me everything. I know she hates me and I forgive her, knowing that I should hate any woman whom *you* loved."

"Are you jealous, dear?"

"Of you, Gerald?" And the fine eyes glanced up at him, full of a brilliancy that looked like the light of love.

"You make a slave of me already. How do you do it? I never obeyed a woman before. Jean, I think you are a witch. Scotland is the home of weird, uncanny creatures, who take lovely shapes for the bedevilment of poor weak souls. Are you one of those fair deceivers?"

"You are complimentary," laughed the girl. "I *am* a witch, and one day my disguise will drop away and you will see me as I am, old, ugly, bad and lost. Beware of me in time. I've warned you. Now love me at your peril."

Coventry had paused as he spoke, and

eyed her with an unquiet look, conscious of some fascination which conquered yet brought no happiness. A feverish yet pleasurable excitement possessed him; a reckless mood, making him eager to obliterate the past by any rash act, any new experience which his passion brought. Jean regarded him with a wistful, almost woeful face, for one short moment; then a strange smile broke over it, as she spoke in a tone of malicious mockery, under which lurked the bitterness of a sad truth. Coventry looked half bewildered, and his eye went from the girl's mysterious face to a dimly lighted window, behind whose curtains poor Lucia hid her aching heart, praying for him the tender prayers that loving women give to those whose sins are all forgiven for love's sake. His heart smote him, and a momentary feeling of repulsion came over him, as he looked at Jean. She saw it, felt angry, yet conscious of a sense of relief; for now that her own safety was so nearly secured, she felt no wish to do mischief, but rather a desire to undo what was already done, and be at peace with all the world. To recall him to his allegiance, she sighed and walked on, saying gently yet coldly, "Will you tell me what I ask before I answer your question, Mr. Coventry?"

"What Lucia said of you? Well, it was this. 'Beware of Miss Muir. We instinctively distrusted her when we had no cause. I believe in instincts, and mine have never changed, for she has not tried to delude me. Her art is wonderful; I feel yet cannot explain or detect it, except in the working of events which her hand seems to guide. She has brought sorrow and dissension into this hitherto happy family. We are all changed, and this girl has done it. Me she can harm no further; you she will ruin, if she can. Beware of her in time, or you will bitterly repent your blind infatuation!' "

"And what answer did you make?" asked Jean, as the last words came reluctantly from Coventry's lips.

"I told her that I loved you in spite of myself, and would make you my wife in the face of all opposition. Now, Jean, your answer."

"Give me three days to think of it. Good night." And gliding from him, she vanished into the house, leaving him to roam about half the night, tormented with remorse, suspense, and the old distrust which would return when Jean was not there to banish it by her art.

CHAPTER VIII
Suspense

All the next day, Jean was in a state of the most intense anxiety, as every hour brought the crisis nearer, and every hour might bring defeat, for the subtlest human skill is often thwarted by some unforeseen accident. She longed to assure herself that Sir John was gone, but no servants came or went that day, and she could devise no pretext for sending to glean intelligence. She dared not go herself, lest the unusual act should excite suspicion, for she never went till evening. Even had she determined to venture, there was no time, for Mrs. Coventry was in one of her nervous states, and no one but Miss Muir could amuse her; Lucia was ill, and Miss Muir must give orders; Bella had a studious fit, and Jean must help her. Coventry lingered about the house for several hours, but Jean dared not send him, lest some hint of the truth might reach him. He had ridden away to his new duties when Jean did not appear, and the day dragged on wearisomely. Night came at last, and as Jean dressed for the late dinner, she hardly knew herself when she stood before her mirror, excitement lent such color and brilliancy to her countenance. Remembering the wedding which was to take place that evening, she put on a simple white dress and added a cluster of white roses in bosom and hair. She often wore flowers, but in spite of her desire to look and seem as usual, Bella's first words as she entered the drawing room were "Why, Jean, how like a bride you look; a veil and gloves would make you quite complete!"

"You forget one other trifle, Bell," said Gerald, with eyes that brightened as they rested on Miss Muir.

"What is that?" asked his sister.

"A bridegroom."

Bella looked to see how Jean received this, but she seemed quite composed as she smiled one of her sudden smiles, and merely said, "That trifle will doubtless be found when the time comes. Is Miss Beaufort too ill for dinner?"

"She begs to be excused, and said you would be willing to take her place, she thought."

As innocent Bella delivered this message, Jean glanced at Coventry, who evaded her eye and looked ill at ease.

A little remorse will do him good, and prepare him for repentance after the grand *coup,* she said to herself, and was particularly gay at dinnertime, though Coventry looked often at Lucia's empty seat, as if he missed her. As soon as they left the table, Miss Muir sent Bella to her mother; and, knowing that Coventry would not linger long at his wine, she hurried away to the Hall. A servant was lounging at the door, and of him she asked, in a tone which was eager in spite of all efforts to be calm, "Is Sir John at home?"

"No, miss, he's just gone to town."

"Just gone! When do you mean?" cried Jean, forgetting the relief she felt in hearing of his absence in surprise at his late departure.

"He went half an hour ago, in the last train, miss."

"I thought he was going early this morning; he told me he should be back this evening."

"I believe he did mean to go, but was delayed by company. The steward came up on business, and a load of gentlemen called, so Sir John could not get off till night, when he wasn't fit to go, being worn out, and far from well."

"Do you think he will be ill? Did he look so?" And as Jean spoke, a thrill of fear passed over her, lest death should rob her of her prize.

"Well, you know, miss, hurry of any kind is bad for elderly gentlemen inclined to apoplexy. Sir John was in a worry all day, and not like himself. I wanted him to take his man, but he wouldn't; and drove off looking flushed and excited like. I'm anxious about him, for I know something is amiss to hurry him off in this way."

"When will he be back, Ralph?"

"Tomorrow noon, if possible; at night, certainly, he bid me tell anyone that called."

"Did he leave no note or message for Miss Coventry, or someone of the family?"

"No, miss, nothing."

"Thank you." And Jean walked back to spend a restless night and rise to meet renewed suspense.

The morning seemed endless, but noon came at last, and under the pretense of seeking coolness in the grotto, Jean stole away to a slope whence the gate to the Hall park was visible. For two long hours she watched, and no one came. She was just turning away when a horseman dashed through the gate and came galloping toward the Hall. Heedless of everything but the uncontrollable longing to gain some tidings, she ran to meet him, feeling assured that he brought ill news. It was a young man from the station, and as he caught sight of her, he drew bridle, looking agitated and undecided.

"Has anything happened?" she cried breathlessly.

"A dreadful accident on the railroad, just the other side of Croydon. News telegraphed half an hour ago," answered the man, wiping his hot face.

"The noon train? Was Sir John in it? Quick, tell me all!"

"It was that train, miss, but whether Sir John was in it or not, we don't know; for the guard is killed, and everything is in such confusion that nothing can be certain. They are at work getting out the dead and wounded. We heard that Sir John was expected, and I came up to tell Mr. Coventry, thinking he would wish to go down. A train leaves in fifteen minutes; where shall I find him? I was told he was at the Hall."

"Ride on, ride on! And find him if he is there. I'll run home and look for him. Lose no time. Ride! Ride!" And turning, Jean sped back like a deer, while the man tore up the avenue to rouse the Hall.

Coventry was there, and went off at once, leaving both Hall and house in dismay. Fearing to betray the horrible anxiety that possessed her, Jean shut herself up in her room and suffered untold agonies as the day wore on and no news came. At dark a sudden cry rang through the house, and Jean rushed down to learn the cause. Bella was standing in the hall, holding a letter, while a group of excited servants hovered near her.

"What is it?" demanded Miss Muir, pale and steady, though her heart died within her as she recognized Gerald's handwriting. Bella gave her the note, and hushed her sobbing to hear again the heavy tidings that had come.

Dear Bella:

Uncle is safe; he did not go in the noon

train. But several persons are sure that Ned was there. No trace of him as yet, but many bodies are in the river, under the ruins of the bridge, and I am doing my best to find the poor lad, if he is there. I have sent to all his haunts in town, and as he has not been seen, I hope it is a false report and he is safe with his regiment. Keep this from my mother till we are sure. I write you, because Lucia is ill. Miss Muir will comfort and sustain you. Hope for the best, dear.

Yours, G. C.

Those who watched Miss Muir as she read these words wondered at the strange expressions which passed over her face, for the joy which appeared there as Sir John's safety was made known did not change to grief or horror at poor Edward's possible fate. The smile died on her lips, but her voice did not falter, and in her downcast eyes shone an inexplicable look of something like triumph. No wonder, for if this was true, the danger which menaced her was averted for a time, and the marriage might be consummated without such desperate haste. This sad and sudden event seemed to her the mysterious fulfilment of a secret wish; and though startled she was not daunted but inspirited, for fate seemed to favor her designs. She did comfort Bella, control the excited household, and keep the rumors from Mrs. Coventry all that dreadful night.

At dawn Gerald came home exhausted, and bringing no tiding of the missing man. He had telegraphed to the headquarters of the regiment and received a reply, stating that Edward had left for London the previous day, meaning to go home before returning. The fact of his having been at the London station was also established, but whether he left by the train or not was still uncertain. The ruins were still being searched, and the body might yet appear.

"Is Sir John coming at noon?" asked Jean, as the three sat together in the rosy hush of dawn, trying to hope against hope.

"No, he had been ill, I learned from young Gower, who is just from town, and so had not completed his business. I sent him word to wait till night, for the bridge won't be passable till then. Now I must try and rest an hour; I've worked all night and have no strength left. Call me the instant any messenger arrives."

With that Coventry went to his room, Bella followed to wait on him, and Jean roamed through the house and grounds, unable to rest. The morning was far spent when the messenger arrived. Jean went to receive his tidings, with the wicked hope still lurking at her heart.

"Is he found?" she asked calmly, as the man hesitated to speak.

"Yes, ma'am."

"You are sure?"

"I am certain, ma'am, though some won't say till Mr. Coventry comes to look."

"Is he alive?" And Jean's white lips trembled as she put the question.

"Oh no, ma'am, that warn't possible, under all them stones and water. The poor young gentleman is so wet, and crushed, and torn, no one would know him, except for the uniform, and the white hand with the ring on it."

Jean sat down, very pale, and the man described the findings of the poor shattered body. As he finished, Coventry appeared, and with one look of mingled remorse, shame, and sorrow, the elder brother went away, to find and bring the younger home. Jean crept into the garden like a guilty thing, trying to hide the satisfaction which struggled with a woman's natural pity, for so sad an end for this brave young life.

"Why waste tears or feign sorrow when I must be glad?" she muttered, as she paced to and fro along the terrace. "The poor boy is out of pain, and I am out of danger."

She got no further, for, turning as she spoke, she stood face to face with Edward! Bearing no mark of peril on dress or person, but stalwart and strong as ever, he stood there looking at her, with contempt and compassion struggling in his face. As if turned to stone, she remained motionless, with dilated eyes, arrested breath, and paling cheek. He did not speak but watched her silently till she put out a trembling hand, as if to assure herself by touch that it was really he. Then he drew back, and as if the act convinced as fully as words, she said slowly, "They told me you were dead."

"And you were glad to believe it. No, it was my comrade, young Courtney, who unconsciously deceived you all, and lost his life, as

I should have done, if I had not gone to Ascot after seeing him off yesterday."

"To Ascot?" echoed Jean, shrinking back, for Edward's eye was on her, and his voice was stern and cold.

"Yes; you know the place. I went there to make inquiries concerning you and was well satisfied. Why are you still here?"

"The three days are not over yet. I hold you to your promise. Before night I shall be gone; till then you will be silent, if you have honor enough to keep your word."

"I have." Edward took out his watch and, as he put it back, said with cool precision, "It is now two, the train leaves for London at half-past six; a carriage will wait for you at the side door. Allow me to advise you to go then, for the instant dinner is over I shall speak." And with a bow he went into the house, leaving Jean nearly suffocated with a throng of contending emotions.

For a few minutes she seemed paralyzed; but the native energy of the woman forbade utter despair, till the last hope was gone. Frail as that now was, she still clung to it tenaciously, resolving to win the game in defiance of everything. Springing up, she went to her room, packed her few valuables, dressed herself with care, and then sat down to wait. She heard a joyful stir below, saw Coventry come hurrying back, and from a garrulous maid learned that the body was that of young Courtney. The uniform being the same as Edward's and the ring, a gift from him, had caused the men to believe the disfigured corpse to be that of the younger Coventry. No one but the maid came near her; once Bella's voice called her, but some one checked the girl, and the call was not repeated. At five an envelope was brought her, directed in Edward's hand, and containing a check which more than paid a year's salary. No word accompanied the gift, yet the generosity of it touched her, for Jean Muir had the relics of a once honest nature, and despite her falsehood could still admire nobleness and respect virtue. A tear of genuine shame dropped on the paper, and real gratitude filled her heart, as she thought that even if all else failed, she was not thrust out penniless into the world, which had no pity for poverty.

As the clock struck six, she heard a carriage drive around and went down to meet it. A servant put on her trunk, gave the order,

"To the station, James," and she drove away without meeting anyone, speaking to anyone, or apparently being seen by anyone. A sense of utter weariness came over her, and she longed to lie down and forget. But the last chance still remained, and till that failed, she would not give up. Dismissing the carriage, she seated herself to watch for the quarter-past-six train from London, for in that Sir John would come if he came at all that night. She was haunted by the fear that Edward had met and told him. The first glimpse of Sir John's frank face would betray the truth. If he knew all, there was no hope, and she would go her way alone. If he knew nothing, there was yet time for the marriage; and once his wife, she knew she was safe, because for the honor of his name he would screen and protect her.

Up rushed the train, out stepped Sir John, and Jean's heart died within her. Grave, and pale, and worn he looked, and leaned heavily on the arm of a portly gentleman in black. The Reverend Mr. Fairfax, why has he come, if the secret is out? thought Jean, slowly advancing to meet them and fearing to read her fate in Sir John's face. He saw her, dropped his friend's arm, and hurried forward with the ardor of a young man, exclaiming, as he seized her hand with a beaming face, a glad voice, "My little girl! Did you think I would never come?"

She could not answer, the reaction was too strong, but she clung to him, regardless of time or place, and felt that her last hope had not failed. Mr. Fairfax proved himself equal to the occasion. Asking no questions, he hurried Sir John and Jean into a carriage and stepped in after them with a bland apology. Jean was soon herself again, and, having told her fears at his delay, listened eagerly while he related the various mishaps which had detained him.

"Have you seen Edward?" was her first question.

"Not yet, but I know he has come, and have heard of his narrow escape. I should have been in that train, if I had not been delayed by the indisposition which I then cursed, but now bless. Are you ready, Jean? Do you repent your choice, my child?"

"No, no! I am ready, I am only too happy to become your wife, dear, generous Sir John," cried Jean, with a glad alacrity, which touched the old man to the heart, and charmed the Reverend Mr. Fairfax, who concealed the romance of a boy under his clerical suit.

They reached the Hall. Sir John gave orders to admit no one and after a hasty dinner sent for his old housekeeper and his steward, told them of his purpose, and desired them to witness his marriage. Obedience had been the law of their lives, and Master could do nothing wrong in their eyes, so they played their parts willingly, for Jean was a favorite at the Hall. Pale as her gown, but calm and steady, she stood beside Sir John, uttering her vows in a clear tone and taking upon herself the vows of a wife with more than a bride's usual docility. When the ring was fairly on, a smile broke over her face. When Sir John kissed and called her his "little wife," she shed a tear or two of sincere happiness; and when Mr. Fairfax addressed her as "my lady," she laughed her musical laugh, and glanced up at a picture of Gerald with eyes full of exultation. As the servants left the room, a message was brought from Mrs. Coventry, begging Sir John to come to her at once.

"You will not go and leave me so soon?" pleaded Jean, well knowing why he was sent for.

"My darling, I must." And in spite of its tenderness, Sir John's manner was too decided to be withstood.

"Then I shall go with you," cried Jean, resolving that no earthly power should part them.

CHAPTER IX
Lady Coventry

When the first excitement of Edward's return had subsided, and before they could question him as to the cause of this unexpected visit, he told them that after dinner their curiosity should be gratified, and meantime he begged them to leave Miss Muir alone, for she had received bad news and must not be disturbed. The family with difficulty restrained their tongues and waited impatiently. Gerald confessed his love for Jean and asked his brother's pardon for betraying his trust. He had expected an outbreak, but Edward only looked at him with pitying eyes, and said sadly, "You too! I have no reproaches to make, for I know what you will suffer when the truth is known."

"What do you mean?" demanded Coventry.

"You will soon know, my poor Gerald, and we will comfort one another."

Nothing more could be drawn from Edward till dinner was over, the servants gone, and all the family alone together. Then pale and grave, but very self-possessed, for trouble had made a man of him, he produced a packet of letters, and said, addressing himself to his brother, "Jean Muir has deceived us all. I know her story; let me tell it before I read her letters."

"Stop! I'll not listen to any false tales against her. The poor girl has enemies who belie her!" cried Gerald, starting up.

"For the honor of the family, you must listen, and learn what fools she has made of us. I can prove what I say, and convince you that she has the art of a devil. Sit still ten minutes, then go, if you will."

Edward spoke with authority, and his brother obeyed him with a foreboding heart.

"I met Sydney, and he begged me to beware of her. Nay, listen, Gerald! I know she has told her story, and that you believe it; but her own letters convict her. She tried to charm Sydney as she did us, and nearly succeeded in inducing him to marry her. Rash and wild as he is, he is still a gentleman, and when an incautious word of hers roused his suspicions, he refused to make her his wife. A stormy scene ensued, and, hoping to intimidate him, she feigned to stab herself as if in despair. She did wound herself, but failed to gain her point and insisted upon going to a hospital to die. Lady Sydney, good, simple soul, believed the girl's version of the story, thought her son was in the wrong, and when he was gone, tried to atone for his fault by finding Jean Muir another home. She thought Gerald was soon to marry Lucia, and that I was away, so sent her here as a safe and comfortable retreat."

"But, Ned, are you sure of all this? Is Sydney to be believed?" began Coventry, still incredulous.

"To convince you, I'll read Jean's letters before I say more. They were written to an accomplice and were purchased by Sydney. There was a compact between the two women, that each should keep the other informed of all adventures, plots and plans, and share whatever good fortune fell to the lot of either. Thus Jean wrote freely, as you shall judge. The letters concern us alone. The first was written a few days after she came.

"Dear Hortense:

"Another failure. Sydney was more wily

than I thought. All was going well, when one day my old fault beset me, I took too much wine, and I carelessly owned that I had been an actress. He was shocked, and retreated. I got up a scene, and gave myself a safe little wound, to frighten him. The brute was not frightened, but coolly left me to my fate. I'd have died to spite him, if I dared, but as I didn't, I lived to torment him. As yet, I have had no chance, but I will not forget him. His mother is a poor, weak creature, whom I could use as I would, and through her I found an excellent place. A sick mother, silly daughter, and two eligible sons. One is engaged to a handsome iceberg, but that only renders him more interesting in my eyes, rivalry adds so much to the charm of one's conquests. Well, my dear, I went, got up in the meek style, intending to do the pathetic; but before I saw the family, I was so angry I could hardly control myself. Through the indolence of Monsieur the young master, no carriage was sent for me, and I intend he shall atone for that rudeness by-and-by. The younger son, the mother, and the girl received me patronizingly, and I understood the simple souls at once. Monsieur (as I shall call him, as names are unsafe) was unapproachable, and took no pains to conceal his dislike of governesses. The cousin was lovely, but detestable with her pride, her coldness, and her very visible adoration of Monsieur, who let her worship him, like an inanimate idol as he is. I hated them both, of course, and in return for their insolence shall torment her with jealousy, and teach him how to woo a woman by making his heart ache. They are an intensely proud family, but I can humble them all, I think, by captivating the sons, and when they have committed themselves, cast them off, and marry the old uncle, whose title takes my fancy."

"She never wrote that! It is impossible. A woman could not do it," cried Lucia indignantly, while Bella sat bewildered and Mrs. Coventry supported herself with salts and fan. Coventry went to his brother, examined the writing, and returned to his seat, saying, in a tone of suppressed wrath. "She did write it. I posted some of those letters myself. Go on, Ned."

"I made myself useful and agreeable to the amiable ones, and overheard the chat of the lovers. It did not suit me, so I fainted away to stop it, and excite interest in the provoking pair. I thought I had succeeded, but Monsieur suspected me and showed me that he did. I forgot my meek role and gave him a stage look. It had a good effect, and I shall try it again. The man is well worth winning, but I prefer the title, and as the uncle is a hale, handsome gentleman, I can't wait for him to die, though Monsieur is very charming, with his elegant languor, and his heart so fast asleep no woman has had power to wake it yet. I told my story, and they believed it, though I had the audacity to say I was but nineteen, to talk Scotch, and bashfully confess that Sydney wished to marry me. Monsieur knows S. and evidently suspects something. I must watch him and keep the truth from him, if possible.

"I was very miserable that night when I got alone. Something in the atmosphere of this happy home made me wish I was anything but what I am. As I sat there trying to pluck up my spirits, I thought of the days when I was lovely and young, good and gay. My glass showed me an old woman of thirty, for my false locks were off, my paint gone, and my face was without its mask. Bah! how I hate sentiment! I drank your health from your own little flask, and went to bed to dream that I was playing Lady Tartuffe—as I am. Adieu, more soon."

No one spoke as Edward paused, and taking up another letter, he read on:

"My Dear Creature:

"All goes well. Next day I began my task, and having caught a hint of the character of each, tried my power over them. Early in the morning I ran over to see the Hall. Approved of it highly, and took the first step toward becoming its mistress, by piquing the curiosity and flattering the pride of its master. His estate is his idol; I praised it with a few artless compliments to himself, and he was charmed. The cadet of the family adores horses. I risked my neck to pet his beast, and *he* was charmed. The little girl is romantic about flowers; I made a posy and was sentimental, and *she* was charmed. The fair icicle loves her departed mamma, I had raptures over an old picture, and she thawed. Monsieur is used to being worshipped. I took no notice of him, and by the natural perversity of human nature, he began to take notice of me. He likes music; I sang, and stopped when he'd listened long enough to want more. He is lazily fond of being amused; I showed him my skill, but refused to exert it in his behalf. In short, I gave him no peace till he began to wake up. In order to get rid of the boy, I fascinated him, and he was sent away. Poor lad, I rather liked him, and if the title had been nearer would have married him.

"Many thanks for the honor." And Edward's lip curled with intense scorn. But Gerald sat like a statue, his teeth set, his eyes fiery, his brow bent, waiting for the end.

"The passionate boy nearly killed his brother, but I turned the affair to good account, and bewitched Monsieur by playing nurse, till Vashti (the icicle) interfered. Then I enacted injured virtue, and kept out of his way, knowing that he would miss me. I mystified him about S. by sending a letter where S. would not get it, and got up all manner of soft scenes to win this proud creature. I get on well and meanwhile privately fascinate Sir J. by being daughterly and devoted. He is a worthy old man, simple as a child, honest as the day, and generous as a prince. I shall be a happy woman if I win him, and you shall share my good fortune; so wish me success.

"This is the third, and contains something which will surprise you," Edward said, as he lifted another paper.

"Hortense:

"I've done what I once planned to do on another occasion. You know my handsome, dissipated father married a lady of rank for his second wife. I never saw Lady H——d but once, for I was kept out of the way. Finding that this good Sir J. knew something of her when a girl, and being sure that he did not know of the death of her little daughter, I boldly said I was the child, and told a pitiful tale of my early life. It worked like a charm; he told Monsieur, and both felt the most chivalrous compassion for Lady Howard's daughter, though before they had secretly looked down on me, and my real poverty and my lowliness. That boy pitied me with an honest warmth and never waited to learn my birth. I don't forget that and shall repay it if I can. Wishing to bring Monsieur's affair to a successful crisis, I got up a theatrical evening and was in my element. One little event I must tell you, because I committed an actionable offense and was nearly discovered. I did not go down to supper, knowing that the moth would return to flutter about the candle, and preferring that the fluttering should be done in private, as Vashti's jealousy is getting uncontrollable. Passing through the gentlemen's dressing room, my quick eye caught sight of a letter lying among the costumes. It was no stage affair, and an odd sensation of fear ran through me as I recognized the hand of S. I had feared this, but I believe in chance; and having found the letter, I examined it. You know I can imitate almost any hand. When I read in this paper the whole story of my affair with S., truly told, and also that he had made inquiries into my past life and discovered the truth, I was in a fury. To be so near success and fail was terrible, and I resolved to risk everything. I opened the letter by means of a heated knife blade under the seal, therefore the envelope was perfect; imitating S.'s hand, I penned a few lines in his hasty style, saying he was at Baden, so that if Monsieur answered, the reply would not reach him, for he is in London, it seems. This letter I put into the pocket whence the other must have fallen, and was just congratulating myself on this narrow escape, when Dean, the maid of Vashti, appeared as if watching me. She had evidently seen the letter in my hand, and suspected something. I took no notice of her, but must be careful, for she is on the watch. After this the evening closed with strictly private theatricals, in which Monsieur and myself were the only actors. To make sure that he received my version of the story first, I told him a romantic story of S.'s persecution, and he believed it. This I followed up by a moonlight episode behind a rose hedge, and sent the young gentleman home in a half-dazed condition. What fools men are!"

"She is right!" muttered Coventry, who had flushed scarlet with shame and anger, as his folly became known and Lucia listened in astonished silence.

"Only one more, and my distasteful task will be nearly over," said Edward, unfolding the last of the papers. "This is not a letter, but a copy of one written three nights ago. Dean boldly ransacked Jean Muir's desk while she was at the Hall, and, fearing to betray the deed by keeping the letter, she made a hasty copy which she gave me today, begging me to save the family from disgrace. This makes the chain complete. Go now, if you will, Gerald. I would gladly spare you the pain of hearing this."

"I will not spare myself; I deserve it. Read on," replied Coventry, guessing what was to follow and nerving himself to hear it. Reluctantly his brother read these lines:

> "The enemy has surrendered! Give me joy, Hortense; I can be the wife of this proud monsieur, if I will. Think what an honor for the divorced wife of a disreputable actor. I laugh at the farce and enjoy it, for I only wait till the prize I desire is fairly mine, to turn and reject this lover who has proved himself false to brother, mistress, and his own conscience. I resolved to be revenged on both, and I have kept my word. For my sake he cast off the beautiful woman who truly loved him; he forgot his promise to his brother, and put by his pride

to beg of me the worn-out heart that is not worth a good man's love. Ah well, I am satisfied, for Vashti has suffered the sharpest pain a proud woman can endure, and will feel another pang when I tell her that I scorn her recreant lover, and give him back to her, to deal with as she will."

Coventry started from his seat with a fierce exclamation, but Lucia bowed her face upon her hands, weeping, as if the pang had been sharper than even Jean foresaw.

"Send for Sir John! I am mortally afraid of this creature. Take her away; do something to her. My poor Bella, what a companion for you! Send for Sir John at once!" cried Mrs. Coventry incoherently, and clasped her daughter in her arms, as if Jean Muir would burst in to annihilate the whole family. Edward alone was calm.

"I have already sent, and while we wait, let me finish this story. It is true that Jean is the daughter of Lady Howard's husband, the pretended clergyman, but really a worthless man who married her for her money. Her own child died, but this girl, having beauty, wit and a bold spirit, took her fate into her own hands, and became an actress. She married an actor, led a reckless life for some years; quarreled with her husband, was divorced, and went to Paris; left the stage, and tried to support herself as governess and companion. You know how she fared with the Sydneys, how she has duped us, and but for this discovery would have duped Sir John. I was in time to prevent this, thank heaven. She is gone; no one knows the truth but Sydney and ourselves; he will be silent, for his own sake; we will be for ours, and leave this dangerous woman to the fate which will surely overtake her."

"Thank you, it has overtaken her, and a very happy one she finds it."

A soft voice uttered the words, and an apparition appeared at the door, which made all start and recoil with amazement—Jean Muir leaning on the arm of Sir John.

"How dare you return?" began Edward, losing the self-control so long preserved. "How dare you insult us by coming back to enjoy the mischief you have done? Uncle, you do not know that woman!"

"Hush, boy, I will not listen to a word, unless you remember where you are," said Sir John, with a commanding gesture.

"Remember your promise: love me, forgive me, protect me, and do not listen to their accusations," whispered Jean, whose quick eye had discovered the letters.

"I will; have no fears, my child," he answered, drawing her nearer as he took his accustomed place before the fire, always lighted when Mrs. Coventry was down.

Gerald, who had been pacing the room excitedly, paused behind Lucia's chair as if to shield her from insult; Bella clung to her mother; and Edward, calming himself by a strong effort, handed his uncle the letters, saying briefly, "Look at those, sir, and let them speak."

"I will look at nothing, hear nothing, believe nothing which can in any way lessen my respect and affection for this young lady. She has prepared me for this. I know the enemy who is unmanly enough to belie and threaten her. I know that you both are unsuccessful lovers, and this explains your unjust, uncourteous treatment now. We all have committed faults and follies. I freely forgive Jean hers, and desire to know nothing of them from your lips. If she has innocently offended, pardon it for my sake, and forget the past."

"But, Uncle, we have proofs that this woman is not what she seems. Her own letters convict her. Read them, and do not blindly deceive yourself," cried Edward, indignant at his uncle's words.

A low laugh startled them all, and in an instant they saw the cause of it. While Sir John spoke, Jean had taken the letters from the hand which he had put behind him, a favorite gesture of his, and, unobserved, had dropped them on the fire. The mocking laugh, the sudden blaze, showed what had been done. Both young men sprang forward, but it was too late; the proofs were ashes, and Jean Muir's bold, bright eyes defied them, as she said, with a disdainful little gesture, "Hands off, gentlemen! You may degrade yourselves to the work of detectives, but I am not a prisoner yet. Poor Jean Muir you might harm, but Lady Coventry is beyond your reach."

"Lady Coventry!" echoed the dismayed family, in varying tones of incredulity, indignation, and amazement.

"Aye, my dear and honored wife," said Sir John, with a protecting arm about the slender figure at his side; and in the act, the words, there was a tender dignity that touched the listeners with pity and respect for the deceived man. "Receive her as such, and for my sake, forbear all further accusation," he continued steadily. "I know what I have done. I have no fear that I shall repent it. If I am blind, let me remain so till time opens my eyes. We are going away for a little while, and when we return, let the old life return again, unchanged, except that Jean makes sunshine for me as well as for you."

No one spoke, for no one knew what to say. Jean broke the silence, saying coolly, "May I ask how those letters came into your possession?"

"In tracing out your past life, Sydney found your friend Hortense. She was poor, money bribed her, and your letters were given up to him as soon as received. Traitors are always betrayed in the end," replied Edward sternly.

Jean shrugged her shoulders, and shot a glance at Gerald, saying with her significant smile, "Remember that, monsieur, and allow me to hope that in wedding you will be happier than in wooing. Receive my congratulations, Miss Beaufort, and let me beg of you to follow my example, if you would keep your lovers."

Here all the sarcasm passed from her voice, the defiance from her eye, and the one unspoiled attribute which still lingered in this woman's artful nature shone in her face, as she turned toward Edward and Bella at their mother's side.

"You have been kind to me," she said, with grateful warmth. "I thank you for it, and will repay it if I can. To you I will acknowledge that I am not worthy to be this good man's wife, and to you I will solemnly promise to devote my life to his happiness. For his sake forgive me, and let there be peace between us."

There was no reply, but Edward's indignant eyes fell before hers. Bella half put out her hand, and Mrs. Coventry sobbed as if some regret mingled with her resentment. Jean seemed to expect no friendly demonstration, and to understand that they forbore for Sir John's sake, not for hers, and to accept their contempt as her just punishment.

"Come home, love, and forget all this,"

said her husband, ringing the bell, and eager to be gone. "Lady Coventry's carriage."

And as he gave the order, a smile broke over her face, for the sound assured her that the game was won. Pausing an instant on the threshold before she vanished from their sight, she looked backward, and fixing on Gerald the strange glance he remembered well, she said in her penetrating voice, "Is not the last scene better than the first?"

Perilous Play

"If someone does not propose a new and interesting amusement, I shall die of ennui!" said pretty Belle Daventry, in a tone of despair. "I have read all my books, used up all my Berlin wools, and it's too warm to go to town for more. No one can go sailing yet, as the tide is out; we are all nearly tired to death of cards, croquet, and gossip, so what shall we do to while away this endless afternoon? Dr. Meredith, I command you to invent and propose a new game in five minutes."

"To hear is to obey," replied the young man, who lay in the grass at her feet, as he submissively slapped his forehead, and fell a-thinking with all his might.

Holding up her finger to preserve silence, Belle pulled out her watch and waited with an expectant smile. The rest of the young party, who were indolently scattered about under the elms, drew nearer, and brightened visibly, for Dr. Meredith's inventive powers were well-known, and something refreshingly novel might be expected from him. One gentleman did not stir, but then he lay within earshot, and merely turned his fine eyes from the sea to the group before him. His glance rested a moment on Belle's piquant figure, for she looked very pretty with her bright hair blowing in the wind, one plump white arm extended to keep order, and one little foot, in a distracting slipper, just visible below the voluminous folds of her dress. Then the glance passed to another figure, sitting somewhat apart in a cloud of white muslin, for an airy burnoose floated from head and shoulders, showing only a singularly charming face. Pale and yet brilliant, for the Southern eyes were magnificent, the clear olive cheeks contrasted well with darkest hair; lips like a pomegranate flower, and delicate, straight brows, as mobile as the lips. A cluster of crimson flowers, half falling from the loose black braids, and a golden bracelet of Arabian coins on the slender wrist were the only ornaments she wore, and became her better than the fashionable frippery of her companions. A book lay on her lap, but her eyes, full of a passionate melancholy, were fixed on the sea, which glittered round an island green and flowery as a summer paradise. Rose St. Just was as beautiful as her Spanish mother, but had inherited the pride and reserve of her English father; and this pride was the thorn which repelled lovers from the human flower. Mark Done sighed as he looked, and as if the sigh, low as it was, roused her from her reverie, Rose flashed a quick glance at him, took up her book, and went on reading the legend of "The Lotus Eaters."

"Time is up now, Doctor," cried Belle, pocketing her watch with a flourish.

"Ready to report," answered Meredith, sitting up and producing a little box of tortoise-shell and gold.

"How mysterious! What is it? Let me see, first!" And Belle removed the cover, looking like an inquisitive child. "Only bonbons; how stupid! That won't do, sir. We don't want to be fed with sugarplums. We demand to be amused."

"Eat six of these despised bonbons, and you *will* be amused in a new, delicious, and wonderful manner," said the young doctor, laying half a dozen on a green leaf and offering them to her.

"Why, what are they?" she asked, looking at him askance.

"Hashish; did you never hear of it?"

"Oh, yes; it's that Indian stuff which brings one fantastic visions, isn't it? I've always wanted to see and taste it, and now I will," cried Belle, nibbling at one of the bean-shaped comfits with its green heart.

"I advise you not to try it. People do all sorts of queer things when they take it. I wouldn't for the world," said a prudent young lady warningly, as all examined the box and its contents.

"Six can do no harm, I give you my word. I take twenty before I can enjoy myself, and some people even more. I've tried many experiments, both on the sick and the well, and nothing ever happened amiss, though the demonstrations were immensely interesting," said Meredith, eating his sugarplums with a tranquil air, which was very convincing to others.

"How shall I feel?" asked Belle, beginning on her second comfit.

"A heavenly dreaminess comes over one, in which they move as if on air. Everything is calm and lovely to them: no pain, no care, no fear of anything, and while it lasts one feels like an angel half asleep."

"But if one takes too much, how then?" said a deep voice behind the doctor.

"Hum! Well, that's not so pleasant, unless one likes phantoms, frenzies, and a touch of nightmare, which seems to last a thousand years. Ever try it, Done?" replied Meredith, turning toward the speaker, who was now leaning on his arm and looking interested.

"Never. I'm not a good subject for experiments. Too nervous a temperament to play pranks with."

"I should say ten would be about your number. Less than that seldom affects men. Ladies go off sooner, and don't need so many. Miss St. Just, may I offer you a taste of Elysium? I owe my success to you," said the doctor, approaching her deferentially.

"To me! And how?" she asked, lifting her large eyes with a slight smile.

"I was in the depths of despair when my eye caught the title of your book, and I was saved. For I remembered that I had hashish in my pocket."

"Are you a lotus-eater?" she said, permitting him to lay the six charmed bonbons on the page.

"My faith, no! I use it for my patients. It is very efficacious in nervous disorders, and is getting to be quite a pet remedy with us."

"I do not want to forget the past, but to read the future. Will hashish help me to do that?" asked Rose with an eager look, which made the young man flush, wondering if he bore any part in her hopes of that veiled future.

"Alas, no. I wish it could, for I, too, long to know my fate," he answered, very low, as he looked into the lovely face before him.

The soft glance changed to one of cool indifference and Rose gently brushed the hashish off her book, saying, with a little gesture of dismissal, "Then I have no desire to taste Elysium."

The white morsels dropped into the grass at her feet; but Dr. Meredith let them lie, and turning sharply, went back to sun himself in Belle's smiles.

"I've eaten all mine, and so has Evelyn. Mr. Norton will see goblins, I know, for he has taken quantities. I'm glad of it, for he don't believe in it, and I want to have him convinced by making a spectacle of himself for our amusement," said Belle, in great spirits at the new plan.

"When does the trance come on?" asked Evelyn, a shy girl, already rather alarmed at what she had done.

"About three hours after you take your dose, though the time varies with different people. Your pulse will rise, heart beat quickly, eyes darken and dilate, and an uplifted sensation will pervade you generally. Then these symptoms change, and the bliss begins. I've seen people sit or lie in one position for hours, rapt in a delicious dream, and wake from it as tranquil as if they had not a nerve in their bodies."

"How charming! I'll take some every time I'm worried. Let me see. It's now four, so our trances will come about seven, and we will devote the evening to manifestations," said Belle.

"Come, Done; try it. We are all going in for the fun. Here's your dose," and Meredith tossed him a dozen bonbons, twisted up in a bit of paper.

"No, thank you; I know myself too well to risk it. If you are all going to turn hashish-eaters, you'll need someone to take care of you, so I'll keep sober," tossing the little parcel back.

It fell short, and the doctor, too lazy to pick it up, let it lie, merely saying, with a laugh, "Well, I advise any bashful man to take hashish when he wants to offer his heart to any fair lady, for it will give him the courage of a hero, the eloquence of a poet, and the ardor of an Italian. Remember that, gentlemen, and come to me when the crisis approaches."

"Does it conquer the pride, rouse the pity, and soften the hard hearts of the fair sex?" asked Done.

"I dare say now is your time to settle the fact, for here are two ladies who have imbibed, and in three hours will be in such a seraphic state of mind that 'No' will be an impossibility to them."

"Oh, mercy on us; what *have* we done? If that's the case, I shall shut myself up till my foolish fit is over. Rose, you haven't taken any; I beg you to mount guard over me, and see that I don't disgrace myself by any nonsense. Promise me you will," cried Belle, in half-real, half-feigned alarm at the consequences of her prank.

"I promise," said Rose, and floated down the green path as noiselessly as a white cloud, with a curious smile on her lips.

"Don't tell any of the rest what we have done, but after tea let us go into the grove and compare notes," said Norton, as Done strolled away to the beach, and the voices of approaching friends broke the summer quiet.

At tea, the initiated glanced covertly at one another, and saw, or fancied they saw, the effects of the hashish, in a certain suppressed excitement of manner, and unusually brilliant eyes. Belle laughed often, a silvery ringing laugh, pleasant to hear; but when complimented on her good spirits, she looked distressed, and said she could not help her merriment; Meredith was quite calm, but rather dreamy; Evelyn was pale, and her next neighbor heard her heart beat; Norton talked incessantly, but as he talked uncommonly well, no one suspected anything. Done and Miss St. Just watched the others with interest, and were very quiet, especially Rose, who scarcely spoke, but smiled her sweetest, and looked very lovely.

The moon rose early, and the experimenters slipped away to the grove, leaving the outsiders on the lawn as usual. Some bold spirit asked Rose to sing, and she at once complied, pouring out Spanish airs in a voice that melted the hearts of her audience, so full of fiery sweetness or tragic pathos was it. Done seemed quite carried away, and lay with his face in the grass, to hide the tears that would come; till, afraid of openly disgracing himself, he started up and hurried down to the little wharf, where he sat alone, listening to the music with a countenance which plainly revealed to the stars the passion which possessed him. The sound of loud laughter from the grove, followed by entire silence, caused him to wonder what demonstrations were taking place, and half resolve to go and see. But that enchanting voice held him captive, even when a boat put off mysteriously from a point nearby, and sailed away like a phantom through the twilight.

Half an hour afterward, a white figure came down the path, and Rose's voice broke in on his midsummer night's dream. The moon shone clearly now, and showed him the anxiety in her face as she said hurriedly, "Where is Belle?"

"Gone sailing, I believe."

"How could you let her go? She was not fit to take care of herself!"

"I forgot that."

"So did I, but I promised to watch over her, and I must. Which way did they go?" demanded Rose, wrapping the white mantle about her, and running her eye over the little boats moored below.

"You will follow her?"

"Yes."

"I'll be your guide then. They went toward the lighthouse; it is too far to row; I am at your service. Oh, say yes," cried Done, leaping into his own skiff and offering his hand persuasively.

She hesitated an instant and looked at him. He was always pale, and the moonlight seemed to increase this pallor, but his hat brim hid his eyes, and his voice was very quiet. A loud peal of laughter floated over the water, and as if the sound decided her, she gave him her hand and entered the boat. Done smiled triumphantly as he shook out the sail, which caught the freshening wind, and sent the boat dancing along a path of light.

How lovely it was! All the indescribable allurements of a perfect summer night surrounded them: balmy airs, enchanting moonlight, distant music, and, close at hand, the delicious atmosphere of love, which made itself felt in the eloquent silences that fell between them. Rose seemed to yield to the subtle charm, and leaned back on the cushioned seat with her beautiful head uncovered, her face full of dreamy softness, and her hands lying loosely clasped before her. She seldom spoke, showed no further anxiety for Belle, and soon seemed to forget the object of her search, so absorbed was she in some delicious thought which wrapped her in its peace.

Done sat opposite, flushed now, restless, and excited, for his eyes glittered; the hand on the rudder shook, and his voice sounded intense and passionate, even in the utterance of the simplest words. He talked continually and with unusual brilliancy, for, though a man of many accomplishments, he was too indolent or too fastidious to exert himself, except among his peers. Rose seemed to look without seeing, to listen without hearing, and though she smiled blissfully, the smiles were evidently not for him.

On they sailed, scarcely heeding the bank of black cloud piled up in the horizon, the rising wind, or the silence which proved their solitude. Rose moved once or twice, and lifted her hand as if to speak, but sank back mutely, and the hand fell again as if it had not energy enough to enforce her wish. A cloud sweeping over the moon, a distant growl of thunder, and the slight gust that struck the sail seemed to rouse her. Done was singing now like one inspired, his hat at his feet, hair in disorder, and a strangely rapturous expression in his eyes, which were fixed on her. She started, shivered, and seemed to recover herself with an effort.

"Where are they?" she asked, looking vainly for the island heights and the other boat.

"They have gone to the beach, I fancy, but we will follow." As Done leaned forward to speak, she saw his face and shrank back with a sudden flush, for in it she read clearly what she had felt, yet doubted until now. He saw the telltale blush and gesture, and said impetuously, "You know it now; you cannot deceive me longer, or daunt me with your pride! Rose, I love you, and dare tell you so tonight!"

"Not now—not here—I will not listen. Turn back, and be silent, I entreat you, Mr. Done," she said hurriedly.

He laughed a defiant laugh and took her hand in his, which was burning and throbbing with the rapid heat of his pulse.

"No, I *will* have my answer here, and now, and never turn back till you give it; you have been a thorny Rose, and given me many wounds. I'll be paid for my heartache with sweet words, tender looks, and frank confessions of love, for proud as you are, you do love me, and dare not deny it."

Something in his tone terrified her; she snatched her hand away and drew beyond his reach, trying to speak calmly, and to meet coldly the ardent glances of the eyes which were strangely darkened and dilated with uncontrollable emotion.

"You forget yourself. I shall give no answer to an avowal made in such terms. Take me home instantly," she said in a tone of command.

"Confess you love me, Rose."

"Never!"

"Ah! I'll have a kinder answer, or—" Done half rose and put out his hand to grasp and draw her to him, but the cry she uttered seemed to arrest him with a sort of shock. He dropped into his seat, passed his hand over his eyes, and shivered nervously as he muttered in an altered tone, "I meant nothing; it's the moonlight; sit down, I'll control myself—upon my soul I will!"

"If you do not, I shall go overboard. Are you mad, sir?" cried Rose, trembling with indignation.

"Then I shall follow you, for I *am* mad, Rose, with love—hashish!"

His voice sank to a whisper, but the last word thrilled along her nerves, as no sound of fear had ever done before. An instant she regarded him with a look which took in every sign of unnatural excitement, then she clasped her hands with an imploring gesture, saying, in a tone of despair, "Why did I come! How will it end? Oh, Mark, take me home before it is too late!"

"Hush! Be calm; don't thwart me, or I may get wild again. My thoughts are not clear, but

I understand you. There, take my knife, and if I forget myself, kill me. Don't go overboard; you are too beautiful to die, my Rose!"

He threw her the slender hunting knife he wore, looked at her a moment with a far-off look, and trimmed the sail like one moving in a dream. Rose took the weapon, wrapped her cloak closely about her, and crouching as far away as possible, kept her eye on him, with a face in which watchful terror contended with some secret trouble and bewilderment more powerful than her fear.

The boat moved round and began to beat up against wind and tide; spray flew from her bow; the sail bent and strained in the gusts that struck it with perilous fitfulness. The moon was nearly hidden by scudding clouds, and one-half the sky was black with the gathering storm. Rose looked from threatening heavens to treacherous sea, and tried to be ready for any danger, but her calm had been sadly broken, and she could not recover it. Done sat motionless, uttering no word of encouragement, though the frequent flaws almost tore the rope from his hand, and the water often dashed over him.

"Are we in any danger?" asked Rose at

last, unable to bear the silence, for he looked like a ghostly helmsman seen by the fitful light, pale now, wild-eyed, and speechless.

"Yes, great danger."

"I thought you were a skillful boatman."

"I am when I am myself; now I am rapidly losing the control of my will, and the strange quiet is coming over me. If I had been alone I should have given up sooner, but for your sake I've kept on."

"Can't you work the boat?" asked Rose, terror-struck by the changed tone of his voice, the slow, uncertain movements of his hands.

"No. I see everything through a thick cloud; your voice sounds far away, and my one desire is to lay my head down and sleep."

"Let me steer—I can, I must!" she cried, springing toward him and laying her hand on the rudder.

He smiled and kissed the little hand, saying dreamily, "You could not hold it a minute; sit by me, love; let us turn the boat again, and drift away together—anywhere, anywhere out of the world."

"Oh, heaven, what will become of us!" and

Rose wrung her hands in real despair. "Mr. Done—Mark—dear Mark, rouse yourself and listen to me. Turn, as you say, for it is certain death to go on so. Turn, and let us drift down to the lighthouse; they will hear and help us. Quick, take down the sail, get out the oars, and let us try to reach there before the storm breaks."

As Rose spoke, he obeyed her like a dumb animal; love for her was stronger even than the instinct of self-preservation, and for her sake he fought against the treacherous lethargy which was swiftly overpowering him. The sail was lowered, the boat brought round, and with little help from the ill-pulled oars it drifted rapidly out to sea with the ebbing tide.

As she caught her breath after this dangerous maneuver was accomplished, Rose asked, in a quiet tone she vainly tried to render natural, "How much hashish did you take?"

"All that Meredith threw me. Too much; but I was possessed to do it, so I hid the roll and tried it," he answered, peering at her with a weird laugh.

"Let us talk; our safety lies in keeping

awake, and I dare not let you sleep," continued Rose, dashing water on her own hot forehead with a sort of desperation.

"Say you love me; that would wake me from my lost sleep, I think. I have hoped and feared, waited and suffered so long. Be pitiful, and answer, Rose."

"I do; but I should not own it now."

So low was the soft reply he scarcely heard it, but he felt it and made a strong effort to break from the hateful spell that bound him. Leaning forward, he tried to read her face in a ray of moonlight breaking through the clouds; he saw a new and tender warmth in it, for all the pride was gone, and no fear marred the eloquence of those soft, Southern eyes.

"Kiss me, Rose, then I shall believe it. I feel lost in a dream, and you, so changed, so kind, may be only a fair phantom. Kiss me, love, and make it real."

As if swayed by a power more potent than her will, Rose bent to meet his lips. But the ardent pressure seemed to startle her from a momentary oblivion of everything but love. She covered up her face and sank down, as if overwhelmed with shame, sobbing through passionate tears, "Oh, what am I doing? I am mad, for I, too, have taken hashish."

What he answered she never heard, for a rattling peal of thunder drowned his voice, and then the storm broke loose. Rain fell in torrents, the wind blew fiercely, sky and sea were black as ink, and the boat tossed from wave to wave almost at their mercy. Giving herself up for lost, Rose crept to her lover's side and clung there, conscious only that they would bide together through the perils their own folly brought them. Done's excitement was quite gone now; he sat like a statue, shielding the frail creature whom he loved with a smile on his face, which looked awfully emotionless when the lightning gave her glimpses of its white immobility. Drenched, exhausted, and half senseless with danger, fear, and exposure, Rose saw at last a welcome glimmer through the gloom, and roused herself to cry for help.

"Mark, wake and help me! Shout, for God's sake—shout and call them, for we are lost if we drift by!" she cried, lifting his head from his breast, and forcing him to see the brilliant beacons streaming far across the troubled water.

He understood her, and springing up, uttered shout after shout like one demented. Fortunately, the storm had lulled a little; the lighthouse keeper heard and answered. Rose seized the helm, Done the oars, and with one frantic effort guided the boat into quieter waters, where it was met by the keeper, who towed it to the rocky nook which served as harbor.

The moment a strong, steady face met her eyes, and a gruff, cheery voice hailed her, Rose gave way, and was carried up to the house, looking more like a beautiful drowned Ophelia than a living woman.

"Here, Sally, see to the poor thing; she's had a rough time on't. I'll take care of her sweetheart—and a nice job I'll have, I reckon, for if he ain't mad or drunk, he's had a stroke of lightnin', and looks as if he wouldn't get his hearin' in a hurry," said the old man as he housed his unexpected guests and stood staring at Done, who looked about him like one dazed. "You jest turn in yonder and sleep it off, mate. We'll see to the lady, and right up your boat in the morning," the old man added.

"Be kind to Rose. I frightened her. I'll not

forget you. Yes, let me sleep and get over this cursed folly as soon as possible," muttered this strange visitor.

Done threw himself down on the rough couch and tried to sleep, but every nerve was overstrained, every pulse beating like a trip-hammer, and everything about him was intensified and exaggerated with awful power. The thundershower seemed a wild hurricane, the quaint room a wilderness peopled with tormenting phantoms, and all the events of his life passed before him in an endless procession, which nearly maddened him. The old man looked weird and gigantic, his own voice sounded shrill and discordant, and the ceaseless murmur of Rose's incoherent wanderings haunted him like parts of a grotesque but dreadful dream.

All night he lay motionless, with staring eyes, feverish lips, and a mind on the rack, for the delicate machinery which had been tampered with revenged the wrong by torturing the foolish experimenter. All night Rose wept and sang, talked and cried for help in a piteous state of nervous excitement, for with her the trance came first, and the after-agitation was increased by the events of the evening. She slept at last, lulled by the old woman's motherly care, and Done was spared one tormenting fear, for he dreaded the consequences of this folly on her, more than upon himself.

As day dawned he rose, haggard and faint, and staggered out. At the door he met the keeper, who stopped him to report that the boat was in order, and a fair day coming. Seeing doubt and perplexity in the old man's eye, Done told him the truth, and added that he was going to the beach for a plunge, hoping by that simple tonic to restore his unstrung nerves.

He came back feeling like himself again, except for a dull headache, and a heavy sense of remorse weighing on his spirits, for he distinctly recollected all the events of the night. The old woman made him eat and drink, and in an hour he felt ready for the homeward trip.

Rose slept late, and when she woke soon recovered herself, for her dose had been a small one. When she had breakfasted and made a hasty toilet, she professed herself anxious to return at once. She dreaded yet longed to see Done, and when the time came armed herself with pride, feeling all a woman's shame at what had passed, and resolving to feign forgetfulness of the incidents of the previous night. Pale and cold as a statue she met him, but the moment he began to say humbly, "Forgive me, Rose," she silenced him with an imperious gesture and the command "Don't speak of it; I only remember that it was very horrible, and wish to forget it all as soon as possible."

"All, Rose?" he asked, significantly.

"Yes, *all.* No one would care to recall the follies of a hashish dream," she answered, turning hastily to hide the scarlet flush that would rise, and the eyes that would fall before his own.

"*I* never can forget, but I will be silent if you bid me."

"I do. Let us go. What will they think at the island? Mr. Done, give me your promise to tell no one, now or ever, that I tried that dangerous experiment. I will guard your secret also." She spoke eagerly and looked up imploringly.

"I promise," and he gave her his hand, holding her own with a wistful glance, till she drew it away and begged him to take her home.

Leaving hearty thanks and a generous token of their gratitude, they sailed away with a fair wind, finding in the freshness of the morning a speedy cure for tired bodies and excited minds. They said little, but it was impossible for Rose to preserve her coldness. The memory of the past night broke down her pride, and Done's tender glances touched her heart. She half hid her face behind her hand, and tried to compose herself for the scene to come, for as she approached the island, she saw Belle and her party waiting for them on the shore.

"Oh, Mr. Done, screen me from their eyes and questions as much as you can! I'm so worn out and nervous, I shall betray myself. You will help me?" And she turned to him with a confiding look, strangely at variance with her usual calm self-possession.

"I'll shield you with my life, if you will tell me why you took the hashish," he said, bent on knowing his fate.

"I hoped it would make me soft and lovable, like other women. I'm tired of being a lonely statue," she faltered, as if the truth was wrung from her by a power stronger than her will.

"And I took it to gain courage to tell my love. Rose, we have been near death together; let us share life together, and neither of us be any more lonely or afraid?"

He stretched his hand to her with his heart in his face, and she gave him hers with a look of tender submission, as he said ardently, "Heaven bless hashish, if its dreams end like this!"

My Mysterious Mademoiselle

At Lyons I engaged a coupé, laid in a substantial lunch, got out my novels and cigars, and prepared to make myself as comfortable as circumstances permitted; for we should not reach Nice till morning, and a night journey was my especial detestation. Nothing would have induced me to undertake it in mid-winter, but a pathetic letter from my sister, imploring me to come to her, as she was failing fast, and had a precious gift to bestow upon me before she died. This sister had mortally offended our father by marrying a Frenchman. The old man never forgave her, never would see her, and cut her off with a shilling in his will. I had been forbidden to have any communication with her on pain of disinheritance, and had obeyed, for I shared my father's prejudice, and made no attempt to befriend my sister, even when I learned that she was a widow, although my father's death freed me from my promise. For more than fifteen years we had been utterly estranged; but when her pleading letter came to me, my heart softened, and I longed to see her. My conscience reproached me, and, leaving my cozy bachelor establishment in London, I hurried away, hoping to repair the neglect of years by tardy tenderness and care.

My thoughts worried me that night, and the fear of being too late haunted me distressfully. I could neither read, sleep, nor smoke, and soon heartily wished I had taken a seat in a double carriage, where society of some sort would have made the long hours more endurable. As we stopped at a way-station, I was roused from a remorseful reverie by the guard, who put in his head to inquire, with an insinuating shrug and smile:

"Will monsieur permit a lady to enter? The train is very full, and no place remains for her in the first-class. It will be a great kindness if monsieur will take pity on the charming little mademoiselle."

He dropped his voice in uttering the last words, and gave a nod, which plainly expressed his opinion that monsieur would not regret the courtesy. Glad to be relieved from the solitude that oppressed me, I consented at once, and waited with some curiosity to see what sort of companion I was to have for the next few hours.

The first glance satisfied me; but, like a true Englishman, I made no demonstration of interest beyond a bow and a brief reply to the apologies and thanks uttered in a fresh young voice as the new-comer took her seat. A slender girl of sixteen or so, simply dressed in black, with a little hat tied down over golden curls, and a rosy face, lit up by lustrous hazel eyes, at once arch, modest and wistful. A cloak and a plump traveling bag were all her luggage, and quickly arranging them, she drew out a book, sank back in her corner, and appeared to read, as if anxious to render me forgetful of her presence as soon as possible.

I liked that, and resolved to convince her at the first opportunity that I was no English bear, but a gentleman who could be very agreeable when he chose.

The opportunity did not arrive as soon as I hoped, and I began to grow impatient to hear the fresh young voice again. I made a few attempts at conversation, but the little girl seemed timid, for she answered in the briefest words, and fell to reading again, forcing me to content myself with admiring the long curled lashes, the rosy mouth, and the golden hair of this demure demoiselle.

She was evidently afraid of the big, black-bearded gentleman, and would not be drawn out, so I solaced myself by watching her in the windows opposite, which reflected every movement like a mirror.

Presently the book slipped from her hand, the bright eyes grew heavy, the pretty head began to nod, and sleep grew more and more irresistible. Half closing my eyes, I feigned slumber, and was amused at the little girl's evident relief. She peeped at first, then took a good look, then smiled to herself as if well pleased, yawned, and rubbed her eyes like a sleepy child, took off her hat, tied a coquettish rose-colored rigolette over her soft hair, viewed herself in the glass, and laughed a low laugh, so full of merriment, that I found it difficult to keep my countenance. Then, with a roguish glance at me, she put out her hand toward the flask of wine lying on the leaf, with a half-open case of chocolate croquettes, which I had been munching, lifted the flask to her lips, put it hastily down again, took one bon-bon, and, curling herself up like a kitten, seemed to drop asleep at once.

"Poor little thing," I thought to myself, "she is hungry, cold, and tired; she longs for a warm sip, a sugar-plum, and a kind word, I dare say. She is far too young and pretty to be traveling alone. I must take care of her."

In pursuance of which friendly resolve I laid my rug lightly over her, slipped a soft shawl under her head, drew the curtains for warmth, and then repaid myself for these attentions by looking long and freely at the face encircled by the rosy cloud. Prettier than ever when flushed with sleep did it look, and I quite lost myself in the pleasant reverie which came to me while leaning over the young girl, watching the silken lashes lying quietly on the blooming cheeks, listening to her soft breath, touching the yellow curls that strayed over the arm of the seat, and wondering who the charming little person might be. She reminded me of my first sweetheart—a pretty cousin, who had captivated my boyish heart at eighteen, and dealt it a wound it never could forget. At five-and-thirty these little romances sometimes return to one's memory fresher and dearer for the years that have taught us the sweetness of youth—the bitterness of regret. In a sort of waking dream I sat looking at the stranger, who seemed to wear the guise of my first love, till suddenly the great eyes flashed wide open, the girl sprung up, and, clasping her hands, cried, imploringly:

"Ah, monsieur, do not hurt me, for I am helpless. Take my little purse; take all I have, but spare my life for my poor mother's sake!"

"Good heavens, child, do you take me for a robber?" I exclaimed, startled out of my sentimental fancies by this unexpected performance.

"Pardon; I was dreaming; I woke to find you bending over me, and I was frightened," she murmured, eyeing me timidly.

"That was also a part of your dream. Do I look like a rascal, mademoiselle?" I demanded, anxious to reassure her.

"Indeed, no; you look truly kind, and I trust you. But I am not used to traveling alone; I am anxious and timid, yet now I do not fear. Pardon, monsieur; pray, pardon a poor child who has no friend to protect her."

She put out her hand with an impulsive

gesture, as the soft eyes were lifted confidingly to mine, and what could I do but kiss the hand in true French style, and smile back into the eyes with involuntary tenderness, as I replied, with unusual gallantry:

"Not without a friend to protect her, if mademoiselle will permit me the happiness. Rest tranquil, no one shall harm you. Confide in me, and you shall find that we 'cold English' have hearts, and may be trusted."

"Ah, so kind, so pitiful! A thousand thanks; but do not let me disturb monsieur. I will have no more panics, and can only atone for my foolish fancy by remaining quiet, that monsieur may sleep."

"Sleep! Not I; and the best atonement you can make is to join me at supper, and wile away this tedious night with friendly confidences. Shall it be so, mademoiselle?" I asked, assuming a paternal air to reassure her.

"That would be pleasant; for I confess I am hungry, and have nothing with me. I left in such haste I forgot——" She paused suddenly, turned scarlet, and drooped her eyes, as if on the point of betraying some secret.

I took no notice, but began to fancy that my

little friend was engaged in some romance which might prove interesting. Opening my traveling-case, I set forth cold chicken, *tartines,* wine, and sweetmeats, and served her as respectfully as if she had been a duchess, instead of what I suspected—a run-away school-girl. My manner put her at her ease, and she chatted away with charming frankness, though now and then she checked some word on her lips, blushed and laughed, and looked so merry and mysterious, that I began to find my school-girl a most captivating companion. The hours flew rapidly now; remorse and anxiety slept; I felt blithe and young again, for my lost love seemed to sit beside me; I forgot my years, and almost fancied myself an ardent lad again.

What mademoiselle thought of me I could only guess; but look, tone and manner betrayed the most flattering confidence. I enjoyed the little adventure without a thought of consequences.

At Toulon we changed cars, and I could not get a coupé, but fortunately found places in a carriage, whose only occupant was a sleepy old woman. As I was about taking my seat, after bringing my companion a cup of hot coffee, she uttered an exclamation, dragged her veil over her face, and shrunk into the corner of our compartment.

"What alarms you?" I asked, anxiously, for her mystery piqued my curiosity.

"Look out and see if a tall young man is not promenading the platform, and looking into every carriage," returned mademoiselle, in good English, for the first time.

I looked out, saw the person described, watched him approach, and observed that he glanced eagerly into each car as he passed.

"He is there, and is about to favor us with an inspection. What are your commands, mademoiselle?" I asked.

"Oh, sir, befriend me; cover me up; say that I am ill; call yourself my father for a moment—I will explain it all. Hush, he is here!" and the girl clung to my arm with a nervous gesture, an imploring look, which I could not resist.

The stranger appeared, entered with a grave bow, seated himself opposite, and glanced from me to the muffled figure at my side. We were off in a moment, and no one spoke, till a little cough behind the veil gave the newcomer a pretext for addressing me.

"Mademoiselle is annoyed by the air; permit me to close the window."

"Madame is an invalid, and will thank you to do so," I replied, taking a malicious satisfaction in disobeying the girl, for the idea of passing as her father disgusted me, and I preferred a more youthful title.

A sly pinch of the arm was all the revenge she could take; and, as I stooped to settle the cloaks about her, I got a glance from the hazel eyes, reproachful, defiant, and merry.

"Ah, she has spirit, this little wandering princess. Let us see what our friend opposite has to do with her," I said to myself, feeling almost jealous of the young man, who was a handsome, resolute-looking fellow, in a sort of uniform.

"Does he understand English, madame, my wife?" I whispered to the girl.

"Not a word," she whispered back, with another charming pinch.

"Good; then tell me all about him. I demand an explanation."

"Not now; not here, wait a little. Can you

not trust me, when I confide so much to you?"

"No, I am burning with curiosity, and I deserve some reward for my good behavior. Shall I not have it, *ma amie?"*

"Truly, you do, and I will give you anything by-and-by," she began.

"Anything?" I asked, quickly.

"Yes; I give you my word."

"I shall hold you to your promise. Come, we will make a little bargain. I will blindly obey you till we reach Nice, if you will frankly tell me the cause of all this mystery before we part."

"Done!" cried the girl, with an odd laugh.

"Done!" said I, feeling that I was probably making a fool of myself.

The young man eyed us sharply as we spoke, but said nothing, and, wishing to make the most of my bargain, I pillowed my little wife's head on my shoulder, and talked in whispers, while she nestled in shelter of my arm, and seemed to enjoy the escapade with all the thoughtless *abandon* of a girl. Why she went off into frequent fits of quiet laughter I did not quite understand, for my whispers were decidedly more tender than witty; but I fancied it hysterical, and, having made up my mind that some touching romance was soon to be revealed to me, I prepared myself for it, by playing my part with spirit, finding something very agreeable in my new *rôle* of devoted husband.

The remarks of our neighbors amused us immensely; for, the old lady, on waking, evidently took us for an English couple on a honeymoon trip, and confided her opinion of the "mad English" to the young man, who knit his brow and mused moodily.

To our great satisfaction, both of our companions quitted us at midnight; and the moment the door closed behind them, the girl tore off her veil, threw herself on the seat opposite me, and laughed till the tears rolled down her cheeks.

"Now, mademoiselle, I demand an explanation," I said, seriously, when her merriment subsided.

"You shall have it; but first tell me what do I look like?" and she turned her face toward me with a wicked smile, that puzzled me more than her words.

"Like a very charming young lady who has

run way from school or *pension,* either to escape from a lover or to meet one."

"My faith! but that is a compliment to my skill," muttered the girl, as if to herself; then aloud, and soberly, though her eyes still danced with irrepressible mirth: "Monsieur is right in one thing. I have run away from school, but not to meet or fly a lover. Ah, no; I go to find my mother. She is ill; they concealed it from me; I ran away, and would have walked from Lyons to Nice if old Justine had not helped me."

"And this young man—why did you dread him?" I asked, eagerly.

"He is one of the teachers. He goes to find and reclaim me; but, thanks to my disguise, and your kindness, he has not discovered me."

"But why should he reclaim you? Surely, if your mother is ill, you have a right to visit her, and she would desire it."

"Ah, it is a sad story! I can only tell you that we are poor. I am too young yet to help my mother. Two rich aunts placed me in a fine school, and support me till I am eighteen, on condition that my mother does not see me. They hate her, and I would have rejected their charity, but for the thought that soon I can earn my bread and support her. She wished me to go, and I obeyed, though it broke my heart. I study hard. I suffer many trials. I make no complaint; but I hope and wait, and when the time comes I fly to her, and never leave her any more."

What had come to the girl? The words poured from her lips with impetuous force; her eyes flashed; her face glowed; her voice was possessed with strange eloquence, by turns tender, defiant, proud, and pathetic. She clinched her hands, and dashed her little hat at her feet with a vehement gesture when speaking of her aunts. Her eyes shone through indignant tears when alluding to her trials; and, as she said, brokenly, "I fly to her, and never leave her any more," she opened her arms as if to embrace and hold her mother fast.

It moved me strangely; for, instead of a shallow, coquettish school-girl, I found a passionate, resolute creature, ready to do and dare anything for the mother she loved. I resolved to see the end of this adventure, and wished my sister had a child as fond and faithful to comfort and sustain her; but her only son had died a baby, and she was alone, for I had deserted her.

"Have you no friends but these cruel aunts?" I asked, compassionately.

"No, not one. My father is dead, my mother poor and ill, and I am powerless to help her," she answered, with a sob.

"Not quite; remember I am a friend."

As I spoke I offered my hand; but, to my intense surprise, the girl struck it away from her with a passionate motion, saying, almost fiercely:

"No; it is too late—too late! You should have come before."

"My poor child, calm yourself. I *am* indeed a friend; believe it, and let me help you. I can sympathize with your distress, for I, too, go to Nice to find one dear to me. My poor sister, whom I have neglected many years; but now I go to ask pardon, and to serve her with all my heart. Come, then, let us comfort one another, and go hopefully to meet those who love and long for us."

Still another surprise; for, with a face as sweetly penitent as it had been sternly proud before, this strange girl caught my hand in hers, kissed it warmly, and whispered, gratefully:

"I often dreamed of a friend like this, but never thought to find him so. God bless you, my——" She paused there, hid her face an instant, then looked up without a shadow in her eyes, saying more quietly, and with a smile I could not understand:

"What shall I give you to prove my thanks for your kindness to me?"

"When we part, you shall give me an English good-by."

"A kiss on the lips! Fie! monsieur will not demand that of me," cried the girl, whose changeful face was gay again.

"And, why not, since I am old enough to be called your father."

"Ah, that displeased you! Well, you had your revenge; rest content with that, *mon mari,*" laughed the girl, retreating to a corner with a rebellious air.

"I shall claim my reward when we part; so resign yourself, mademoiselle. By-the-way, what name has my little friend?"

"I will tell you when I pay my debt. Now let me sleep. I am tired, and so are you. Good-night, Monsieur George Vane," and, leaving me to wonder how she had learned my name, the tormenting creature barricaded herself with cloaks and bags, and seemed to sleep tranquilly.

Tired with the long night, I soon dropped off into a doze, which must have been a long one; for, when I woke, I found myself in the dark.

"Where the deuce are we?" I exclaimed; for the lamp was out, and no sign of dawn visible, though I had seen a ruddy streak when I last looked out.

"In the long tunnel near Nice," answered a voice from the gloom.

"Ah, mademoiselle is awake! Is she not afraid that I may demand payment now?"

"Wait till the light comes, and if you deserve it *then,* you shall have it," and I heard the little gipsy laughing in her corner. The next minute a spark glowed opposite me; the odor of my choice cigarettes filled the air, and the crackle of a bon-bon was heard.

Before I could make up my mind how to punish these freaks, we shot out of the tunnel, and I sat petrified with amazement, for there, opposite me, lounged, not my pretty blonde school-girl, but a handsome black-haired, mischievous lad, in the costume of a pupil of a French military academy; with his little cap rakishly askew, his blue coat buttoned smartly to the chin, his well-booted feet on the seat beside him, and his small hands daintily gloved, this young rascal lay staring at me with such a world of fun in his fine eyes, that I tingled all over with a shock of surprise which almost took my breath away.

"Have a light, uncle?" was the cool remark that broke the long silence.

"Where is the girl?" was all I could say, with a dazed expression.

"There, sir," pointing to the bag, with a smile that made me feel as if I was not yet awake, so like the girl's was it.

"And who the devil are you?" I cried, getting angry all at once.

Standing as straight as an arrow, the boy answered, with a military salute:

"George Vane Vandeleur, at your service, uncle."

"My sister has no children; her boy died years ago, you young villain."

"He tried to, but they wouldn't let him. I'm

sorry to contradict you, sir; but I'm your sister's son, and that will prove it."

Much bewildered, I took the letter he handed me, and found it impossible to doubt the boy's word. It was from my sister to her son, telling him that she had written to me, that I had answered kindly, and promised to come to her. She bade the boy visit her if possible, that I might see him, for she could not doubt that I would receive him for her sake, and free him from dependence on the French aunts who made their favors burdensome by reproach and separation.

As I read, I forgave the boy his prank, and longed to give him a hearty welcome; but recollections of my own part in that night's masquerade annoyed me so much that to conceal my chagrin I assumed a stern air, and demanded, coldly:

"Was it necessary to make a girl of yourself in order to visit your mother?"

"Yes, sir," answered the boy, promptly, adding, with the most engaging frankness: "I'll tell you how it was, uncle, and I know you will pardon me, because mamma has often told me of your pranks when a boy, and I made you my hero. See, then, mamma sends me this letter, and I am wild to go, that I may embrace her and see my uncle. But my aunts say, 'No,' and tell them at school that I am to be kept close. Ah, they are strict there; the boys are left no freedom, and my only chance was the one holiday when I go to my aunts. I resolved to run away, and walk to mamma, for nothing shall part us but her will. I had a little money, and I confided my plan to Justine, my old nurse. She is a brave one! She said:

" 'You shall go, but not as a beggar. See, I have money. Take it, my son, and visit your mother like a gentleman.'

"That was grand; but I feared to be caught before I could leave Lyons, so I resolved to disguise myself, and then if they followed I should escape them. Often at school I have played girl-parts, because I am small, and have as yet no beard. So Justine dressed me in the skirt, cloak and hat of her granddaughter. I had the blonde wig I wore on the stage, a little rouge, a soft tone, a modest air, and—*voilà mademoiselle!*"

"Exactly; it was well done, though at times you forgot the 'modest air,' nephew," I said, with as much dignity as suppressed merriment permitted.

"It was impossible to remember it at all times; and you did not seem to like mademoiselle the less for a little coquetry," replied the rogue, with a sly glance out of the handsome eyes that had bewitched me.

"Continue your story, sir. Was the young man we met really a teacher?"

"Yes, uncle; but you so kindly protected me that he could not even suspect your delicate wife."

The boy choked over the last word, and burst into a laugh so irresistibly infectious that I joined him, and lost my dignity for ever.

"George, you are a scapegrace," was the only reproof I had breath enough to make.

"But uncle pardons me, since he gives me my name, and looks at me so kindly that I must embrace him."

And with a demonstrative affection which an English boy would have died rather than betray, my French nephew threw his arms about my neck, and kissed me heartily on both cheeks. I had often ridiculed the fashion, but now I rather liked it, and began to think my prejudice ill-founded, as I listened to the lad's account of the sorrows and hardships they had been called on to suffer since his father died.

"Why was I never told of your existence?" I asked, feeling how much I had lost in my long ignorance of this bright boy, who was already dear to me.

"When I was so ill while a baby, mamma wrote to my grandfather, hoping to touch his heart; but he never answered her, and she wrote no more. If uncle had cared to find his nephew, he might easily have done so; the channel is not very wide."

The reproach in the last words went straight to my heart; but I only said, stroking the curly head:

"Did you never mean to make yourself known to me? When your mother was suffering, could you not try me?"

"I never could beg, even for her, and trusted to the good God, and we were helped. I did mean to make myself known to you when I had done something to be proud of; not before."

I knew where that haughty spirit came from, and was as glad to see it as I was to see how much the boy resembled my once lovely sister.

"How did you know me, George?" I asked, finding pleasure in uttering the familiar name, unspoken since my father died.

"I saw your name on your luggage at Marseilles, and thought you looked like the picture mamma cherishes so tenderly, and I resolved to try and touch your heart before you knew who I was. The guard put me into your coupé, for I bribed him, and then I acted my best; but it was so droll I nearly spoiled it all by some boy's word, or a laugh. My faith, uncle, I did not know the English were so gallant."

"It did not occur to you that I might be acting also, perhaps? I own I was puzzled at first, but I soon made up my mind that you were some little adventuress out on a lark, as we say in England, and I behaved accordingly."

"If all little adventuresses got on as well as I did, I fancy many would go on this lark of yours. A talent for acting runs in the family, that is evident," said the boy.

"Hold your tongue, jackanapes!" sternly. "How old are you, my lad?" mildly.

"Fifteen, sir."

"That young to begin the world, with no friends but two cold-hearted old women!"

"Ah, no, I have the good God and my mother, and now—may I say an uncle who loves me a little, and permits me to love him with all my heart?"

Never mind what answer I made; I have recorded weaknesses enough already, so let that pass, as well as the conversation which left both pair of eyes a little wet, but both pair of hearts very happy.

As the train thundered into the station at Nice, just as the sun rose gloriously over the blue Mediterranean, George whispered to me, with the irrepressible impudence of a mischief-loving boy:

"Uncle, shall I give you 'the English good-by' now?"

"No, my lad; give me a hearty English welcome, and God bless you!" I answered, as we shook hands, manfully, and walked away together, laughing over the adventure with my mysterious mademoiselle.